Let Love Find a Way

Let Love Find a Way

Mary Georgina de Grey

Mary Georgina de Grey.

The Silent Room

First published in Great Britain in 2024 by The Silent Room

Paperback ISBN
978-1-9168875-2-7
The Silent Room

About the Author

Mary Georgina De Grey is a linguist and novelist living in Torquay. She is currently engaged on a series of romantic novels, each of which features an independent young woman making her way in a different European country.

Then the Earth Moved, set in Italy, was published by American publisher The Wild Rose Press in 2023 and **Then Time Stands Still**, which plays out in Spain, will be released in 2024.

Mary Georgina has always been interested in history. Over the gin and tonics one warm night, on a veranda in South America, she listened to the story of a family tradition. It stayed with her until she felt compelled to write it. The result, set in 1966, was this book, **'Let Love Find a Way,'** published by The Silent Room.

DEDICATION

To my editor and all those who willingly spent time reading the first draft – and helped me improve it.

Chapter 1

Colombia, South America. March 1966

Tegan had forgotten about Luís, and he'd be here any moment. She heaved an exhausted sigh. Her father had fallen ill again, and during the night, she'd taken his place, assisting with the difficult birth of a calf. Now it was mid-morning, and she was filthy and stinking of the cowshed. This wasn't how she wanted to meet the man she loved, but she had no choice. The calf was about to be born, and her job was to help it on its way.

She grasped the nose in one hand and the spindly legs in the other and tugged gently. When the mother moved, the little animal slid out and plopped onto the ground, straight into a puddle. A spray of green mud splashed onto Tegan's cheek, and she raised a weary hand to clear it away. She smelled badly enough, without being given this shower, courtesy of the newborn.

Fumes of ammonia swirled in the air and tears pricked at the back of her eyes. It wasn't the strength of the chemicals but the birth itself that made her want to cry. How could she not react to the wonder of it? To how beautiful it was?

‘He’s perfect.’ The exhausted mother started licking the little creature clean.

‘I’ll leave you to it, Julio. Take care of her – she’s had a tough time.’ She stood a moment where she was, watching the cow begin to bond with her new calf. ‘Right, I’ve got to go – I’m late already.’

The fresh air smelled sweet as Tegan hurried out of the barn, wishing the calf could have timed it better. The hot Colombian sun caressed her skin, and she stretched her arms to loosen her shoulder muscles. Then she narrowed her eyes against the glare and focused on a distant cloud of dust which was growing bigger by the second. Almost straight away, she made out the dark green of a large car. Damn. Luís was on his way already. That was too bad. He’d have to wait for her to shower, but she’d speak to him first.

A moment later, he was driving into the yard. She ran over to greet him and reached the car as he slammed the door shut.

‘Luís!’

He swung around, a smile on his face. But it vanished when he saw her. ‘Ugh, Tegan, what’s that smell? What on earth have you been doing?’ His perfect features twisted in a moue of disgust.

‘Delivering a calf. Sorry, I’ll have to change.’

‘Yeah. That stinks …

‘Give me a few minutes, Luís. Go in through the front door when you’re ready, and you’ll find Dad in the sitting room.’

Her father had scarcely moved from the room during the weeks of his illness, sometimes too weak to mount the stairs. Tegan was already heading to the back of the house. 'He'll be glad to see you. I'll be as quick as I can.'

She went into the mudroom, dragged off her boots and hurried barefoot towards the stairs, pausing only to stick her head around the door and speak to her father. 'It all went well, Dad. Got to change. Luís is here.'

In her room, she flung off her clothes, leaving them where they fell for Pilar to pick up later. Just now, she needed that shower, and if her boyfriend didn't like waiting … well, it was hardly her fault.

With the rains still a couple of weeks away, the rate of water flow was set at minimum, to eke it out until the tanks began to fill again – but this morning's efforts called for more, and she turned the knob to full power. Smears of mud, and of other substances, covered her hands and arms up beyond the elbows, and there were spots of some greenish stuff in her hair. She glanced in the mirror; those streaks on her face weren't doing anything to improve her appearance. Working up a lather on a bar of her favourite gardenia soap, she luxuriated in the cool water.

Luís had looked shocked by the dirt and the smell. She'd never seen him in anything but the most perfectly-cut clothes, even when they were out riding, or if they met casually with friends. Better not make matters worse; it wasn't as if she didn't care about smelling like this. She scrubbed hard for five minutes and then stepped out of the shower and enveloped herself in a thick white bath towel.

Well, it had been time for him to meet this other Tegan: the one who worked with animals, who sometimes had to deliver a calf and occasionally got covered in smelly excretions. The problem was that he saw her as a fine possession, not a living, breathing woman who helped run a successful cattle ranch. It was a sore point, but one she generally tried to smooth over.

Roused by the banging on the door at five that morning when the cow had begun to calve, she'd pulled on jeans and a man's thick flannel shirt, before slipping her feet into tough work boots. Now, the silky underwear was deliciously cool against her warm skin and this pale, floaty dress was great, so lightweight, it scarcely felt she was wearing anything, pure bliss after hours in the sticky atmosphere of the barn. She wriggled, enjoying the sensuous caress of the material. These clothes were perfect for the drive into Santo Domingo. Could she remember where she'd put those new sandals with the high heels, though? They were on the delicate side, but she wouldn't be walking anywhere much today.

After applying a pale pink lipstick, her only concession to make-up, she took a long, assessing look in the mirror, tweaked a lock of red-gold hair, and congratulated herself on a remarkable transformation in a mere fifteen minutes. A couple of spritzes of Miss Dior, and she was ready. She grabbed jacket, bag and hat and walked quietly out onto the landing. From here, the view over the balustrade into the wide hall was unobstructed. Luís hadn't heard her come out, and she enjoyed a moment gazing down at him. It was always a pleasure to look at a very handsome man.

Unusually, he wasn't sitting relaxed in the deep chair he'd favoured on previous visits. Instead, he was pacing. And were those worry lines on his brow? Maybe something had happened to upset him.

He raised his head as she started down the stairs, a remote expression on his face, and she had the distinct impression he was irritated that she hadn't been ready. That was a pity, but it couldn't be helped.

'There you are, Luís! I'm sorry I've kept you waiting, only it's been a busy morning.'

They kissed. Hmm! he did smell good, his musky cologne expensive but discreet. She sniffed appreciatively and hoped the shower and the perfume she'd applied afterwards had chased away any lingering traces of the calving shed. The charms of playing midwife to an overdue cow were limited, even for an enthusiast like her. It had been a difficult birth, or she wouldn't have been involved. It felt good now to be getting away for the afternoon.

Hand in hand, they went out to the big Chevrolet. It was a practical replacement for the little red MG he loved so much, but there was no way he'd use an open-top and expose them to the dust it would churn up at this time of year.

'Did you speak to Dad?'

'Er – no. I didn't see him.'

Which was odd. Had he bothered to look? She glanced up but could read nothing on his face and she decided to ignore what he'd said.

'You can't believe how hard it was to get the calf out,' she was saying as they drove through the gate. 'Dad's still not very well, so he asked me to keep an eye on things, although I do think Pedro and Julio could have done it between them. I thought Pedro would burst a blood vessel at one point, he was pulling so hard. Then Julio had a go and fell backwards into a stinking puddle. He was really fed up – you should have heard him swearing.'

She grinned as she turned towards Luís. His mouth had turned down in a grimace at this last item of information, but she persevered.

'So, in the end, I just stuck in my arm, grabbed the nose and legs, and pulled. And out it came, making it look as if I'd worked a miracle, when in fact it was all down to them. It was *time* – we'd been in there for over five hours by then.'

'I wish you weren't involved in these things.'

'But I don't mind at all. It's so satisfying, so beautiful, when an animal is born.'

She'd wanted to make him laugh with her story, to share with him the emotion of the birth, but he was pre-occupied and looked very serious, and she knew it wasn't going to happen. His knuckles showed white as he gripped the wheel and he made no reply, his usual charm conspicuously missing.

They reached the main road and for a while, Luís kept his attention on negotiating the many potholes, but then he began to talk about his father's recent visit to the capital city, Bogotá. It sounded as if things were going well for him.

'That's great, Luís. How does your mother feel about the possibility of being a senator's wife?'

'My mother knows what's expected of her and she has a lot of friends among the political families. I think she's looking forward to what this will open up for us.'

My Goodness, he sounded so … pompous.

'Do they know yet where they'll live?'

'Papá's in Bogotá right now, researching possible houses. He'll need a base if all this works out.'

They talked a while longer about the inevitable changes but then sank into an uneasy silence. Nothing felt right today. A niggling worry sprang up at the back of Tegan's mind, but she pushed it away.

Hadn't he said he wanted to discuss their engagement when he'd rung the evening before? About a month earlier, they'd agreed they would marry, but they lived in a very traditional society, so the first step had to be an engagement, everyone invited to a party to underline the importance of the moment, especially as the two families occupied positions of importance in the area.

'Why couldn't we just tell people we're engaged and set a date for the wedding?' she'd said. 'It would be so much simpler.'

'It's not about what's easy. The party will be a huge event in the area, you know that. We have to think of our position.' She hadn't liked his repressive tone and was hard put to hide her irritation. Sometimes he sounded older than her father.

'All sorts of important people will attend. Just think what Mari-Dolores and Sofía would think if you didn't have a party to celebrate.'

She'd smiled then; actually, that was true. It was ironic that at nineteen, the down-to-earth, hardworking member of the trio of friends would be the first to settle down. And a party would certainly make the point.

'Okay, you're right. We do have to have a party.'

*

They were approaching the outskirts of Santo Domingo now. There was some business she had to conduct on behalf of her father, who still wasn't well enough to go into town, and Luís had arranged a short meeting with one of his father's tenants.

'I'll meet you at the Corazón in half an hour,' he said as he dropped her off in the square five minutes later.

Chapter 2

Her chores finished, Tegan wandered slowly through the centre. She loved this purposeful little town with horses at its heart – many horses of many different kinds – but sometimes it felt claustrophobic. Today, the place was buzzing as people went about their business. The wooden buildings baked in the sun, and the equine visitors, tied up on either side of the main street, outnumbered the cars and the jeeps five to one. And then, there were the mules and the donkeys.

She glanced at her watch. It was still early, so she could take her time, looking into the shops. Every second or third outlet catered to the riding and agricultural community. Feed, tack, clothing, farm machinery, camping gear and guns. She'd grown up on the ranch, and this kind of thing was interesting to her. Up to a point. The little town provided everything that people needed. Not that she couldn't appreciate something more sophisticated; if she was looking for finery, she'd drive into Cartagena or even fly south to Bogotá.

Sandwiched between the merchant outlets were enough saloons for parched riders to slake their thirst ten times over. And every one of them appeared to be full. About half of these establishments were owned by Luís's family, but such rough watering holes were not the sort of place he'd consider taking Tegan.

They arrived at the same time at the front of the "Restaurante Corazón Roja," the only stone building at that end of the town. Its whitewashed walls brilliant in the sun, it stood at the corner of the street that led down to the Morales forge. Luís ushered her through the door into the cool, shadowy interior, which was empty of customers at this hour. Then, shoulders back and not speaking, he strode to a booth near the back of the room, where he gestured for her to sit.

What had happened to bring this on?

'Señor, señorita,' said the bar manager, recognizing them. *'Cómo le va?'*

'Bien, Miguel. Tráiganos una coca cola y una cerveza, por favor.'

The man came back with the drinks and proceeded to engage them in conversation but, receiving little encouragement, he soon went away. Luís took a long drink of beer, wiped his mouth, and then banged the glass down on the table. Tegan looked at him.

'Is something wrong, Luís? Is there a problem?'

He picked it up again and stared into it before looking up. 'I guess we're the problem, Tegan. You and me. The way we are, I don't see things working out.'

'Things?'

'Us. Our engagement. I've tried, Tegan, I really have, and I do love you, *querida*. But we're so different.'

He was speaking quickly and watching her with close attention. Something stabbed at her heart, but Tegan kept her face expressionless.

'You see, you think the only things that matter are the horses and the ranch,' he went on. 'That's one thing.'

'But there's more?'

'What bothers me even more is that you don't respect what I do. That's not a good basis for a marriage. We have to change it – one way or another.'

What was all this? She couldn't quite grasp what it signified. What did he mean by "one way or another"?

Despite the heat, goosepimples sprang up along her bare arms, and his words clanged through her mind like a death knell. Heat began to build in her chest, but she mustn't overreact.

She had to stay calm. 'That's because I'm not really sure what you do, Luís.' Her voice was cracked, and she cleared her throat. She didn't know where this was going but it felt like dangerous ground – which didn't mean she should keep silent. 'You could try explaining to me.'

His exasperated look was condemnation, but Tegan waited for the answer.

'I told you. I work for my father.'

'Yes? But what work do you do for him, exactly? Surely, he's got people to do the running around.'

He sighed. 'Of course, but he needs me as a secretary and close confidant. There are things he cannot entrust to others. The *Senado* is within his grasp, Tegan, and if he succeeds in these elections, it will mean we have to live a life of a certain standard – you and me, not just my parents.

You'd be the daughter-in-law of a senator, one of the most important men in Colombia.'

She stared past him at the distant street. Of course, she'd known for a long time that Roberto Morales Blanco had his eye on the Capitolio Nacional. Winning one of the hundred-odd seats would catapult him right into the top one per cent of Colombian society. It was a prize well worth fighting for, to a man like him. And clearly, his son would support him and benefit from that.

If only she were more interested in the status that he longed to achieve; but that world felt artificial and even unworthy to her. She forced herself to concentrate on what he was saying. 'There's always a price to pay for getting what you want, *querida.*' He paused, looking into her eyes. Then, he turned away and said, 'But I realise now that you don't want to be a beautiful and cherished woman with an important position in the world, do you?'

'No, no, you've got that wrong. It's just that I … need to be other things as well.'

'So why don't you even try to fit in, Tegan? When was the last time you went to a charity event? Or met with the women's circle for coffee? My mother invited you to a gathering last week and you found some excuse not to turn up. Do you understand what message that sends out?'

A tide of heat rose in her cheeks. It was true she'd neglected the things he'd suggested because she could find no enthusiasm for them. But the excuse to his mother had been genuine. She would never have insulted her in that way, ignoring a direct invitation. And his mother had been gracious in replying. Sometimes, Tegan thought his mother understood her better than Luís did.

'I didn't – '

'You see, these things will be expected of you.'

'I don't have the time just now, with Dad being ill. I thought you knew that. And I explained to your mother.'

He looked away. Of course he knew she'd told his mother, knew how hard things were at the moment, but he'd wanted to bolster his argument with the cutting words. That was unfair.

'And you've always said you appreciated me for what I am. You said you liked that I'm independent.'

'I did. I do. It's what attracted me to you in the first place. But someone in our position has responsibilities. You have to make the time, but it doesn't mean you can't retain your independence.' He stopped a moment, and it looked as if he was trying to work out what to say next.

She waited. 'Naturally, you couldn't continue working on the ranch full time, but you could still run your little horse affair, although you'd have to get someone to manage it, of course. But this business this morning – stinking like a farm hand. That's totally disgusting and it's just not possible to go on like that. You do see what I mean?'

A shiver ran through her. This was leading somewhere she hadn't expected. It was beginning to look serious.

'Yes … no. No, I don't, Luís. What do you mean?'

He stared at her, marshalling his words. 'That you don't really care about me if you can't make the effort. When I tell you these things, you don't listen. You shrug it off as if it doesn't matter.'

Her thoughts were rushing around in her head, a chaotic assembly that made no sense. She seemed to be looking down on the two of them, as they stared at each other across the table, as if they were actors in a play. All the lines had been written already, giving her no control over what happened next. But that wasn't true. She could take control. And she would.

She stayed quiet a moment, thinking, and then decided; it didn't matter if she didn't fully understand what he wanted of her. Because now, she knew she couldn't give it – whatever it was.

'I am listening, Luís and I hear clearly what you're saying. It's finished. That's what you've just told me. That you don't want me anymore.'

Already she was rising from the table, but he grasped her arm and pulled her back down. 'No! Not finished, *querida* … I want to suggest we have some time apart, that we don't meet while we take time to consider what we want, to work out the compromises that are going to be necessary – from both of us.'

She slumped down in her seat, feeling defeated. She was a fool. They both were. Everything he said was sound common sense, things they should have discussed long ago. 'No.'

'You love those horses more than you love me. You'd die if you were parted from that mare. How could I marry you when you feel like that?'

He was wrong about the horse. But his words were helping her to see things more clearly. 'I think – '

'You still don't understand. We can't have a marriage based entirely on a shared love of horses.'

Of course they couldn't, but she wanted to tell him about all the times he hadn't made the effort to understand her, how he tried to mould her into the person he wanted her to be, as if he thought because she was younger than he was, he could change her, change her character; how he didn't listen when she talked to him about the things that were important to her, didn't recognize that her "little horse affair" was a successful and growing business, something she worked at every day, not the whimsical pastime of a bored young woman.

And then came the cold explanation of his behaviour: her parents' wealth, earned in the silver mines sixty years earlier, would certainly help the ambitious Morales family attain their political dreams. To say nothing of the inheritance she had from her grandmother. Why hadn't she seen it before?

So, something must have happened to change things, or he wouldn't be abandoning such a lucrative match.

'You've found someone else, haven't you?' The look in his eyes was answer enough. 'No, don't deny it, Luís.'

'How can you possibly think …'

She was certain of it, could even make a reasonable guess as to who it was.

'Luís, I know.'

'There's no-one else, I swear.'

'There is.'

She leaned forward, the desire to wound very strong. 'As it happens, I was getting bored. Perhaps you even sensed that, in which case, there's no harm done to either of us. I'm glad we're having this conversation because it gives me a way out before it's too late.'

His jaw went slack, and he made to speak, but she gave him no opportunity. She forced her facial muscles into the semblance of a smile.

'Don't worry, *querido* – I wouldn't want to tarnish your father's image. I won't stand in your way.'

She was on her feet now, gathering her things.

'Tegan, please! Please don't walk away.'

'Why not? You want me to beg you to stay with me? Should I kiss you fondly? Or perhaps I should cry – is that what you want?' Her eyes had grown hard, like the tone of her voice. 'Go to your new love if you want kisses. I'm sorry it's ended like this. But it is over.'

A moment later, she was out on the street, and her eyes were blurring with the tears she'd managed to hold back until she'd turned away from him. She wasn't going to let him see her weep. My little horse affair, she thought, stiffening her spine. How insulting that was. How did he dare?

The galleried wooden sidewalk was crowded. She blundered along and nearly cannoned into someone walking towards her, swerving at the last moment.

'Woah!'

As her ankle started to twist and her foot slipped over the edge, a hand grabbed her arm and pulled her back upright.

'*Señorita* Tegan. You all right?'

Hastily, she brushed away the tears with the back of her hand. 'Yes, I'm fine, Miguel, fine. Just did myself an injury, that's all.' She kept her head down as she rubbed her ankle, taking a moment to gather her wits. 'Say, Miguel, you going back to the ranch any time soon?'

'Right now, *señorita.* You want a lift?'

'*Gracias. Es perfecto.*'

Chapter 3

'I don't want to talk about this just now, Mamá. I'll go and stay with Idris for a few months if that'll make you feel better. I'll even go to that college, although what for, I really don't know. But I am not going to Wales.'

As always, when it was just the family, they were speaking Welsh. The argument was still rumbling on three weeks after that day in Santo Domingo. It was all the more annoying because she was sure her mother was secretly pleased that things had fallen through with Luís, although she *had* been careful not to say so. When she'd learned the news, she'd simply folded her daughter in her arms, offering the comfort she needed, and let days pass before bringing up the difficult question of what Tegan was going to do next.

College was what her mother wanted for her, but it didn't make a lot of sense; they'd been trusting her with major decisions on the ranch for the last six months, and now they wanted her to go back to school.

Mamá was right, of course. Girls were getting a proper education these days, instead of the six months' genteel "finishing" she'd had at seventeen, and she couldn't spend the rest of her life working on the ranch. At least, not without experiencing different places and things first.

And she needed time to get over him. Even that fleeting thought sent a quiver of sorrow through her. How had she got things so completely wrong? As she climbed the stairs to her room, the heavy sensation in her chest seemed to increase. Listlessly, she took out her riding clothes and began to change.

'Of course you can travel, Tegan,' her mother had said. 'We can always get someone in to help. Besides, we would like to go over to the old country ourselves and you can come with us, have a holiday if nothing else.'

'That's right,' Dad said. Her parents seemed to be in complete agreement about this. 'You can't sacrifice yourself just because I've not been well. Anyway, I'm getting better.'

Which was true. But she couldn't leave the ranch, could she? While Dad was recovering, her work was essential to keep things running smoothly. Mamá was heavily involved with the domestic side of things, running the accommodation for the single men, feeding the cowboys and other farm hands. And she did two days a week teaching at the local school. Even if she gave that up, it wouldn't be nearly enough without Tegan's input. How would Dad manage?

And what about her horses? She couldn't walk out on all that. Tegan swallowed the painful lump in her throat and hurried down onto the terrace.

'Señorita!'

Deep in thought, she continued towards the steps.

'Señorita, teléfono.'

She raised her head and looked, unseeing, at the girl.

'Not just now, Pilar. Say I'll ring later.'

It could wait. She couldn't speak to anyone in this state of mind. She came to a halt. *Dios,* what if it was Luís? No matter, she didn't care. He was finished and she had to think about the future. Which, she was coming to see, might mean travelling halfway across the world.

To Wales, *Madre de Dios!* Some damp, cold little country of no account, filled with sheep.

The discussion had been painful on both sides.

'No, I'm not going over there to pick up a husband, just because you did – and Grandma. Now, it's some sort of family tradition. Well, if it is, this is where it ends.'

It was so demeaning. She flushed. How could they think she would accept such a thing? Controlling her anger, she'd walked away. She could turn her back, but it was obvious that things were going to change.

Now she dragged a large handkerchief from her pocket and wiped sweat from her brow. It was too hot, oppressive as well, and the sky was filled with heavy, grey clouds, the afternoon matching her gloomy mood.

The paddock was empty, so Tegan crossed the paved yard into the extensive stable block where her mare, Bonita, greeted her with a welcoming nickering sound. How soft and sweet she was. She laid her head against the horse's neck and stroked the velvety, black nose, the animal responding with affection and enthusiasm as usual. Dealing with animals was so uncomplicated. If only humans were as easy.

'It's going to be hard without you, Bonita. How am I going to manage?'

If she went away, what should she do about the horse breeding? The fledgling business would need an experienced person just to keep it going, never mind expanding as she'd hoped.

The little mare was quivering at the thought of a ride. 'I'm taking her out, Pedro,' she said, as she spotted the stable hand, who was wiping down her father's big stallion. 'Dad been out this morning, has he?'

'*Sí,* first time in months.'

'*Bueno.* And Bonita? Do you think she'll be okay?' She'd been rather worried about Bonita recently.

'*Sí, señorita*. Been waiting for you.' A big toothless grin spread across his face. 'Much better. She needs exercise now.'

*

Ten minutes later, they were cantering across the fields, heading for the open country. She needed to go up to Monte Verde. It was her favourite ride, the place she always went to when she wanted to clear her mind. With clouds of pale grey dust billowing behind her, she bent low in the saddle and gave herself up to the speed and the unique pleasure of the gallop. The mare was as keen as she was, and slowly, her spirits lifted, though she couldn't quite abandon the topic that had occupied so much time in the last few weeks.

Of course, her parents wanted her to find someone else, now Luís was out of the picture. She understood that. But didn't they realise times had changed? This was the nineteen-sixties, not the medieval period, and she certainly wasn't going to be married off to some "suitable" person.

God, she'd been so immature, so … innocent about Luís. She passed her hand in front of her eyes, as if to blot out the picture of her behaviour over the past few months. She took a deep breath to stop herself from breaking into tears at her own naivety, but that Tegan was in the past; she would not be that stupid again. It would be better to keep right away from emotional entanglements for a time. They made you weak, and it just hurt too much.

Chapter 4

One minute, there was the brown, unending plain and the wide sky and the next, a white cow appeared in front of her, and she was in the middle of a life-threatening incident. Tegan grabbed the reins in one hand, pulling Bonita's head hard to the left to get around the obstacle, well aware that if she made the horse stop dead, she'd be catapulted straight over its head.

With inches to spare, they passed the skeletal beast, but stricken with terror, Bonita bolted along the narrow path. God, she was going to cut her legs on those sharp rocks. Tegan hung on tight, praying she could get back out onto the flat.

She swerved around a large boulder, sure the horse would fall and break a bone, but she could do nothing. Now she was sliding sideways, and suddenly, she too was in danger. An image of the hooves thudding inches from her head flashed into her mind while her fingers, slippery with sweat, began to lose hold of the reins.

Her pounding heartbeat pushed up a notch and threatened to choke her, but she exerted every ounce of power in her muscles to inch her way back up into the saddle, and a few moments later, she'd taken control of the animal once again. Finally, Bonita slowed, blowing loudly. Although the horse was still tossing her head and showing the whites of her eyes, Tegan gradually got her down to walking pace. She stroked her neck.

'You're all right, girl. That was a shock but you're all right.' She repeated the words over and over again, needing the soothing effect as much as the horse did. She'd done something stupid. The break-up with Luís had undermined the poised young woman she'd believed herself to be, taken away her ability to make rational decisions. And this dangerous situation was the result.

After a few minutes, they came to a halt, and she slid from the saddle. Keeping a firm hold on the reins, she walked around to Bonita's head and continued talking to her, rubbing and stroking her, until she felt the animal calm. Then she looked closely at each leg for damage. If her carelessness had done anything to cause injury … but there didn't seem to be anything wrong. Relieved, she sank onto a stone in the shade of a huge boulder.

Adrenaline was making her feel sick and dizzy. She took deep breaths, waiting for the sensation to pass, while perspiration trickled down her neck and back.

Idiot! She should know better. She couldn't go on like this, not concentrating, risking serious injury. More disturbed by the incident than she'd expected, she sat on the rock for a long time.

Finally, things became a little clearer. She had to make some decisions for herself, and the first thing was that she wouldn't live with her recently married brother and go to college in Bogotá.

‘Stay with us, Tegan,’ he’d said. ‘We have plenty of room, haven’t we, Carmen?’

‘Yes, of course we have.’

It had sounded as if Carmen had even less enthusiasm for this idea than Tegan. If anyone had mastered the art of smouldering eyes and putting her man at the centre of the universe, it was Carmen. And she wouldn’t welcome his attention on anyone else, not even his sister. Now, there was a passion! – if Tegan had loved Luís like that, things would be completely different.

But she hadn’t. Anyway, it couldn’t be worse than playing wallflower to newly-weds.

And although he’d demurred when she’d said she wouldn’t be accepting the invitation, Idris hadn’t protested much. So, what if she did go to Wales?

She’d returned to this idea again and again, and the last time they’d talked about it, once the heated discussion had died down and she was listening properly, her mother had said: ‘Your aunt might be able to find you work, a real job at one of the local farms. Or perhaps you could look after someone’s children, even teach them to ride. That would make you feel better about staying over there. You’d be independent, earning your own money.’

That had sounded more attractive than just living with them, true. It was so hard to imagine living with people you didn’t know in a completely strange environment and having nothing specific to do. She’d been four years old when the relatives had come over to Colombia, and she didn’t remember them at all.

She let out a long sigh. Finally, she was really thinking about it, and she was going to take responsibility. Instead of asking Mamá to talk to them about finding work for her, she'd speak to her aunt herself. And she'd start a search for someone to look after her horses, someone who could at least keep a holding pattern until she got back.

Her aunt lived on a farm, and she could relate to that. In some ways, Wales was beginning to sound like a good idea … but a whole year? She thought long and hard about it. The pain of the breakup with Luís was still sharp but that affair couldn't be resurrected now.

She would go to Wales.

*

Tegan got to her feet and looked back towards the ranch. Any desire for a gallop up the hill had gone, and she turned towards home, leading her mount carefully down the steeper part of the slope before getting back in the saddle.

Pedro came out to greet her and ran his expert eye over the dark patches of sweat on the mare's coat.

'She got spooked – one of the wild cattle,' Tegan said quickly, trying not to sound defensive. 'I didn't expect them to be so close but they're getting a bit desperate. Can you rub her down for me?'

Tossing him the reins, she hurried towards the house.

Even as she went up to her room to change, she was overwhelmed by a deep ache of longing for the man she now accepted she'd lost.

Misery engulfed her and tears began to fall. At some level, she had loved him.

Chapter 5

The Black Mountains, South Wales. Six weeks later.

This was Tegan's tenth day in Wales, and she itched to get to work. Soon, her parents would be leaving her to begin her new life. It had been exciting that Aunt Mona was able to offer her a genuine job on her own farm. Having a proper reason for being in Wales made everything about the visit feel better.

When she'd telephoned her aunt all those weeks ago, they'd discussed the possibility of working for a local riding school, but then things had changed, and Mona had said, 'You can work for me, be my secretary, Tegan. Mary has left. It was completely unexpected and now I'm desperate for help. Please say you'll consider it.'

'Of course, I will. Just let me know what you want me to do.'

'I'll pay you a proper wage, and I promise you the work won't be too difficult.'

'It's not the amount that's important. I want to earn my living, not be a burden to you.'

‘I’d never think that of you, Tegan, dear. I’m really looking forward to having you stay.’

It was a great opportunity, and the important things was that she’d pick up new ideas she could use when she came back to the ranch.

*

Now it was April, and this Wednesday morning, she was about to take on her new role. Uncle George, who was going up to London, was driving her parents into Bristol, just over the Severn Bridge, where they’d be taking a train to Birmingham, the beginning of a tour visiting friends and relatives.

‘We’ll be returning direct to London Airport,’ her mother said. ‘We’ll be ready to go back by then. I don’t want to spend too long away, and you know *papá* still gets tired easily.’

‘But won’t we meet up again before you go?’ Panic now threatened.

‘No, I’m sorry.’ Bronwen kissed her daughter. ‘He’s a lot better but we don’t want to prolong things. And I can see you’re fine with your aunt and uncle.’

She was, but she wouldn’t be seeing them again for almost a year. It was only now that she was really thinking about it. Her heart began to hammer. What if something happened to them? What if Dad became ill again? A sickening sense of finality hit her … oh, why had she agreed to this?

‘Dad is going to be all right, isn’t he?’ she said then, clutching her mother’s arm a little desperately as they walked towards Uncle George’s car. The surgeon had cut out the cancer some months earlier and said the operation had been completely successful. Dad did seem stronger, and he'd been very keen to make this journey back to the old country. But how could they be sure? 'Take care of him, Mamá. He always does too much.'

'I will, *querida*. But you know as well as I do how stubborn he can be.'

Tegan did know, and that was what was worrying her. She turned to her father, determined to make him think about his health.

'How will you manage, Dad, when you get back? You mustn't overdo it. You know what the doctors said.'

'We'll manage the way we're doing at the moment, Tegan. I have Hernandez there and he's contracted for at least another couple of months. It's not going to be a problem, Tegan. Just forget about everything and enjoy yourself. And with Alfonso looking after your horses, I'll be able to call on his help when the man leaves.'

He'd brought in the ranch manager on a short contract to cover their absence in Europe and give him time to recuperate, and maybe they'd keep him on longer. Her cousin Alfonso's help would leave her mother free to carry on with her own responsibilities.

'Just look after yourself, Dad.'

She kissed them both and clung to her father as Uncle George urged them to get into the car. As the big vehicle drove off, and the rear lights glowed red in the darkness of the dawn, she wiped away a few tears.

*

Despondent, Tegan followed her aunt back to the breakfast table. Everything was flat and she had a sinking feeling that made her afraid.

‘I don’t know about you,’ Mona said, ‘but I’d like another cup of tea.’

‘That would be nice.’

Tegan sat down and sipped the freshly made brew. Politeness had made her accept, but it did taste good, even though she didn’t really want it. She’d never been so far away from home before and was going to miss her parents. At the same time, there was a sort of desperation to start work, as if the job might disappear before she managed to get to it. She smiled at how ridiculous she was being.

The thing was, after years of being protected, she was more than ready to launch herself on the world and organise her own life. She’d been self-reliant and cool-headed, and had shouldered responsibilities no-one had noticed, but this was different. She thought about the ranch. She’d pretty much been running things in the last few months, but this wasn’t her own immediate family she’d be working for, and that meant she had to develop a more professional approach to things, although she wasn’t sure what that would entail. A surge of excitement filled her, and she sprang to her feet. ‘I’ll clear, shall I?’

Mona replaced her cup on the saucer and stood up.

‘No, leave that to Bethan. If you’re ready, I’ll show you where you’ll be working.’

‘Are you sure I can do this, Aunt Mona? I don’t have any training.’

‘Of course, you can. I’m just so grateful you’re here. It was such a shock when Mary became ill. She’s been with me for years.’

‘Won’t she want her job back eventually?’

'I don't think so. She's moved in with her daughter in Newport and she told me it's very unlikely she'll be coming back. I'm exhausted, trying to keep up with everything and the paperwork's mounted over the last few weeks, so there'll be plenty to keep you occupied. There was nobody suitable available and I didn't know how I was going to cope. You've arrived at just the right moment. Just remember that if you think I somehow invented this job for you. You're helping me.'

'That's good to hear. I wanted to do something worthwhile.'

'It is worthwhile. I'm sorry if I seem more concerned about the work than Mary's health. I'm not, but this is a business, and the staff are important. One can't let things go, or everyone suffers – including the other employees.'

As they came out of the house, the sun was still behind the clouds, no more than a faint glimmer of brighter light here and there. Thick swirls of white mist dramatically hid the lower part of the valley, and the dynamic grey shapes of hills marched like ghosts in front of her, coming into view and then vanishing again. Tegan shivered in the chilly, damp air. She closed the jacket she'd borrowed around her and glanced at her watch. At home, they'd already be feeling the heat.

How was her cousin managing? Her parents would be back there in a few weeks, so it should be all right. They'd be able to pick up the normal routine. But from now on, for her, things were going to be very different.

Chapter 6

The office was housed in a single-story building to one side of a paved courtyard. It was neat and business-like, with its brick walls, slate roof and green-painted woodwork. Mona pushed open the door, and a blast of warm air enveloped them as they entered. A portable heater occupied the centre of the space.

'Here's a desk for you.' A simple wooden table with a chair and some shelves behind it occupied one side of the room. She indicated a surface spread with papers and office paraphernalia. 'I tend to work over there, by the other window.'

This was going to be a nice workplace. All those multi-paned windows on both sides were attractive, although they were small. Wondering how come there was so much light, she glanced up and saw another window set in the ceiling. Despite the thick, white cloud, light was pouring in, filling the whole space.

She'd have a decent view from her desk. She walked over and sat down, looking around, pleased that she could see the courtyard on one side and look down into the valley on the other. When the sun burned off the mist, there'd be the sweep of the hills, gentle, rounded humps, unlike the spikey teeth of the range that was the backdrop to her own home. It looked inviting and she longed to get out there to explore on horseback.

'What do you want me to do?'

'Answer the phone, place orders for foodstuffs, keep charts on various animals, help with the organisation of the market-garden side, get cheques ready for signature to pay the bills – the list is endless, and you can only learn by doing it. I'll try to be with you as much as I can during this first week. At least you know the basics of how a farm works, so I expect it won't take you too long.'

'Are there particular hours you want me to work?'

'I'm flexible. For instance, if you have something you want to do, you say so, and providing there's nothing too urgent, I'll give you the time off. But if you set something up, say an inspection with the vet, you will need to deal with it. I must be able to rely on you.'

'Yes, of course.'

'Shall we say mornings, Monday to Saturday, eight until one, to start with, and we'll see how that goes?'

Okay, that was organised, a more formal way of doing things than at home. It *was* a real job, not just something the families had cooked up between them. So much the better.

'Can you type?'

'No.'

The rather monstrous, upright machine that sat brooding on the middle of what was now her desk must be thirty years old and it looked complicated. Would she ever get the hang of it?

‘Well, you’ll need to learn – and this will help.’

Mona reached up to a shelf and took down a book with a red and yellow cover. Tegan caught sight of the title: “Typing Made Simple”, and wondered just how true that would turn out to be. Mona flicked through and placed it on the desk, open at a page that showed a diagram of a keyboard.

‘It will take you about a week to master the basic finger positions – and several months to get up to speed, depending on how much you practice. And you must try, Tegan. Otherwise, you’ll be typing with two fingers for ever more.’

‘Of course, I’ll work at it.’

Finger positions. That didn’t sound much fun. Learning to play the piano had been hard and she hadn’t enjoyed it. Okay, maybe she should just think of this as work and get on with it. You couldn’t expect to like every aspect of your job, and at least it was only the keyboard to learn, unlike with the piano.

‘If you don’t get on top of it, you’ll soon be bored because everything will take too much time. In fact, that’s the first task I’m giving you: learn the fingering and then build up speed. Now, let’s have a look at a few things, and then I’ll take you around the yard and introduce you to some of the staff.’

Before her parents had left, there’d been little contact with the yard staff, but now two hours passed in a blur of activity with constant interruptions from people who worked on the farm, and those who had questions to ask. By far the largest number of visitors to the little office were people who dropped in to have a sight of the new girl, their excuses for being there thin, to say the least. Curiosity rippled through the small community. The telephone rang as well, but her aunt handled the calls.

'It's coming up to eleven. Let's have a rest,' she said a little while later, laying down the pen she'd just filled and screwing the cap back on a bottle of blue Quink.

'I'm exhausted already,' said Tegan, slightly ashamed of the fact.

'That's because it's all new to you. You'll soon settle down.'

They walked back into the house and entered a small, blue morning room she'd not been in before. A pale cream and blue Chinese rug spread across the polished parquet floor and two blue, silk-covered armchairs flanked the fireplace. A couple of small landscapes hung on the wall, but much of the wall space was taken up with bookcases packed with volumes of all shapes and sizes. This was different from their workmanlike office. A fire crackled and sparked behind a guard which Mona removed as she invited her guest to sit down. But Tegan twirled around, taking everything in and peering at some of the books.

'This is my personal sitting room,' Mona was saying as the door opened, and the coffee was brought in.

'It's beautiful,' said Tegan, 'and it's so feminine.'

The shelves were crammed with literature of all kinds. Several of the books lay in small piles where they couldn't fit in, and very few were in pristine condition. These were books that were read and cherished, not just decoration. She caught sight of a whole shelf of poetry. Her aunt was evidently a great reader. When did she find the time?

‘Oh, you’ve got Byron and Keats, my absolute favourites. I love them.’

Back in Colombia, during their early teens, Tegan and her two best friends had mined the English romantic poets for the excitement and exoticism they longed to find in their own lives, pouring over translations into Spanish, while Tegan read the original English.

‘There are some modern writers as well. You’re welcome to borrow any books. Come on, do sit down.’

‘You’re very organised. Do you always have coffee at the same time?’

‘Yes – and I do have to be organised. Bethan knows my routine.’ She smiled at the grey-haired housekeeper who said, ‘I certainly do.’

‘And she makes sure she’s got everything ready when I come across.’

The woman set things down and went out, leaving Mona to pour the coffee.

‘Bethan would bring all this to the office if I asked her, but I feel it’s a good idea to have a break – and everyone knows they won’t find me there between eleven and half past.’

‘What about Uncle George? I haven’t seen him out in the fields or the stables. Is he a farmer too, or does he leave it to you?’

Mona’s infectious laugh rang out.

‘George! Oh, no. George is in business and does rather well out of it. If forced, he can just about get on the back of a horse – that’s as far as he goes with the farm. But now, he wants to be an MP – Member of Parliament,’ she added, at Tegan’s questioning look. ‘He’s going to try to get elected in this constituency. It worries me a little because we don't have unlimited funds and, no matter what he says, these things cost money. With the elections early next year, he's very busy learning the ropes, and you'll find he's often up in London during the week.'

'It sounds as if it's a good thing that you like the farming.'

'Oh, yes. It means he can stay away and be certain he'll come back to a smooth-running household and no unexpected worries to deal with. No, George was never meant to be a farmer.'

'Like my brother,' said Tegan. 'He's very clever. He's only a few years older than me, but he already has a doctorate and works at the university in Bogotá. He'd be hopeless on the farm and hates to organise people. He doesn't even ride that well.'

She tried to keep the scorn from her voice because she loved her brother and admired him for lots of things. But it really was a drawback, a mystery in a boy brought up in the country. How was it he didn't ride?

'It's a good thing your parents recognize that he's different and aren't trying to push him into farming. You have to love the life, don't you agree? You can't just do it like any other job.' She took a sip of coffee. 'But you do like the farm, I take it?'

'I do. I already help Papá with it. He's had a temporary farm manager in, while he's been over here, and my cousin's replacing me while I'm in Wales, but Alfonso, well, he's great with horses but he's a bit lazy, so I'm not sure how the rest of the year will work out.'

Twenty minutes later, they were back in the office. There seemed to be a lull in the activity, so Tegan opened the typing book and studied the diagram of the keyboard for a few moments. It didn't look too complicated. She'd soon master it.

'Aunt Mona, can you show me how to put the paper into the typewriter properly, and I'll have a go at this.'

Full of confidence, she got down to work straight away, tapping away at speed, but after the tenth time of producing utter rubbish, it came to her that it really was like the piano – your fingers learned the various configurations, and gradually, you put it all together. Heaving a sigh of frustration, she went back to the beginning, a frown on her face as she practised again a few simple little exercises. This time, there was a determined set to her shoulders.

'Sorry, I didn't hear,' she said half an hour later, when her aunt spoke to her as she replaced the telephone receiver on its cradle.

'Could you run an errand for me tomorrow morning, Tegan? I usually go to see Olive Jones on a Thursday, to check she's all right. She's getting quite elderly, you see. But I've just had a call which means I may be stuck here most of the day. Could you help me?'

'Of course. How do I get there? Shall I ride?'

Relieved to find horses on the farm, Tegan had chosen Thunder, a big grey animal with white markings. She was used to the dainty bay mare she rode at home and had thought him quite an ugly brute. But as they got to know one another, she found she was enjoying his personality – now that she'd worked out that she had to be firm with him.

'I think it'll have to be the Land Rover because I want you to take some things up there for her. Can you drive a Land Rover?'

'Yes, Dad imported a couple. I've often driven them.'

'I thought you'd have Jeeps out there.'

'No. I know there's very little difference, and it probably cost him twice as much to get them over there, but he wouldn't be swayed.'

'Anyway, that's good. It means we can pack in quite a lot of food. We've had a freezer installed in her house and Bethan's made up a few meals. Each meal is labelled and dated. Perhaps you'd be kind enough to put them away for Olive when you've unloaded? Make sure she knows what's there and can get at it easily? Oh, and remind her about taking a meal out early in the morning to defrost before she puts it in the oven.'

Tegan went back to her typing, pounding away at the keyboard until it sounded as if a herd of wild animals was running through the office. Finally, she rolled out the sheet and stared at it critically. Yes, that was a bit better – almost coherent. She'd get this right.

But then, she slowed down, her thoughts on the next day's trip up the mountain. It would be the first time away from the estate since the visit to Cardiff with her parents. And she'd be on her own. She relished the unexpected freedom to come.

Chapter 7

The road was pitted and potholed. In places, it fell steeply away down the mountainside, so it was a good thing she was driving a Land Rover. Any other vehicle wouldn't have been of much use, especially as it had rained in the night. Water ran in rivulets diagonally across the track, filled up potholes the depth of which you couldn't imagine, and dripped from the branches that closed overhead, forming a gloomy, wet tunnel of dark shadows under the trees.

It was good to see a few rays of light were now finding their way through, so the sun must be shining above the tree canopy. Tegan steered around a patch of sodden ground, and the vehicle rose over a large stone before thudding down on the far side. She changed gear and the engine whined as she followed the road around the next corner, but she had to stop almost immediately. Every foot of the track was choked with sheep, making it completely impassable. In seconds, the vehicle filled with their bleating and baaing, and their particular sour smell soon stung her nose.

It was so concentrated, a smell she'd noticed quite a lot since she'd come to Wales, up here in these hills. There were sheep everywhere, but at least her aunt's large garden was fragrant with spring flowers, and the animals were kept well away from the house.

A movement caught her eye across the space. A man in a wax jacket stood at an open gate. A black and white dog, with brown patches of fur at its head and neck, was running crazily around after the sheep. It took a few moments before she realised the dog was driving the flock forward into a field and then running back down the track to round up those that escaped, and they seemed intent on doing just that. It was amazing, the way the animal worked, apparently without needing instruction from its owner. They sometimes used dogs with the cattle at home, but this creature was in a class of its own.

The man seemed not to have noticed her. He was working with the dog, his full attention on the flock. Suddenly, he took off his jacket and hooked it onto a post and was soon heading towards a section of fence further up, on the right side of the road. Tegan watched what was going on, absently admiring the wide shoulders and the athletic way he hopped over the wooden bars. She couldn't help but be curious.

He looked good, in the tough, masculine way she associated with cowboys and ranch workers, well put together, tall with floppy black hair – and younger than she'd first imagined. Clean-shaven, too, which was a plus. In her country, a substantial number of men appeared not to be able to grow a beard at all, so she wasn't used to it. There were a lot of hairy men in Wales.

And he was sexy. Her heart gave a little flip, and her attention became more focused. Maybe life on a remote Welsh farm was about to get a bit more interesting.

This was intriguing. What on earth could he be doing? His head descended and then disappeared down the slope. She had to know what was going on, and it was perfectly reasonable to go and find out, since she was stuck here for the moment. And he was the reason she couldn't move on.

She checked the handbrake and got out. Water everywhere. Picking her way around the puddles across to the spot where he'd vanished, she took great care to avoid damaging the stylish new boots she'd bought in London during her brief stay there with her parents. To her dismay, the fine tan leather was already getting stained a darker brown, and she stooped to wipe the toes, but it achieved nothing. In future she'd find something more suitable to tuck her jeans in – maybe like the green wellingtons the farmer was wearing. That was probably normal footwear around here since it rained all the time. She hadn't really given it any thought this morning.

It *was* a damp little country, at least so recent experience led her to believe.

Looking over the railings, she saw only the tops of bushes and trees. The bank descended steeply, and she leaned further over the fence but there was no sign of him. Then, came a flickering movement a long way below where she stood, suddenly he reappeared, head down, climbing back up the slope with a lamb under his right arm, using his other hand to catch at bushes and branches and haul himself up towards the track.

'Want some help?' she called as he came closer.

He looked up and Tegan was startled by the current that seemed to hover between them as she gazed into the fierce blue eyes immediately below. He didn't answer for a moment as he pulled himself up to her level, but then he said, 'Well, you can take this little chap for me, if you don't mind. It'll save me a walk to the stile.'

She'd spoken in English, and he'd replied in the same language. He had a delicious voice, unexpectedly deep, with a definite lilt that told of his Welsh origins. Gosh she'd been staring! How embarrassing. Looking away, she said weakly, 'Yes, all right,' and held out her arms.

Having reached the top of the bank now, he gently handed over the little lamb. It was bleating with all its might, distressed no doubt at being parted from its mother. How could so much noise come from such a small creature? She'd never been close to a sheep before. It was filthy and it stank. But although Tegan didn't consider herself the sentimental type, she had to admit it was the sweetest little animal.

He was watching her. '*Cwtch*,' he said, climbing up onto a flat stone by the fence post. 'Sweet.'

'*Cwtch*,' she agreed, smiling.

A moment later, he vaulted the fence again with the ease of long practice. '*Diolch.* Thank you.'

Okay, they were speaking Welsh. Fine.

'Why have you got them all out here on the road.'

'I'm driving them up from the valley to the farm for the summer.'

'Why's that? Don't they stay all year on the farm?'

'It's too cold, especially during lambing. You risk losing quite a few of them.' He shrugged on his jacket. 'Come on, let's get this little chap back to mother – if you want to see, that is.'

'Oh yes. It's fascinating.'

He laughed. 'I've never thought of it like that before!'

Then he whistled. The dog, who had now got all of the sheep through the gate and was standing guard, turned its head momentarily and pricked up its ears. But she could see its eyes went straight back to the sheep. It had responsibilities and it wasn't going to default on them. The silly animals milled around, obviously ready to come pouring back out through the gate again, if he gave them the chance. She followed the farmer, pushing through the tightly-packed bodies, and he uttered some low-voiced command. The dog stayed where it was.

She could tell straight away which ewe had lost her baby. A piteous bleating greeted them, and the lamb began to struggle in her arms. He took it from her and placed the tiny creature on the ground, and straight away, it bounded up to its mother, clearly responding to her voice. A moment later, it was under her flank, sucking vigorously at a dangling teat.

'You're not familiar with sheep, I take it.'

She grinned. 'I think it's safe to say that.'

'Are you staying hereabouts?'

'Yes, at Court Farm. Do you know the people there?'

'Of course. Mona's my nearest neighbour, except for Olive – who I assume you're on your way to visit.'

She noticed George didn't get a mention. Perhaps, not being a farmer, he wasn't important in this supremely agricultural area.

She held out her hand. '*Tegan Lewis dw i.*'

'Hywel Davies.'

They shook hands. His palm was warm and dry. As they touched, a tingling sensation went straight up her arm and seemed to invigorate her whole being. Her heart gave a lurch. He was an attractive man, not handsome like Luís, but something more … she couldn't find the word, but she most definitely felt the force of his appeal.

'Sorry. I have to get on with this.'

As he spoke, he nodded in the direction of the sheep, and the dog waiting patiently at the gate. 'Shall I be seeing you again?'

'Yes,' she said. 'Probably. I'm going to be with them for a while.'

As he turned away to lock the gate, she walked slowly back to the Land Rover, disgusted with herself. How pathetic! Where was the sparkling girl that usually had boys – and men – hanging on her every word? Suddenly, she'd forgotten how to command the situation, or even the right words to use. Instead, she felt weak and a little trembly.

And she'd utterly failed to hold his attention when it mattered. And it did matter. She couldn't deny the attraction she'd felt. She had to see him again. She had to. She must find out about him and then she'd make sure to meet him. No-one had affected her like that before.

It was only a few moments before a sense of reality trickled into her thoughts, and with it a few unpleasant ideas. She really was stupid not to think of it – of course, he must already have a girlfriend. This unwelcome possibility popped into her mind as she reached the Land Rover. Surely, such a good-looking man could not live alone, could he? There must be many girls living in the valley and at least a few of them had to have found their way to his mountain eyrie. Although, come to think of it, she hadn't met any. Ah – what if he was already married? In farming country, people married young.

Where did he say he lived? Had he even said?

Suddenly, the visit to Olive Jones acquired a new importance and she wondered what she might be able to find out. Maybe the old woman would enjoy having a talk. Old ladies were partial to a good gossip, so she would encourage that. Reminded of her errand, she glanced at her watch; it was almost midday, and she hadn't even got there.

She looked down as she prepared to get back inside the vehicle. A brown slime was stuck to the front of her new suede jacket.

She found an old rag on the floor and tried to clean it off, but the stuff seemed to cling – and it stank. Disgusted, she pulled the jacket off and threw it onto the passenger seat. Then, she turned on the ignition and released the handbrake. As the Land Rover moved cautiously forward, she was suddenly keen to arrive at her destination.

The lane twisted and turned, climbing all the time. Although the distance was relatively short, the many hair-pin bends meant that she had to take it slowly. No doubt the farmer and his dog would be able to follow a more direct route on foot through the fields, but it was all she could do to keep the vehicle on the track.

Finally, a stone-built cottage appeared on her right. An electricity cable looped over the trees before it swooped down to the building, and she remembered what her aunt had said about the freezer. Then it snaked on, slung from post to post, up to a point where it disappeared over a col. Maybe that was where the sheep farm was situated, down the other side.

She'd come back up here on horseback and explore, just as soon as she could get the time to do it.

Chapter 8

As the Land Rover drove off, Hywel Davies shut the gate and strode up the field, his dog at his heels. He was not going to look back – why should he? But after a moment, that's exactly what he did. She'd gone, but her green-eyed gaze and strawberry-blonde hair were as clear to him as if she stood right there in front of him, and that fact disturbed him.

He clicked another gate shut and stood there for a moment, lost in thought.

Where had she come from? Mona hadn't said anything about taking anyone on. But now he remembered something about her secretary being ill. It was a big farm and Mona would need the help. Maybe this girl was standing in for Mary.

She seemed utterly unlike any of the girls he usually met, no mere farm girl; she was kind of poised, as if she had a lot of confidence but at the same time, she had a fresh open manner that was very appealing. Too much so for his peace of mind. He didn't have time for this.

Hurrying across the grass, he arrived at the quarry fence in time to snatch up another lamb intent on jumping to its death. He rejoined Finn and the flock.

What had she said when he'd suggested they might meet again? Probably. That wasn't too encouraging. Yet she didn't appear shy. Maybe it meant she didn't like the look of him. She'd had the sheen of money and worldly experience. He looked down at his mud-covered boots and worn jacket. That was it – he wasn't in her league.

He sighed as he worked out what his next step might be. But what on earth was he doing, thinking about next steps, when he could barely cope with what was going on in the present? He frowned, trying to push away the inconvenient thoughts. Yet he knew there'd been an instant connection between them. If he wanted proof, he could still feel the warmth in his hand from her grasp. Or was that just imagination?

No, he wasn't wrong about it. For the first time in a very long time, he had that heightened awareness that told him this was something special, but he shrugged his shoulders, remembering the expensive clothes and the glow of good health, the way she looked as if she'd been reared on only the best that life could offer. He couldn't be doing with someone high maintenance. His life was difficult enough as it was. It was best to forget her.

Finn barked again, returning him to the present. Unlike his master, the dog had been working all the time and was now calling him over to open the next gate. They needed to move the flock up the hill quickly. This field had far too many holes in the hedges, and the dry-stone walls had fallen in places, even though he'd repaired yards of fencing after a particularly bad winter. Of course, the priority had been the boundary that corralled the animals higher up the mountain.

But a deep quarry began just a few hundred yards away from where they stood, and the work wasn't finished yet. Finn was now pushing the wanderers towards the gate, and when Hywel signalled to him again, they drove the sheep forward together.

Half an hour later, they arrived. He cast a glance over to the edge of the field. Here, too, it bordered the quarry, and the danger to the sheep was all too obvious, reminding him of the need to check this stretch as soon as he could find the time. Dan had been working on it, and had said he'd finished, but he could be a bit slow. The weather constantly eroded this part of the mountain surface, the quarry evidence of an ancestor's enterprise. Now, where the stone had been cut away, the fence work was ongoing.

Half past twelve. The old man would be up by now. It was time he got back.

The broken leg, encased right to the top of the thigh, was proving a major problem. Not only could his father not work but he even needed help to get around the house. He was supposed to be lying flat on his bed, but he was a difficult patient, and confining him to his bed was a complete impossibility.

Hywel sighed again and rubbed his eyes. A bone-deep weariness came from carrying the work of the farm on his own during the last weeks, with just the one labourer to help – and one who was none-too-quick on the uptake, at that. It was no use thinking about the bewitching eyes of the girl with the red-gold curls because he was never going to have time to do anything about it. He had to get back to work. He made for the final gate at the top end of the field and opened it. Spotting what looked like a break in the fence, he went over to check, but Dan had repaired it. He walked back to where Finn was channelling the last of the sheep through, and sighed as he closed it behind the last one. It would be nice not to have to do this.

She hadn't answered his question about Olive, he thought a couple of minutes later, unable to tear her from his mind. She'd probably just been exploring, couldn't have been around long or he'd have met her before. There'd been a Young Farmers social down in Crickhowell just a couple of weeks ago – before Dad's accident, when he'd still had time to go to such things – and she'd not been at that.

Again, he forced his thoughts back to work.

'Could you have a go at the accounts, Dad?' he'd said the evening before. 'If you're not in too much pain.' He'd get Dad set up with them this afternoon. There was nothing wrong with his brain and the sooner they could get them down to the accountant in Newport, the better. Especially as he had plans for the farm and wanted to know where they stood financially. It would help if his father could take that task off his hands.

Finn trotted ahead of him along the narrow path and then waited, casting a look which told him he'd better get a move on. The dog was hungry. They both were.

It'd been good of Mona to provide the freezer. She'd had to pay an undisclosed amount to the electricity board to get a powerline up the mountain and his dad had got them to extend it through to their own property by paying another, all-too-noticeable sum, which had practically emptied the account. At least, they'd been able to say good-bye to the oil lamps, and the generator was now just insurance, in case the power failed.

This was the right time to think of building the lambing shed on that plot behind the house. That had been their main reason for bringing in the electricity.

'We could keep the sheep up on the farm the whole year round and feeding them in winter would take half the time, Dad. Just think of the difference lambing in the shed would make to the survival rate. We might make some money for once.'

That's why good accounts were so important: they'd have to borrow money.

Those plans had been a breath of fresh air, a sign of hope after months of difficulties. It was a pity about Dad's accident. It didn't look now as if there was much chance of a new shed, at least not if things continued the way they were. There was no money for big projects and the accident had shaken his father's confidence. It was a hard life on the mountain and Hywel wondered privately if he'd ever be fit enough to get back to work.

*

Finn came bounding up, eager for a rub around the ears, recognition that he'd done a good job. Together, they went into the house.

'Hi Dad, you in there?'

Hywel took off his boots and walked in stockinged feet through to the huge farm kitchen at the back.

'Yeah, the food's ready.'

With its thick stone walls and a floor made of slate, it would have felt very cold had it not been for the large kitchen range fitted into the ancient fireplace. Although they were nearly into May now, they were still lighting it every day. It was the last thing they'd done to the house before his mother died, when he was twelve. She'd struggled for years with the original range, using it for heating and for cooking as well. Before the new one, she'd rarely managed to get the temperature of the house up to a decent level in winter. It was sad she'd died just a year after it was installed, and never really enjoyed the benefit of it.

Tom Davies was seated in a deep chair by the fire. It was an old thing, the brown leather cracked and buttons missing from decades of use. Hywel had intended to throw it out, but with the broken leg, it was the only place his father felt reasonably comfortable, and he'd retrieved it from the barn.

'You managed on your own, Dad?'

Hywel pushed his feet into the house shoes he kept warming by the range.

'Of course, I did.'

'That's good. I hope you haven't been doing too much. You have to rest.'

'Can't rely on you for everything, son. Get all the sheep up, did you?'

'Yes, that's the last of them.'

'I've been thinking. You know, maybe it's time for me to retire and you to take over. You're pretty much running things as it is.'

‘You’re not there yet, Dad. You’ll get better.’

He wanted to shut down the discussion because he had to think through all the issues, but maybe his father was right. He was only fifty but looked twenty years older. His black hair, once identical to Hywel’s was now thinning and streaked with grey. They were about the same height, just under six feet, but his father’s shoulders were bowed. It was too hard a life.

‘Maybe, instead of building a lambing shed, we should just sell up.’

‘What are you talking about, Hywel?’

‘Look, the farm could interest some weekend farmer with romantic ideas about the countryside. I’ve heard of people doing that over in North Wales.’

And what would he do then? He was a farmer and the family had worked this land for three hundred years, if the records were to be believed, and probably centuries before that. How could he give it up? He had no other skills, and to be honest, he liked farming, and he was good at it. But it killed so many men before their time.

‘It would be a big risk, true. We’ll have to think hard about whether it could work.’

No woman in her right mind would accept a life like this. He had a fleeting vision of the girl with the green eyes. Then he thought of Caitlin who hadn’t hesitated for a second to take him on.

But his father hadn’t finished. ‘No, you can’t do that, boy. This is our home and livelihood. We’ll find a way.’

That was all very well, but he couldn’t let things go on as they were. It was time for a radical rethink. And, whether his father retired or not, he'd be no help for weeks yet. He'd start by paying a visit to Mona to see if he could hire a labourer from her. Most of the single men didn't mind a summer up in the hills. And they had more than enough room in the house to put a man up.

'Can you have a look at those accounts, Dad? It's becoming urgent.'

'Of course. You have to stop worrying about everything, son. At the moment, your job is the animals. Leave the rest to me.'

So he would. And he mustn't forget to drop in on Olive later in the day, to check on how she was getting along, just in case – what was her name? – Tegan hadn't in fact been on her way to pay her a visit. Damn, he was going soft in the head. He should have asked her again and maybe saved himself a journey.

Later, as he stood under the shower he'd rigged up, he felt just a little more cheerful.

Chapter 9

'Come in! Come in!'

Without giving Tegan a chance to explain about the food she'd brought, Olive ushered her down a narrow hallway into a room at the back of the single-story building and had her sit down straight away, while she brought the kettle to the boil.

Tegan looked around. It was a dark, pokey little house, the windows too small, the ceilings too low, and the floor was covered in a linoleum that imitated parquet blocks. They were probably placed over stone flags, not allowing them to breathe, which would account for that smell of damp. The old woman had spread an assortment of coloured rugs across the tiny living room floor, in an attempt to brighten it up. It looked clean and tidy, and every available surface carried pictures of babies, children, and young people.

'My nieces and nephews,' said Olive, seeing the direction of Tegan's gaze. 'I never married myself, but I have seven nieces and four nephews. The eldest is thirty-eight now, with three of his own. He manages the Boots shop down in Newport. Here he is.' Full of pride, she handed Tegan one of the few coloured photographs in the sea of black and white.

Olive went into the kitchen and reappeared with a tray. The tea looked like tar. Tegan watched her ladling in spoonsful of sugar and followed suit, feeling it was the only way she'd be able to drink it. The old lady prised open a biscuit tin, her swollen fingers quivering.

'Help yourself. I like to offer visitors my own cooking, but I just haven't been up to it, so it'll have to be these,' she said, dismissing Court Farm's best efforts. 'Must say, it's nice to see a fresh face. Mona's niece, did you say? The one from South America? What's brought you over here, then?'

The colour rushed into Tegan's cheeks. What did the woman know about her and her family? If she started on about finding a husband in Wales, they'd soon fall out.

'Well, my parents were keen for me to see a bit of the world and understand something of my background. I didn't want to come at first but now I'm here, I'm enjoying it.' Change the subject.

'How do you know my family?'

'Mae'n iawn. It's all right,' she said. 'We all know each other around here. I worked for your da's family and then at Court Farm all my life. I remember him as a little lad. He always had it in him to do some great things, and I understand from the Lady Mona that he's doubled the size of your farm out there.'

'That's certainly true,' said Tegan. 'It's expanding all the time. That's why he needs me, especially as my brother isn't interested.'

Relieved at the direction of the conversation, she took a sip of the tea, but her lip burned, and she put the cup down quickly. 'So, what did you do, before you came to live in this house?'

'I was personal maid to the Lady Mona when she was just plain Miss Mona and your da was still here in the valley. That was in the days when people still had personal maids, mind, back in the thirties.'

'I can't imagine my aunt having a maid. She works so hard.'

'Yes, but things were different before the war, and people like us considered ourselves lucky if we could get that sort of job, especially with a decent family like hers. It was clean work, and we got to handle the fine objects and dresses – not like the lower orders, the kitchen maids and such-like Then she married Sir George when she was eighteen and, though he had the grand house and title, he didn't have a penny to his name, so she's had no choice but to work hard.' She paused to draw breath and then rattled on. 'Mind you, Mona never had no time for titles and all that flummery. She just seemed to fall for him.'

It was obvious the old lady couldn't get her mind around such a strange idea.

'You're right," said Tegan. 'She's very straightforward. I noticed everyone calls her Mona or Missus, even the farm hands.'

'Anyway, she couldn't afford luxuries like personal maids so eventually, I had to go and work in the kitchen.'

'That must have been hard for you – a bit of a come-down, as well.'

'Wasn't so bad. I was still young, and I worked my way up to housekeeper in no time, mind you. By the time the war broke out, we'd become a military convalescent home and were hosting RAF officers. Oh, and some of the scientists from that place down the road. All very secret it was. And I was in charge of the catering.'

There was pride and more than a trace of regret in her voice. It must have been an exciting time in her life. The Second World War had ended almost exactly twenty years earlier. Olive couldn't be much beyond sixty now, although she looked a lot older. She would've been in her prime during the war and she'd have loved the bustle and the sense of contributing. Probably, nothing since had come up to that level of interest and excitement.

'It sounds as if you've had an interesting life, but it must have given you a lot of work.'

'Oh, it did but we all enjoyed it. So many people around, so many nice boys. And the younger girls – well, there was quite a buzz, I can tell you.'

Her eyes twinkled and colour came into her cheeks, as she told her stories to her new audience.

Tegan had to be patient. If only she could steer the conversation onto the surrounding area and to wherever the young man of her morning encounter lived. But the old lady needed a chance to talk about what she had on her mind. Probably, she spent a lot of time on her own. Tegan tried to concentrate on what the woman was saying, and it was truly fascinating to hear about the various people in the area, some of whom she'd already met, but it was almost impossible not to think of the young farmer.

'It was a different world then, but don't go getting any romantic ideas about the relationship between masters and servants. Our life was hard.'

It sounded as if it had not been that different from the way they treated people who worked for them on the ranch at home – not badly, just always ensuring there was a certain distance between them. For the first time, she asked herself what it felt like if you were that other person, the worker?

One thing she'd discovered on arriving in her aunt's house was that the housekeeper, the farm hands, everyone who worked there got the same respect from her aunt. She was friendly and she cared for them if they were in trouble. The distance was about allowing people their privacy rather than underlining her superiority. And in return, they all worked hard for her. South America was way behind Europe in the way things were done, but the world was changing, and she'd learn from her aunt.

'Then, a couple of years ago, it was all getting a bit much for me, what with the arthritis, so I stopped working and the Lady Mona looks after me. She's a lovely woman.'

'Yes, I heard about the freezer. Look, that reminds me. I've brought a whole lot of food to fill it, made in the kitchens at the farm, so you can feed yourself until you're feeling better. Show me where things are, and I'll put it away. We shouldn't leave it outside to defrost.'

She made her escape and returned with two large cool boxes. Olive took her into the very old-fashioned kitchen she'd glimpsed from where they'd been sitting. There was a dresser with the good china, but otherwise, there were no cupboards, just worktops with the area below them hidden by red and white gingham curtains matching those at the tiny window. A mottled blue, cast iron gas stove on iron feet with a white oven door stood half-way along one wall and a single tap brought water to a large white porcelain sink. Red quarry tiles covered the floor. It was dated rather than charming. But once again it was clean.

A relatively small freezer had been placed on the workbench, so that the old lady could easily reach inside without the need to bend down to floor level. It lent the kitchen an incongruous note of modernity, but it would certainly do the job. While she transferred the food packs, Olive put the kettle back on and made more tea, leaving it to brew until Tegan had finished.

Sitting opposite her hostess, she stirred the contents of her cup, which looked even blacker than the previous one, and gave it a try. Mmm … not bad. She could learn to drink tea like this.

'Of course, there's always Mr Davies if I have a problem. He keeps an eye on me.'

'Mr Davies? Would that be the sheep farmer I saw on the way up here?'

'Yes, that'll have been the son, of course. Old Tom's no good for anything now he's had the accident …'

She was off again, and Tegan waited until at last, she apparently ran out of words. It took a long time, and they'd finished the second cup before she managed to say, 'The farm must be close if he visits you so often.'

'Yes, this cottage is on the edge of his land. About half a mile from the farmhouse, just over the mountain. He and Mona set it up for me between them. It's good of him to come, I grant you. I get frightened sometimes, you know, when I'm not feeling so good. At least I can be sure someone will find me if I have a fall.'

She was so vulnerable, despite that stubborn streak of independence.

Then, Tegan looked at her watch. Oh, no! Several hours had gone by. She'd wasted so much time and it was now mid-afternoon. But it didn't matter – she was using her own time, although she really hadn't intended to be away so long. She glanced out of the window; it would get dark quickly under the trees. If she didn't get on the road soon, she might lose her way or drive straight over the edge on those hairpins. She stood up.

'I'll have to go now. It's late.'

'So, I'll be seeing you again, will I? I've enjoyed our little talk.'

'I'll look forward to it,' said Tegan, clasping the frail old woman's gnarly hand. 'Is there anything I can bring you when I come next time?'

'I'm running out of canvas and silks for my embroidery, if you can get hold of some for me,' she said. She pulled a half-finished piece of work out of a wicker basket which stood on the table. 'See here, this is for Mona's birthday, a surprise, so it's better if I don't ask her to get them. It's a couple of months yet but I want to make sure I finish it in time. Anyway, she's already got too much on her plate to be running errands for me. It's a picture, see,' she said as she spread it flat on the table. 'Mind you, she'll have to get it framed.'

While Olive cut strands of different colours and a little square of the material so she would know what to look for, Tegan took the work in her hands. As she studied it, it shimmered in the late afternoon light now slanting through the narrow window. This was no printed piece of canvas with a sew-by-numbers picture. The intricate design of flowers with curling tendrils looked like the classic work on old tapestries. It must have been drawn on the fine linen by Olive herself.

'You did this?' she asked. 'It's beautiful.'

The old woman had to be in a lot of pain from her arthritis, and yet the work was exquisite.

'It's just something I've always done.'

'I'll get some silks when I go into town. I hope I'll see you soon, but it all depends on my aunt and whether she can give me time off.'

That was true, of course, but she wasn't being completely honest. There was something else exerting its pull on her now. She had every intention of finding her way back up the mountain, and the sooner the better – however much work her aunt had in store for her.

Chapter 10

Over several days, Tegan had received half a dozen postcards from her parents, and when the telephone rang one evening, she hurried to pick up, certain it would be for her. They would still be in York, and it would be lovely to have a talk with them.

'Hello, Dad. Tell me what you've been doing. Have you seen our Yorkshire cousins yet?'

When she'd caught up with what they'd been doing, they wanted to know how she was getting on.

'Everyone's looking after me and it feels like being at home. And I love Aunt Mona, Dad. She does remind me of you. She makes me laugh, just like you do.'

She wanted to give them all her news and reassure them that, yes, she really was all right.

'… honestly, Mamá, I'm fine. Dad sounds well, too.'

She'd thought often about her mother and father, and wondered how the tour was going, but she'd been here without them for several weeks now, and strangely, she didn't miss life on the ranch. In the end, it was the people who mattered. Her mother demanded a minutely-detailed account of how she was spending her days. Maybe allowing their daughter to live on the other side of the world for a year was harder for them than for her, now that both their children had left home. Tegan had never given that any thought.

'Please don't worry. I'll be fine and I'll write lots.'

She murmured further reassuring words and again promised to write. Slowly, she replaced the receiver, her mind on the conversation. It was true that she had settled in. And the last couple of weeks had been great; she was enjoying the moment and learning new skills. What a struggle it had been with the typing at first! She grinned at how inept she'd been and how frustrated when it wouldn't go the way she wanted.

But her aunt had been right, and she was glad now that she'd persevered. She could type a letter with no mistakes in just a few minutes. It was a tiny victory, important to no-one but her, but she was quite proud of it. Already she was doing more things in the estate office without supervision. Aunt Mona could leave her to compose a letter, and these days, though it took her a long time, she almost never had to hand it back to redo before signing. And, listening in on how Mona dealt with callers, Tegan had soon got the hang of business telephone calls.

She admired Mona and considered her a good farm manager. 'I'm so envious of how you talk to people and how much they like you.'

'It's all about giving them the respect they deserve. And you do learn from working with people. You're doing very well, Tegan.'

Tegan had found herself copying her aunt's manner, friendly but professional, particularly when dealing with the people who worked for her, or someone who might drop into the office with an invoice. Although the farm and the environment were so different from at home, all this experience was going to be very useful when she went back to Colombia. She'd be able to take on more of the administrative side of things.

For the first time since the idea had been put forward, she was grateful to her parents for persuading her to come to Wales. And she worked hard because to do anything less would be an insult to her energetic boss.

But she also rode out at least once a day and was gradually meeting new people. In fact, everything was perfect. Except that she'd seen nothing further of the intriguing Mr Davies.

How could she get to see him? There had to be a way.

She mused on those intelligent blue eyes. What a pity she'd not had a chance to meet him again. There was definitely a spark of interest. She'd felt it. But she hadn't seen him even once since that meeting on the track, and now she wondered if she'd got things wrong.

'Penny for them,' said Mona.

'Sorry?'

'It's what we say when someone's lost in thought – a penny for your thoughts. Is anything wrong?'

Tegan felt the colour rise in her cheeks. 'Oh, no – I … er, I was just going over the telephone call with Mamá and Dad last night, thinking how good you are to me.'

'I'm not having to work too hard at that, my dear girl. You've been an absolute godsend. And you've learned so quickly.'

'I'm really enjoying myself.'

It was great she could say that with complete honesty. A few short weeks ago, she couldn't have imagined she would feel so comfortable here.

It was Wednesday, and they were indulging in their morning cup of coffee in the elegant, little sitting room, taking a breath after a busy couple of hours.

'I've decided to lend Joe to the Davies farm for the summer to help Hywel out.'

This was interesting.

'Oh?' She tried not to sound as if it mattered too much. 'Is that because of Mr Davies having an accident? I heard about that from Olive.'

'That's right. Hywel's desperate and wants him to start as soon as we can let him go.' The name Hywel had a good sound; it was a strong, Welsh name she hadn't come across before meeting him.

But Mona was telling her what she wanted doing. She'd better pay attention. 'Could you check the schedules? Move people around where you have to and make sure things are covered here. You'll need to talk to everyone concerned, so it'll take you a little while to sort that out. I'll find Joe and tell him he's okay to leave on Friday morning.'

'Won't he mind being sent away like that?'

'No, he's worked for Tom Davies before, and we've already talked about the possibility. Now, to save time and allow him to put in a full day's work, I want you to drive him over there first thing. He lives on his own so he might as well stay up there for the next few weeks. He'll need to take some things with him. I'm sorry but you will have to make an early start.'

Tegan could have hugged Mona. She was sending her up to the farm – and was apologising for it. She'd have started at four in the morning if it meant visiting that farm. 'How early should we leave?'

'Well, shall we say six? Get yourself a hot drink before you go, and have breakfast when you get back.'

Energized by the news that she now had a legitimate reason to go to the Davies farm, Tegan went off, humming a favourite tune. Oh, wait a minute! Maybe the situation wasn't that good. Hywel Davies must have been at Court Farm in the past few days in order to set this up with Mona. And she hadn't seen him. It was possible he had a telephone, but she didn't think so, since the electricity had only recently arrived up the mountain.

So why hadn't he made more of an effort to see her? Did that mean he wasn't interested? Or had he dropped in, and she'd missed him? It was true, if he was desperate for help on the farm, he wouldn't have hung around. And of course, she'd been out riding every afternoon, for quite long periods of time. It was probably her fault she'd not seen him. But she couldn't stay in every day in the vain hope that he'd turn up.

The image of Luís suddenly floated into her mind. It was funny how she'd completely forgotten his existence until this moment. Weeks had passed since she'd thought of him. How was that possible when she'd loved him? But so much had happened since she'd left Colombia, and she'd spent every moment processing the events. There hadn't been time to think about what had gone before, which was a bit sad. But it did mean he belonged in the past.

Hywel didn't have his smooth, slim good looks and vivacious manner, and he was probably a few years older than Luís. His hands were calloused, and the beginnings of lines around his eyes were evidence of his hard, outdoor life. He looked as if he had some life experience, but that only added to what was already a very attractive face. Even thinking about him made her heart beat faster. She had well and truly outgrown Luís, and now she wondered what she had ever seen in him.

*

Several hours later, Tegan closed the door to her room and plumped down on the stool in front of her dressing table. The day had been very busy with a lot to organise to cover the fact that they were going to be a man down on the farm.

Her mind still on Hywel, she stared into the mirror. They'd met exactly once, and suddenly he filled her life. What was it about Hywel Davies that had affected her so deeply? He was different, and that had aroused her curiosity, but it was something more than that; she hadn't been mistaken about the fizzle of electricity between them. Her stomach clenched as she thought of how that had felt. She was sure he'd felt it too.

That resolve she'd made only a few weeks earlier to avoid all romantic entanglements – she seemed to be abandoning it. It was hard to judge, but this had the look of something serious.

She was still thinking about her changed circumstances as she set her alarm clock later that evening. So far, every day had been different. She liked working on a farm in a small community. There was plenty going on and she'd met a lot of people as she rushed about on her aunt's behalf. But sadly, no girls of her own age.

Still, she'd written to her friends in Colombia, catching them up on what she was doing, though she hadn't mentioned Hywel. She'd keep him to herself for the time being. Besides, there was nothing to report. She'd been so busy, and the work was so varied that she rarely had to spend a full morning at her desk. That was just the way she liked things.

She got into bed, switching on the little transistor radio her parents had given her as a present when they left, but keeping the volume low. There was a Beatles number playing. It was a bit soppy: 'I wanna hold your hand,' they sang. But it hit exactly the right note, and she gave herself up to her thoughts.

Chapter 11

There was another whole day before the much-anticipated drive up the mountain. On Thursday morning, Mona had an early appointment in Swansea, and was on her way out, as Tegan came down the stairs.

'Walk over to the office with me, will you, Tegan.'

Tegan followed her across the courtyard.

'I'm going to be away all day, so I've left you instructions here for a few letters,' she said, pointing to a small pile of papers and a written list. 'If you could get them ready, you can send them all out yourself, except for the one to Williams & Sons. I'll just give that one a quick readthrough when I get back. Now, I must go.'

While Tegan checked through the pile, Mona hurried out, and two minutes later, the sound of her car engine was fading down the drive.

After breakfast in the main house, Tegan returned to the office. A big tractor trundled by, and then silence rushed in, the courtyard empty. No mist this morning. Sunlight slanted through the windowpanes by Tegan's desk, and she gradually became aware of the electric heater whirring gently, sending dust motes into the air.

It was good to feel she knew what she was doing now. She heaved a big sigh, telling herself that it meant getting on with her work, not idling away the time thinking about Hywel Davies. Anyway, with luck, she'd be seeing him tomorrow, and this time, she wouldn't waste the opportunity. At least she'd find out if he had a wife.

She sat down and completed the letters, checking them through carefully before folding them so that the addresses showed correctly through the envelope windows. She stuck on the stamps. Then she tackled a few jobs, dusted the shelves and tidied the items in her drawers. A tractor engine throbbed in the distance, but it was very quiet. Had everyone realised that Mona was away and decided not to come in? She telephoned the vet and arranged a time for his visit. What now?

That monstrous typewriter was sitting there, beckoning to her in the middle of her desk, so she'd better get down to it. She pulled it toward her. Twenty minutes of exercises each day did seem to increase her speed, and she tried to keep to her schedule, even when she didn't much feel like it.

She didn't feel like it today but told herself she had no choice. She was pretty good at getting words down without mistakes, but the punctuation and numbers nearly always pulled her up short. She sighed again, knowing only further hard practice would do the trick, so she worked on with concentration for half an hour.

Was that an engine outside? She looked up. A white van making its way slowly around the estate office, before stopping by the back door of the main house. The baker.

She lost interest and returned to her exercise but suddenly, someone knocked, and before she could say anything, the door slammed back into the wall and a girl came sauntering in.

Wow! What a surprise. Surely this exotic creature didn't live on the farm.

She was like a fashion plate from the latest Vogue magazine. It was just so weird to see her in the country setting. She wore a geometric-style shift dress, like a Mondrian painting, except it was just black and white, no colour at all. Dark, back-combed hair was held in place by a white band of some stretchy material and the features of her face, admittedly quite lovely, had been enhanced by make-up, long, thick lashes sweeping her cheeks. On her feet were shiny white boots that went up to her knees. It was all so beautifully put together.

'Er … can I help you?' asked Tegan. Was this a business person? But she looked too young for that.

'Hello, I'm Angharad.' She had a wide, warm smile. 'And you must be Tegan, Mona's niece.'

'That's right. I …'

'So, I wondered if you'd like to come out with me for the day. You must be so bored up here, you poor thing. Get to see a bit of the area, maybe go to Newport?'

What a lovely idea. 'That's nice of you. Do you live up here on the farm?' she asked. 'I haven't seen you.'

'Oh, no, I couldn't stick it out here, in the middle of nowhere. I got a lift up with my dad, so I've only got a few minutes. He gets mad if he has to wait around.'

Did this girl work in his shop or on a farm? She was trying to imagine that and totally failed.

Saying nothing further, Angharad began to wander around, touching various objects, lifting things off Mona's desk, which made Tegan feel uncomfortable. Then she turned her back, saying, 'I don't know how you can stand to live in this godforsaken place.'

'It's all right.'

She was trying to see what the girl was doing. Why didn't she leave the desk alone? She was opening Mona's diary now.

'Please don't touch that. It's Mona's.' She waited until she'd replaced the diary. 'Actually, I don't just live here. I work here as well and get paid for it. And it's a pretty good job. But you're right. It would be nice to get away for a while.' Which was true.

Angharad was sitting on Mona's desk now, her legs crossed at the ankles, displaying the beautiful leather boots. Tegan relaxed a little; at least the girl wasn't rifling through her aunt's personal possessions anymore.

And it would be lovely to get together with someone her own age. It would be good to have a friend to exchange gossip with, particularly since she now had something very interesting that she wanted to talk about. She gave a little sigh, sure she wouldn't be able to discuss it with this girl. It didn't sound as if they had much in common, and probably, she couldn't be trusted. But she ought to give it a try.

'What about tomorrow?'

'I'll ask my aunt … Oh, no, I can't. I've already agreed to do something for her.'

'Just say you can't. Say there's something else you have to do.'

‘No, I really can’t do that. She’s relying on me, and I won’t let her down. I already promised.’

A deep frown now marred the flawless features and the corners of the girl’s mouth turned down. She was silent for a moment, clearly working something out. Then she smiled and said, ‘What about Saturday, then? Could you make that? Meet me at half past nine at Abergavenny station. The train gets in at quarter to ten.’

‘That’d be great, I’ll be there.’

‘Good. Oh, there’s Dad. Got to go.’

She gave a little wave and flounced out into the courtyard. The frame shuddered as she flipped the heavy door shut behind her. Tegan stared after her. It was an impressive performance, but not the way she did things.

But how could she know what the girl was like if she didn’t give it a try? She didn’t much like how Angharad had acted. It felt superficial, and she wondered who she was trying to impress. Surely not her? She’d promised to be there on Saturday morning, but already, she had misgivings, wondering what they’d find to talk about, together for a whole day.

On the other hand, it was nice to be invited. She should do her best to make something of the opportunity.

Chapter 12

Joe hadn't said anything for half an hour. Tegan was equally silent as she concentrated on negotiating the difficult mountain road in the dark. She'd gone down to the kitchen just before six and found the man already there, waiting. Downing half a cup of tea, she gathered her things and said, 'If you're ready, Joe, we can go.'

Silent, he picked up a small, blue cardboard suitcase and followed her out to the barn. She'd got the Land Rover ready the evening before, familiarizing herself with the lights and checking there was enough fuel. Once they opened the huge doors, she drove straight out into the yard and onto the track and waited while he closed up. A man of few words and possibly a great deal of trust, Joe clambered in, propped his feet on top of his bag and immediately fell asleep.

The rain, which had continued throughout the night and was still falling, had left everything soaked. It'd been very heavy and had done considerable damage to the road, so Tegan drove slowly and carefully, her headlights occasionally picking out the glassy eyes of animals staring from between the looming trunks of the trees. Twice, she had to wake her passenger for help to remove a fallen branch. On the second occasion, the rain suddenly stopped, and the sky began to grow lighter.

Everything was drenched. God, it was so dreary in the first glimmerings of dawn. But a little while later, her excitement increased. Soon, she'd be seeing Hywel Davies again and this time, it would all go well. She was determined she would leave a better impression.

They passed Olive's cottage. Maybe she'd pop in there on the way back down, just to make sure the old lady was all right. Still rising, they arrived at the col a few minutes later. As they began to drop down the far side, the track twisted around boulders and then opened onto windswept moorland, high up in the mountains.

There was the low-slung, white-washed farmhouse, with clouds scudding across the sky from left to right as the sun finally made a reluctant appearance. The house stood with a group of barns on the right of the track, and over to the left, closer to the next peak, a small cottage was just visible. She drove into the yard as the main door to the house opened. Her heart was beating fast.

It wasn't Hywel. The disappointment was crushing. How could this happen? It was a much older man with hair that was beginning to grey, who'd opened the door as she was bringing the vehicle to a halt. It had to be Hywel's father, waiting there to greet them, but where was his son? The man must have heard their engine labouring along the track, and now he stood, propped up against the door frame, where a light hung from a lintel just above his head. He looked grey with fatigue and pain. A plaster cast encased his left leg, his trouser leg rolled high up the thigh.

Tegan wound down the window and he said, ‘I’m sorry but Hywel’s not here. All this rain’s caused a mudslide, and he’s had to go out to get some of the sheep off the quarry slopes.’

So that was why he was absent.

‘Can we help?’ asked Tegan.

‘Not you, miss.’ He raised his voice. ‘Joe, he said to tell you to get over there as soon as you arrived. You’ll find he’ll have gone down by the burnt tree. I think we may have lost a few head,’ he added, referring to the wandering sheep.

Without comment, Joe pushed his bag across to Tegan for her to put in the house, jumped down from the Land Rover and hurried across to a field gate on the opposite side of the farmyard. Tegan’s eyes followed him for a moment, and then the rain started spitting again as she turned to look at the older man. He was easing himself back into the house and she saw how painful the process was for him.

If Hywel had left in the early hours of the morning, had the invalid had anything to eat or drink? She didn’t know what he could do for himself, encumbered as he was, but at least she could help. She might as well make the best of the situation.

She jumped down, carrying Joe’s bag. ‘Can I put the kettle on?’ she called, hurrying over to follow him in. ‘I wouldn’t mind a cup of tea before I head back if you don’t mind. I didn’t have time for breakfast before we set out. Maybe you’d like something too?’

‘That’s right, miss, I would. Come on in and we can get acquainted.’

The house was very clean and tidy. She liked that. But it was sort of masculine and dark, with none of the pretty fabrics and rugs you'd find if a woman lived here.

Stark. No wife. Not unless she was different from any woman Tegan had ever met.

Ten minutes later, Mr Davies was seated at the kitchen table, his leg propped on a low stool to one side. And somewhat perplexed, Tegan was looking at the gas stove that stood in the corner. She'd never seen such a thing before. How did you get it going?

'Now, light one of those long matches and then press and twist the button at the same time. It's a bit tricky if you don't know the stove.'

With the grill going, she put the kettle on and sorted out cups and plates. Right, now it was glowing red. She popped the slices of bread he'd cut for toast onto the grill tray and slid it underneath.

He'd already given instructions about how to stoke up the big range and a pleasing warmth was beginning to permeate the freezing atmosphere. Tegan glanced at her host, who seemed open and pleasant, and quite relaxed about having this stranger rummage about in his kitchen. He wasn't that old, although at first glance, he'd looked it. But her father had aged very quickly after they'd diagnosed the cancer. Pain could have that effect, though Dad was looking much better these days.

Finally, with a pot of tea and a heaped plate of toast between them, she sat down. For a minute of two, they worked silently through the pile, spreading the butter and thick strawberry jam on chunky pieces of toast. After the early morning journey, she was famished, and her mouth was watering, so the slices disappeared quickly.

Between bites, they chatted about life at Court Farm, and when she mentioned she'd come from Colombia, he wanted to know about the journey from her home.

'They sent me away to broaden my mind and learn more about farm management. I wasn't that keen, at first, but everyone has made me feel so welcome, I really love being here.'

If Tom Davies was aware of how her mother had come to Wales and found herself a husband, he had the good manners not to make any indelicate suggestions.

Mind you, she thought, picking up Olive's favourite phrase, if he knew of her interest in his son, what would he say then? Maybe he wouldn't be quite so friendly. For a start, he'd probably think she was too young. But she dismissed these thoughts; she was enjoying the warmth of this new relationship with the farmer, so it was a good thing he didn't know. And she had no intention of informing him.

The greyness had now left her host's face and it looked as if the food had done him some good.

'When do you think they'll be back?'

'There's no telling. If he's had to climb down into the quarry, it could take the whole morning. You can get into difficulties there. With the weather as bad as it is, I'm relieved Joe's arrived.'

'It's a hard life, I think, for farmers up here.'

'Yes. I worry about the boy. I wanted him to stay at the university, finish his course and get out of farming, but he left after one year.' She desperately wanted to know more, but she held her tongue. He'd provide further information, if he wanted to. 'He was studying law, but there were big storms that year and we lost more than half our sheep. There was just no money and I had to lay people off. So Hywel came back.'

Tegan felt she'd forced the farmer into revealing something too private for her to hear. A little embarrassed, she looked out the window. The rain was stopping again and there was a whole heap of work waiting for her on her desk at Court Farm. She had to go. She turned to him and smiled. 'It's been lovely meeting you, Mr Davies. Tell your son, I was asking after him.'

The farmer was smiling at her.

'I'll do that.' He began to struggle to his feet.

'Please don't bother to move. You haven't even finished your tea. I'll see myself out.'

Chapter 13

Olive was reluctant to let her go and it was late morning when she got back, but the office was empty. Where was everyone? There was a note from Mona to say she'd already had the expected telephone call, so she'd be out somewhere on the farm. Tegan looked at the pile of letters and sat down with a sigh, wondering about her mysterious visitor of the previous day. An hour later, she was hungry; she would get some lunch and could have a conversation with Bethan at the same time. The housekeeper would probably be able to tell her about the girl.

Bethan wasn't there. Disappointed, Tegan sampled the vegetable broth that had been left out for her to heat up. She dipped her roll into the steaming liquid and took a bite. It was delicious – as was the bread, brought by Angharad's father. Now she remembered the housekeeper had asked for time off and was going to be away for several days.

For a while she thought about the chance of seeing Hywel soon, but the next day's excursion loomed large. What sort of thing might she and Angharad do? Her aunt had said, 'You have to watch your step in Newport. It's a port and there are definitely a few unsavoury characters around, but it's no problem as long as you keep to the town centre and stay together.'

Of course, Tegan didn't know much about small Welsh towns, but how dangerous was Newport likely to be for a girl who came from a country where there were armed gangsters and killings every day, and drug smuggling was the norm in certain coastal areas? Where the police often turned a blind eye for a kickback. She'd been taught to take care of herself, and the other girl must have visited Newport often enough to know how to look out for them.

Anyway, she hadn't made up her mind yet. Maybe she wouldn't go, though it would be shabby not to turn up. She ought to make the effort, however little she wanted to do it.

The kitchen darkened and a few seconds later, a hard rain pounded the flagstones in the courtyard and blurred the windows. Thunder would be disappointed because they couldn't go out in this. Although it was almost the end of May, those clouds had been closing in all morning. Summer hadn't come yet to South Wales, and this was an afternoon to stay indoors.

Perhaps she'd write again to Mari-Dolores. The young woman was the same age as Tegan, but infinitely older in terms of experience – or so she would have her friends believe. Tegan grinned as she thought of her friend and the efforts she'd made in the early days to develop a love life outside the very restricted circle of potential suitors her parents allowed. She had fallen violently in love at least six times in the last two years, and Tegan fancied she'd taken things rather further than her parents would like.

The daughter of an old-fashioned family of Spanish Colombians, Mari-Dolores was well-chaperoned every time she left the house. But she'd worked out a system which enabled her to meet young men without her parents knowing. She would probably understand what was happening to Tegan.

'They'll drop us off at the store and we'll promise to be there a couple of hours later,' she'd say to her friends. 'They won't mind at all – after all, what can three girls like us get up to in a department store?'

And the following Saturday, she'd put it into practice for the first time; the girls had descended from the Rolls Royce and waved goodbye to Mari-Dolores's chauffeur, disappearing into the vast shop, with its goods laid out over five floors. Soon the routine was established.

'*Hasta luego, mis queridas,*' she would say, and already changing her appearance with a different hat and scarf, would exit the store at the other side. They never saw anything of her until a couple of hours later.

It didn't occur to Tegan and Sofía, who were both judged to be sensible girls, that they shouldn't collude with this behaviour. Instead, they spent their allowances and enjoyed the stories. Tegan thought now those stories had been highly embellished, and she smiled at how quickly Mari-Dolores had worked out how to get her own way. Maybe she wasn't that experienced, but she'd certainly kept them entertained.

Sometimes, one of the boys from the other families in their circle met them in the store, and they'd have coffee and cake together in the elegant coffee room – which was how Tegan had first met Luís. Mari-Dolores, who always arrived back at the last minute, the rosy glow on her cheeks telling its own story, would never reveal any details about who her current love was, nor where she'd met him.

‘If you don’t know anything,’ she’d said to her friends, ‘you can’t give me away and you can’t be blamed.’ Which was generous of her. But what she did divulge, were her thoughts and feelings, and not a little of what she got up to on the romantic front: how many times he’d kissed her, what little presents he’d bought, how he’d sworn she had to be his. It sounded as if she used the time well. Or maybe, she had a lively imagination.

Tegan longed to unburden herself, and wished she had a friend to talk to. She definitely wouldn’t be able to talk about Hywel with Angharad in the same way.

She went up to her room and took out her writing case. A pleasurable hour passed as she laid out all her concerns to her friend. She wanted to post it straightaway, given that letters took anything between two and six weeks to arrive, according to Mona. Weak sunlight lay across her desk, and by the time she’d sealed and stamped the letter, the weather had cleared. She needed to go down to the village.

Chapter 14

'That's a very nice girl,' the farmer said to his son. 'Knew how to make a good cup of tea, too. You don't often find that with the youngsters.'

'What are you talking about, Dad?' said Hywel absently, wondering if the old man had finally lost it, being on his own so much since he'd had the accident. Maybe they both needed to get out and see more people. It couldn't be good for him, cooped up all day in the house. He sighed and wished things were a little less difficult. Never mind – another few weeks, and the plaster cast would come off. Then they'd see.

'The girl. The driver who brought Joe up.'

At least, he was talking sense now. It was a good thing someone had got Joe up to the farm early. They'd worked a straight six hours after he'd arrived, with no break for food or drink, and they'd not lost a single sheep. And now, they were both exhausted. Joe had gone straight off to have a sleep and said he'd come down later for something to eat.

He was a good man. Maybe he could persuade Mona to let him go permanently. She'd always been clever at choosing good workers and Joe had some real skills. If he brought him on, gave him more responsibility …

Ultimately, he'd have to find a partner if the farm was to continue and there was no reason it couldn't be someone like Joe – if Dad's heart really had gone out of things and he didn't want to continue working the farm. Of course, Joe wouldn't have much money to put in but there were other things that were important too; it wasn't all about money. Hywel put the pan on to heat up and the rich smell of lamb and onions began to fill the kitchen.

'That beautiful hair,' his dad continued. 'She's a real strawberry blonde. You don't often see that, do you? I could tell straight away whose daughter she is.'

'Yes, I know it's a mess but there's not been the time,' Hywel said, latching onto the word "hair" as he stirred the bubbling stew. 'I'll get it cut when I'm next in Chepstow – or maybe you could do it for me?'

He turned back to the stove, testing the simmering potatoes with a sharp knife and hoping they were ready. It was a relief the stew was done. If he had to wait much longer, he'd be fainting from hunger.

With the potatoes drained, he brought the dish over, and then began serving the stew his dad had made straight onto their plates. The old man was tough. Okay, he was at a low ebb at the moment, but he'd soon be better.

He sat down and stretched across for the vegetables. When he looked up, he caught an amused smile on his father's face.

'What?' he said. 'What are you laughing about?'

'You haven't been listening to a word I've said, have you? I wasn't talking about your hair.'

‘Sorry, Dad, I’ve got a lot on my mind.’ He heaped potatoes onto his plate. ‘What were you talking about?’

‘The girl. Lovely, intelligent. I think you should try to get to know her before she falls for the dubious charms of Dai Thomas or, God forbid, Chris Jones,’ he said, mentioning two hopefuls from the Young Farmers. ‘If I weren’t an old man, I wouldn’t be able to resist that hair along with the green eyes.’

This was great, coming from the man who hadn’t even looked at another woman in the fifteen years since his wife had died, despite a number of attractive ladies who’d made clear their interest.

‘You mean it was a girl with long blonde hair and green eyes who drove Joe here? That one?’

‘Strawberry blonde, but yes, that’s what I said. So – you’ve already met her?’

‘Well, yes. I was blocking the lane with the sheep the other day when she was driving up there. She helped me rescue one.’

‘And you didn’t notice her?’

Suppressing any sign he was interested in the girl, Hywel narrowed his eyes and didn’t answer the question. ‘What are you up to, Dad?’

‘Looking after your interests, my boy. You’re twenty-seven years old – too young to be a hermit. It’s time you found yourself someone else.’

A look of real pain crossed Hywel’s face. He hadn’t always been on his own. Caitlin had died, and rarely a day went by when he did not think of her in some way or other. Since then, he’d devoted himself to the farm, striving to find ways of pulling it into the modern world, and he’d ignored the interest shown by local girls who'd found all sorts of reasons to come calling. He'd not been very responsive; the Davies men were nothing if not faithful.

But recently, he'd forced himself to go to a couple of social events where he'd met up with other farmers and downed a few pints. He'd even had a couple of dances, but he usually left early, and he'd not once felt the pull of attraction – not until that day on the mountain road.

Dad was right. The farm couldn't always come first.

'Yeah, you've got a point, Dad – but hell knows what I'll be able to do about it.'

Chapter 15

'Just put it all there on the counter, over by the parcels, will you, Tegan *bach*. Is it all stamped?'

'Yes, it's already done, except for the parcel, and I've put airmail stickers on the letters going abroad.' Tegan handed over her package and paid the postage. 'I'll be back in a minute. I want to buy a couple of things.'

The post office was part of a little general store and, even after such a short time in the village, Tegan felt welcomed whenever she went in, a recognized member of the community. She wandered around, picking up one or two items, while several elderly folks talked to the post mistress as they collected their pensions.

A couple of other customers were standing in the queue by the time she re-joined it, including a man with thick, blonde, curly hair who was carrying a large box. That was interesting – he looked young from where she was standing, and she hadn't met many young people in the village. But he'd gone by the time she reached the counter again. She paid for her purchases and wandered out into the street. The sun was now warm on her bare arms, and in the mood for exploring a little, she walked farther, down past the Ancient Briton pub and the Church of Wales, towards the river.

After the busy week, the prospect of a free weekend was good. Angharad had phoned and said that they'd have to postpone their visit to Newport until the following Saturday. Tegan didn't particularly mind. She still wasn't sure she could find enough in common with the girl to justify spending a whole day with her.

She stopped at the bridge and looked down at the water. They called it a river, but it was little more than a stream. It gurgled noisily as it tumbled over the stones through the two narrow arches, the water so clear you could see down to the riverbed, where there were white and black markings on golden-brown pebbles. These things tugged at her. The stones linked far back in time; during millennia, the water had been cascading over them, rubbing them smooth, endlessly eroding and polishing, to reveal their beautiful colours and patterns.

She watched carefully and could see quick, darting movements in the water. Perhaps there were fish in there, but the water looked too turbulent for that, and there was no sign of the ducks she'd been told to look out for, not even up ahead, where a quiet pool had formed.

'I say, I think you dropped this.'

The voice startled her. It was the blonde man from the post office queue, and he was holding out a letter.

'Back there in the street. I saw it lying there.'

'Oh, thank you. I don't know how that happened. I was sure I put everything on the counter. I didn't realise I'd dropped it.'

He was just over average height, only a little taller than she was, his smile open and charming. Now, he held out his hand. 'I'm Daffyd ap Llewelyn. I think you must be new around here.'

'Tegan Lewis,' she replied, shaking the proffered hand. 'I've been here about a month. I'm staying with my aunt and uncle at Court Farm.'

'Ah, well, that explains it. I've been away.'

He stood at her side, looking over the bridge.

'Look, there's a Young Farmers' Dance this evening at the Browns' Barn. Any chance you're going? Everyone does. Maybe see you there?'

'Yes, maybe. Thanks for letting me know about it. And for the letter.'

She smiled and was already turning away when he said, 'Could I pick you up? I know your farm. And you won't know where to go.'

She'd already decided she wouldn't go, unless someone from Court Farm was going to the dance as well, and that had seemed unlikely. Anyway, she was really tired after the morning's drive up the mountain. She'd risen at five-thirty and concentrating on getting up there safely through the darkness and rain had worn her out. She suppressed a yawn, torn between having a quiet evening in and taking the opportunity offered.

'Oh! Oh, yes, that would be nice.'

Somehow, she'd agreed to go. They began to talk about the arrangements.

As she returned to the post office, she glanced down at the address. It was the letter she'd written to her parents, and she distinctly remembered placing it on the top of the pile on the side counter. She smiled. He'd purloined it with the sole intention of getting to speak to her. That was so easy to work out, he had to know she'd see through his ruse, but it made her feel good. It showed he'd wanted to get to know her.

She'd just worked out who Daffyd was. He had to be the son of the big landowner thereabouts, a baronet named Sir John Ap Llewelyn. That was just the sort of person her parents would like her to marry. It was flattering, of course, that he seemed keen to know her, but it was a pity he was the wrong man. Still, she should be sensible and cultivate him. And maybe she could have some fun.

But he wasn't Hywel Davies. There'd been no spark between her and Daffyd. It had just been a pleasant conversation with a nice young man. Of course, she hadn't seen anything of Hywel since that single encounter on the track to Olive's house, but the memory was frequently in her mind. She ought to accept that he wasn't interested in her, or he'd have been in touch by now. Never mind, she'd enjoy the evening with Daffyd. He was rather good looking, and quite boyish in appearance like Luís, although a very different body type.

And maybe Hywel would be there, and she'd get a chance to talk to him.

It was nice that this handsome man found her attractive. Personally, she thought her face was too long and thin, and she hated the freckles that spread across her nose and cheeks. Real Welsh looks, people at home used to say, not always as a compliment, a big contrast to the olive skin and black hair of most Colombians. But here, she was quite ordinary – not a beauty like the dark-haired Angharad.

She was going to enjoy this evening. She'd already made a mess of one relationship, so she had to take things slowly and apply a bit of common sense. But then, going to a barn dance was hardly committing to anything long-term, was it? This time she would be careful.

She was smiling anyway as she returned to the farm, determined to be sensible *and* have a good time.

Chapter 16

They were just three dances into the evening. Tegan was already exhausted and looking around for a chair. Daffyd said, 'I'll get you a drink. Would you like beer or cider'

'I've never had either but I'm very thirsty. Do you think they have any coca cola?'

'I'll ask but I don't think so,' he said doubtfully, clearly unfamiliar with the drink.

She watched him head over to the corner where a couple of casks of cider were being emptied fast, a queue of young men holding out their glasses. As he arrived, the man who'd just taken over the bar indicated he'd have to change the cask. Daffyd would probably be there a while.

Tegan was glad she'd listened to Mona's advice on what to wear. Dress was casual. Nearly all the men wore jeans and checked shirts with the sleeves rolled up. The girls' fashions were more varied, jeans or flouncy dresses, one or two with several layers. She smoothed down her long, swirly blue skirt which went nicely with the embroidered blouse and felt completely at ease in the crowd. The carefully restored brown boots looked perfect too.

A red-haired boy, who must have been about fourteen, came up to her. 'Want to dance, miss?'

That was confident. She smiled, her tiredness disappearing. 'I was having a rest, but I think Daffyd's going to be a while, so yes, thanks.'

She'd danced with him and then with two of his friends by the time her escort arrived back.

'Sorry about that. You must be desperate for a drink.'

It was cider, apparently, a pale, cloudy yellow colour, and incredibly strong. She took tiny sips, sure she'd be drunk if she got through it too fast, though no-one around her appeared to be showing the effect of strong drink yet.

'That's right, treat it with respect. It's good stuff,' he said, watching her.

'So, tell me who's who.'

He embarked on an amusing commentary. She laughed at his spikey humour, and he wasn't too critical of anyone. Then he introduced her to one or two people.

Someone set up a square dance and a few minutes later, she'd forgotten her tiredness and was whirling around, passing from partner to partner. This was all new to her. It looked like a good way to meet people, but she found she didn't get time to talk. It all moved fast, and she had to keep the patterns in her head or risk going completely wrong.

The barn was hot and stuffy, and very loud. Several dances later, she plumped down on an upturned crate and began massaging her calves. She couldn't think of anything she'd like more than to lie down in a cool, quiet place. She checked her watch and found it was already after eleven. It wasn't surprising she was so tired, after her early start, but it had been such a good evening, well worth going.

A few latecomers had just arrived and now they crowded around the bar, getting in pints of beer. Tegan looked up and something caught her eye. She stared at the group, couldn't take her eyes off them, determined to see who the tall man with the black hair was. He had his back to her, but it could easily be Hywel Davies. But Daffyd must have realised her focus was no longer on him. He took the half-full glass out of her hand, placed it on a table and pulled her to her feet. A new song was starting up.

'Come on, last dance. Then we should go. I can see how tired you are.'

Wrenching her gaze away from the group with difficulty, she smiled and allowed him to lead her into the dance. It was a dreamy, slow song by Elvis: "I can't help falling in love with you." More people surged onto the floor, holding each other in a clinch and Daffyd soon had his arms around her.

'It's been a great evening,' he said as she looked up at him. 'I've enjoyed every minute. I want to see you again.'

And he dropped a light kiss on her lips before Tegan could stop him. She lowered her head, blushing. She hadn't intended to lead him on.

As they moved around, her gaze swept the barn and her eyes met those of Hywel Davies. Quickly, he turned away. Then he drained his glass, placed it on the table and strode out through the nearest door.

Tegan's bubble of pleasure was instantly deflated. Why had she let Daffyd kiss her? She was sure Hywel had seen him do so. How could he have put her in such a situation? She pulled away, angry with him without reason.

'I really am tired, Daffyd. I was up at five this morning. Do you mind if we go home now?'

*

He left her at the front door twenty minutes later. 'I'll give you a call soon, Tegan. Maybe we could do something?'

'I'd like that.' Suddenly, she was not keen for Hywel to imagine she'd just hung around waiting for him to come to her. She had some pride. And Daffyd was fun. 'I've got a busy week coming up, but I should have some free time Thursday or Friday. Just give me a call.'

She turned away and inserted her key in the lock. He was nice, but having seen Hywel so recently, she didn't feel like kissing Daffyd. If that was what he had in mind.

Chapter 17

On Thursday, Hywel was about to turn off the main road onto the lane that went up past Court Farm to his own place. As he slowed for the corner, the roar of a powerful engine reached his ears and a car appeared at the junction. It took up most of the width of the little road and he was forced to stop. It was a beautiful, white sports car. He had little interest in cars, but he still knew he was looking at a rare beauty.

It didn't surprise him to see Daffyd ap Llewelyn driving. And when the man executed the turn, Hywel recognised the passenger; the girl with the red-gold hair was seated beside him, laughing at something Daffyd had said, and she was clearly enjoying herself.

A well of sadness opened up. Meeting her had changed something deep within, but he'd lost his opportunity, and if proof were needed that Tegan wasn't interested in him, here it was. Of course, he'd seen Daffyd kissing her at the barn dance. And now there she was, off on a jaunt with the most eligible man in the area – which was just as it should be. She was a very eligible young woman, he reminded himself, and deserved only the best.

It was almost pitiful the way he was in equal parts angry and stirred, just by the sight of her. And he had no right to feel that way because she'd given him not the slightest bit of encouragement. He'd just assumed that maybe … no, there wasn't a chance. But it was the fact it was Daffyd that rubbed salt into the wound.

They'd be off to Cardiff or Swansea, and no doubt this evening, he'd be wining and dining her. Was this their first date or had there been others since the dance? He shook himself and resolutely pushed that thought out of his mind. What could he do about it? There was no way he could compete. Although he was loath to admit it, Daffyd wasn't a bad person. He and Daffyd had been at loggerheads for a very long time, but the man was fundamentally decent. And she was going to go with that, wasn't she? Especially when it was coupled with all that money, and the exalted life style. What girl wouldn't?

The car had long since disappeared. It was time for him to get moving – Joe and his dad would be waiting.

*

The car was incredible, a creamy white that had been polished to gleaming perfection. She'd never seen one quite like it, with its slim but curvaceous form and wheels that were so delicate it looked as if they were made from the metal fretwork that covered them. It had to be some sort of Jaguar because there was the iconic model of the beast on the bonnet.

Daffyd's hand caressed the door as he held it for her, and he gently clunked it shut once she was seated, as if it were a delicate creature he must tend with the utmost care. She guessed he hadn't had it long. Despite it being open to the air, a delicious smell of leather emanated from the black seats, and it was mixed with the lemony scent of the polish that had been applied to other parts of the vehicle. 'It's beautiful, Daffyd.'

'Not nearly so beautiful as the passenger.'

While she pondered on his gallant words, he walked around the long bonnet and slipped in beside her, grinning. 'Present from my Dad for my birthday – and for getting my degree, actually.'

'You have a very indulgent father.'

He smiled. 'I have indeed.'

She settled back and prepared to enjoy the experience. 'Are we still going to Swansea?'

He'd suggested she'd find the trip interesting. A different world, he'd said. 'We are, but via Merthyr Tydfil.'

'Oh, what's there?'

'My father's business interests, for a start. Now I've finished my education, I'm working for him.'

She'd learned he was twenty-six, so he'd obviously had quite a lot of time out before taking the plunge into work. What had he been doing? – travelling probably. He continued, 'He has a development idea for the land he report back. I have a list of questions he wants an answer to, and I'll be taking some photographs, but we won't be there long. Anyway, I'm sure we can find more interesting things to talk about owns there and wants me to have a look at things and.'

'Of course, but it does interest me, Daffyd. What does he want to do with the land?'

'Okay. Well, he already sold off a few fields to the Coal Board and now he wants to develop the remainder for housing and also extend his dairy capacity – and with that in mind, we're going to be looking at some farm buildings which he says are in a very poor state. At the moment, the land's lying fallow, including the fields the Coal Board took on. It's mining country, you see. Those will never be cultivated again.'

The journey was quickly done – only about twenty miles. Tegan gasped when they were drawing close, and she realised what she was looking at. This was so different from the beautiful land she was living in, just a short distance away.

'Not a pretty sight, is it?'

'Oh, Daffyd, it's horrible. What have they done?'

‘Well, these are called slag heaps – slag is what’s left over after the coal’s dug out, the waste product. They have to put it somewhere. And people need coal for heating and electricity.’

‘I know they do.’ It was so ugly. The heaps brooded over the whole valley, and watching the rain, Tegan felt uneasy.

‘Someone has to live near it, and actually, it’s convenient for the miners, easy to get to work. It’s true there’s sometimes a bit of a landslip, especially if they dump the slag over stream beds – which they aren’t supposed to do. But no-one has ever come to harm that I know of, so no need to fret. And it’s not actually on our land anymore. Dad’s proposing to put the dairy farm on the adjoining fields.’

They were very close now. The buildings he wanted to survey had appeared to be at the foot of the tip, but the massive height distorted things and she soon saw that wasn’t the case.

‘Don’t you care about these people, Daffyd?’

Daffyd looked over at her, seeming a little shocked at her words. ‘Well, obviously, I don’t want anyone to get hurt. We do care, and it’s one of the reasons Dad has refused to sell them the fields close to where we intend putting the houses. We could turn all the proposed cattle land over to the Coal Board and make a lot of money, if we didn’t care – and they would build the houses there without a second thought.’

Well, that sounded good. At least they had thought about it. Tegan turned her head away, pondering this. But his father *had* sold that land to the coal people, and he must have known at the time that it would allow them to make their horrible heaps even higher, so that they overshadowed everything around.

She gazed over to the looming blue-black hills, man-made, the result of a desperation to extract everything from the bowels of the earth, so close they appeared to be about to drop onto the rows of cottages below. It was the first time she'd given any attention to this sort of thing. She wanted to protest, to tell him how wrong all this was.

But then she thought about the ranch at home and wondered if her family had been guilty of such things. Had there been forest there before they cleared the land to make the ranch? People cut encroaching forest on a regular basis all over that area. And what about the indigenous people? Where had they gone? Or had her great grandfather literally set up in the desert? It seemed unlikely.

She didn't know now how she felt about Daffyd, but she was grateful he'd opened her eyes to how things were done, not just by individuals like his father, but by companies and governments. Is this what Uncle George was trying to address by becoming an MP? Or was it almost impossible to do anything about it, given the society they lived in? She was going to find an opportunity to talk to him about it.

Daffyd stopped the car by the huddle of stone buildings. 'You're very serious today, Tegan.'

‘It’s all so new to me, I … I’m just trying to take it in.’

He placed a hand over hers. ‘Do you want to have a look? I brought boots for you.’

She wanted to know everything about this place. Now she was here, it was important to understand how it worked. They got out. Rain was already spotting, and he closed the roof.

Even with thick socks, the boots were big, as she found when they clumped over the slimy, black mud, which seemed to suck at her feet. The sun had disappeared now, and before they reached the first of the stone structures, heavy rain began to fall. She looked over at the slag heap.

‘Let’s be quick, Daffyd.’

‘I’ll just take a few photos. I won’t be long.’

They soon returned to the car and the main road. It twisted and turned but the superb vehicle handled it well, and two hours later, they were eating lunch in Swansea town centre.

Chapter 18

Mona dropped Tegan off at Abergavenny station at a quarter past nine the following Saturday, well in advance of the agreed time. 'Give me a ring this evening, just before you leave Newport. Don't make it too late, will you.'

A busy woman, Mona let in the clutch and sped away.

The sky was already changing. It was a good thing she was wearing her pale trench coat over the warm tunic and slacks, because those fluffy little clouds were probably going to mean rain later. The outfit was practical for a day in town, and the well-polished boots matched exactly with the soft, brown leather shoulder bag. She wasn't interested in fashion, but after seeing the splendid outfit Angharad had worn on the day of her visit to the farm, Tegan had felt obliged to make an effort.

Her head full of the time she'd spent with Daffyd, she stood by the news stand out of the wind, content to watch the passengers as a train arrived. It was coming up to the half hour, but there was no sign of Angharad. Was she going to make it? She walked up and down the platform, but ten minutes later, the girl still hadn't arrived. Soon, a faint buzzing along the line announced the incoming train.

She'd have to let it go and continue to wait. The train, one of the new diesels, slid quietly out of the station.

The timetable showed there would be another train in fifty minutes. Something must have happened to delay Angharad. She turned out of the station and headed towards the town centre. It was a long, boring stretch of dusty road, but eventually she passed the town hall. Now there were shop windows to look at and people in the street. This would be an interesting place if she had the time to see it properly.

Some strange old buildings appeared just down the road. A lot of them were painted white with all the windows boldly outlined in a thick black band. She had never seen a town that looked like this, and she wanted to take in all the detail but … surely, that clock was wrong. She'd have to run. She'd come back one day to get to know this fascinating old place better.

*

Angharad was gazing up the line. Again, Tegan immediately felt somehow inferior, and wondered where she got her fashion sense? Today, Angharad wore a short cream dress with black piping, Mary Quant style. It was topped by a red leather coat, and her long legs were encased in matching red boots. She looked like a rare flower among the other passengers on the platform. How could she afford such things?

Tegan raised her hand and the girl hurried forward.

'Sorry, I must have got the times mixed up. Have you been waiting long?'

‘Well, you said half past nine and when you missed the train, I walked into town. It’s an interesting place.’

It wasn’t worth talking about it further, not if she was going to spend the day with this girl. Things did go wrong at the last moment, but how could she be so casual about it? She gave a quick smile and turned away to hide her annoyance. It didn’t give her a good feeling about the day.

The train came to a halt, and they got in. Tegan asked about the town they were going to visit and mentioned again that she’d liked the look of Abergavenny.

‘It’s all right, I suppose, but Newport’s much more interesting. You wait – you’ll see.’

Everything looked interesting from the train, expanding her knowledge of the country in which she now lived: the brooding mountains, the narrow valleys and the dazzling green fields that looked so small. This was so different from home, where acres of land stretched flat right up to the foothills. Finally, they arrived in the bustling port town. As the train slowed for the station, they passed warehouses and industrial-looking areas. Then came large, imposing buildings. A few minutes later, they got out.

Away from the station, the buildings were impressive, as if the people who lived there were proud of their town. Vehicles of all sorts filled the streets. This place was important, with none of the rural charm of Abergavenny. Her spirits lifted with the buzz of the atmosphere, a huge contrast to the quiet of Court Farm and the village.

They’d decided to go shopping, so now Angharad led the way into the centre, chattering all the time. Tegan tried contributing her thoughts to the conversation, but Angharad never stopped talking, and she soon gave up.

In a department store, they wandered around for a while, commenting on the items on display, deciding which they liked and which they didn't. A scarf caught her eye. She ran her hand over the fine silk, thinking of her aunt, who did everything possible to make her stay in Wales as good as it could be. It would surely appeal to Mona, with its abstract design reminiscent of a climbing plant.

'Are you going to get anything for your mum?'

'No. I come into Newport all the time so I can buy something for her any time if she wants.'

Wouldn't her mum enjoy receiving a present? Angharad didn't seem to think of it. At the counter, Tegan talked to the assistant as she wrapped the purchase in tissue paper. She looked around to comment to Angharad, but she was alone. That was odd. As the woman was taking her money, the girl reappeared, hurrying across from the lifts.

'Come on, we have to go!'

'Won't be a moment.'

Angharad stayed at the doors as Tegan said to the assistant, 'I'm sorry. I haven't much time.'

The woman handed over her change. 'Your friend does seem to be in a bit of a hurry.'

Tegan turned to speak to Angharad, but she'd gone, probably already waiting in the street. She hurried down the wide staircase, through two floors, and emerged at the doors by which they'd entered, resigned to hanging about again. It was no surprise that the entrance area was empty.

Should she stay put or walk along and hope to see her? Then, her eye was caught by a small shop immediately opposite, that sold dressmaking materials and haberdashery. In the centre of the window display, she spotted an embroidered canvas and remembered Olive. Here was her opportunity. Keeping an eye on the doorway of the department store, she hurried across to buy the silks and linen for the old lady.

When she returned to the store entrance, there was still no sign of Angharad. Where was she? How could the girl do this to someone she'd invited to accompany her? Tegan wanted to walk away – but she didn't know this town. And what if something had happened? There could be a perfectly good reason for her absence. So she remained where she was, watching the scene around her.

This was annoying. How much longer was she going to be? Another ten minutes passed. It was cold, and she went into the store again and stayed back a little, looking through the glass panes of the door, moving out of the way each time someone came in. She'd give her another five minutes, and then she would leave. It was perfectly possible to visit this place on her own.

'Oh, there you are!'

Angharad somehow managed to give the impression that it was Tegan who was late, that she'd been searching for her. Tegan looked at the several bags she was now carrying; it was more likely she'd been indulging in a mad shopping spree. Those shiny, black patent leather boots were new, too. Well, what she did was up to her, and Tegan couldn't have cared less.

She wasn't much enjoying herself. Was she going to be left hanging around the whole time while Angharad disappeared again? This was not how she'd thought they'd spend the day.

'Would you mind not going off and leaving me on my own. I don't know this town. How would I find you?'

'Don't be like that! I just had to see a friend and pick these things up for someone else – and you were going to be there for ages. Anyway, let's eat.'

They hurried along the street as if someone were after them. Angharad was quiet now, but she looked behind frequently. What was the problem? What was going on?

So far, it hadn't been a pleasant morning, and the town turned out to be rather gloomy and dirty. Perhaps they could spend more time in the centre itself.

'Could we go into that museum.'

But Angharad ploughed on past it with a disdainful look and no explanation. This was getting strange – they began to zigzag through the streets, almost running, dodging around traffic, until Tegan lost all sense of direction, but had the sensation of having gone in a complete circle. Finally, the girl stopped in front of a café and announced, 'This is a Wimpy Bar. Do you like hamburgers?'

It didn't seem like it could be lunchtime yet, but Tegan looked at her watch and saw it was already half past twelve. 'I expect so. It looks like it's beef, and that suits me.'

The menu was in a large frame hanging on the wall. There was so much choice, the problem was how to decide. The more expensive burgers were about three and sixpence although they could buy the basic for two shillings. For a little extra, some were served with fried potatoes and other items. Ah, that was interesting – the Bacon Burger came with two slices of bacon and a tomato in addition to the beef. All that meat was perfect for a girl brought up on a cattle ranch, and just reading the descriptions made her hungry. She'd scarcely eaten any beef since coming to Wales, and the bacon would be a nice extra. She made her order, and Angharad decided on an Egg Burger.

They paid and sat down. Curious, Tegan ran her fingers along the back of the shiny orange seat, wondering if the material could be leather, but it turned out to be a fake of some kind.

'Leatherette,' said Angharad, noticing her interest. 'It's quite popular, and cheaper than leather.'

That was a strange idea. Leather was so plentiful at home that she couldn't imagine why anyone would want to make a synthetic version.

They were early for lunch and drank coffee while they waited, but it was the instant kind, a poor version of the real drink. Meanwhile, the sizzle from the kitchen was making her mouth water, and moments later, the server plonked the food down on the Formica surface of the table with a sharp bang. Tegan dived in. Coming here was a good decision.

'What do you think?' asked Angharad after a few bites. 'I've been eating here for a while now.'

'Pretty good, especially the bacon with it. Thanks for suggesting this place.'

'I'm trying to say sorry for going off earlier. I realise you were a bit put out.'

The girl sounded genuine. She must have been over-critical, and now she ought to make an effort to patch things up. 'I expect you had things to do. Where did you go?'

Angharad gave an enigmatic smile that made her look like a female spy in the films.

'As I said, I had to collect some things for a friend, and I thought I'd be able to do it before you finished, but the girl at the counter really took her time.'

'That's okay.' She'd be friendly if the other girl was.

They talked about what they'd do in the afternoon and decided on the cinema. Having just finished the book, Tegan wanted to see "The Ipcress File", but she was beginning to get the measure of Angharad and didn't think the new-found niceness would go as far as allowing her to have her preference. And any film would be a nice treat, so she said, 'No, you decide. I really wouldn't know one film from the other.'

'What? – don't you go to the cinema?'

'I do when I can, but we live so far from the city, I almost never get the chance. What would you like to see?'

Half an hour later, they were at the Odeon, buying tickets for "The Ipcress File."

Chapter 19

The sky had clouded over, and it was a lot darker when they came back out onto the street.

'That was a really interesting film – a good choice.'

'Well, I didn't like it that much,' said Angharad. 'I think we should have gone for the James Bond.' That week, "Thunderball" was showing at the Gaumont. 'It would have been much more glamorous and exciting.'

'Honestly, it was great, but maybe we ought to go back to the station now,' said Tegan. 'There's a train soon and I promised I'd try to be home by eight.'

'Oh, they won't mind – you're not a little girl anymore. Anyway, you've loads of time. Come on, we'll meet some friends of mine and have a drink first. It's not far away and I'm dying for a beer.'

Beer? Had she said beer? Leaving Tegan to ponder on this, Angharad took off around the corner. Sighing, Tegan followed her, and they entered a part of the town they hadn't been in before. In the distance, the tops of cranes behind tall, bulky buildings showed where the dock area was, but surely, they weren't going there. Hadn't Mona warned against it? She hurried to catch up. 'This all looks a bit run down.'

'It's a grotty area, but all the best pubs are in places like this. You'll see. It's all right,' she added, perhaps picking up on Tegan's unease. 'We won't be going inside, if you don't want.'

As they marched along, Tegan looked to right and left. The grimy, unkempt appearance of the long street was truly off-putting. Was it even safe? She didn't want to be here, but it was still early in the evening, so they probably weren't in too much danger, and her companion seemed to have no misgivings. They ploughed on.

The street was lined at its upper end by dingy terraced houses, their front doors opening directly onto the pavement. There were little white cards in some of the windows, advertising that there was accommodation to let. On several, she read "No blacks" or "No Irish". And even "No dogs". If they were letting rooms, why were they turning people away? She got that dogs might be a nuisance but why didn't they want black or Irish people?

Gaps occurred, even in the middle of a terrace, and in the place of a house were piles of bricks, overgrown with weeds and bushes. Sometimes, an adjacent house was propped up with a triangular wooden structure, giving the whole street a ramshackle look. She didn't want to be there.

'Why are there spaces between the houses? It looks as if the buildings have been destroyed.'

'That's right,' said Angharad. 'They're bomb sites – from the war, you know. Quite a lot of bombs were dropped on Newport, like with most big ports. Sometimes, they still find a bomb and it causes a lot of excitement.'

The war? Of course – World War Two. It had happened before Angharad was born, yet she talked about it as if it were recent. Maybe it felt that way if you were surrounded by all the evidence. Since coming here, she'd seen a few TV films that concentrated on the war. People were reminded all the time of what had happened.

The houses gradually gave way to small industrial buildings and crumbling warehouses. A lot of streetlamps had been broken, and glass and paper were strewn about in the gutter. It was eerily quiet but occasionally, a car, driven far too fast, went by, or a motorbike roared off towards the docks and then silence returned.

Tegan's uneasy feeling was growing. It was darker, the shadows lengthening. All she wanted was to go back to the station, to leave this town. She was on the point of saying she was going home, that she could easily find the way on her own, when Angharad grabbed her arm. 'Here they are!'

*

The road had widened gradually as they approached a crossroads, and the Palace Hotel straddled the two sides of the far left-hand corner. It bore no resemblance to a palace or a hotel, not to her mind, anyway. Next to it was a shabby pub called "The Grapes of Wrath", the name over the windows picked out in gold letters on shiny black tiles. Motor scooters filled a wide area of badly-laid concrete, where tufts of grass grew in the cracks.

'It's a Mods pub.'

What was she talking about? Tegan was confused about what they were doing here, but Angharad said, 'What do you want to drink? I'll get you something.'

'Oh … er, lemonade, I think.'

She didn't like lemonade unless it was made with real lemons, and this wouldn't be. A crisp white wine would be nice, but she wasn't going to get that here. Besides, she had no intention of drinking alcohol in this grimy place. The sooner she could get away, the better – even if that meant leaving her difficult companion behind.

There were lots of things she'd rather be doing than this. For a moment, the image of Hywel Davies floated into her mind and she thought wistfully of how nice it would be to see him. Well, it was no use dwelling on him; he'd made it clear he had no interest in her.

Before long, she was being introduced to various boys and one other girl. They were friendly enough, giving her curious looks, but soon she was standing alone. The group had been drinking for some time, that much was clear, and Angharad was making every effort to catch up with them. How could she drink so fast? Already, someone was handing her a second glass of beer. Voices rose as they drank steadily. They began passing something around.

'Purple Hearts,' said Pete, one of the scooter boys who had been sidling up to her. Now, he held out his hand on which there were blue, triangular pills. 'Here, you have one – go on,' he insisted as she stepped back. He popped one into his mouth and swallowed beer. 'It'll blow your mind if you haven't tried before.'

'No, thanks. Not my scene,' said Tegan, borrowing a phrase Angharad had used several times that morning.

Dios, it didn't feel good here. How was she going to persuade Angharad to leave? The girl was sitting sideways on the seat of one of the scooters on the opposite side of the bike park, shrieking with laughter as she talked to a tall boy, Brian, whose barbered blonde hair and well-made parka set him apart from the others. It was impossible to hear what was being said, but her grin widened and then the boy whispered something into her ear, looking directly across at Tegan.

What were they talking about? How rude they were being. She'd had enough of it. If she was becoming an object of fun or if they were planning something that included her without telling her, it wasn't going to be anything she'd enjoy.

'I have to go,' she said, turning to Pete.

But at that moment, the blonde boy climbed onto the extraordinary scooter with its dozens of mirrors and badges and started the engine. Angharad swung her legs around and clasped him around the waist.

'Hey, where're you going?' Tegan shouted.

'Brian's place. Pete'll bring you.'

Giving a jaunty wave, she turned her back and the scooter left the pub in a cloud of blue exhaust. How could she do this? Others were starting up their machines now, with a lot of revving and shouting and smelly fumes.

'Come on,' said Pete. 'You can come with me.'

'I can't.' She wasn't alarmed yet but was desperate to get away. 'I've promised to get back by eight. I'll be fine on my own.'

There were rain clouds piling up overhead that made the sky charcoal. That was a bit scary, but she would find her way back. After leaving the centre, they'd walked quite a long way, but it had been along that one straight road. Back on the High Street, everything would be signposted. There'd be no problem in finding the station.

'Well, I'll come with you,' said Pete.

No, she really didn't want him to – she didn't need anyone looking after her. It would make things difficult.

'We can go on my scooter,' he added, blocking her way out of the bike park. She sidestepped him.

'No, I'm walking. Thanks.'

If she got on that scooter, she'd have no control over where they went. He'd drunk rather a lot and taken that weird pill, and she was sure he'd be a danger on the machine. What if he followed the others instead of taking her back to the station? She couldn't risk it.

She put down the half-drunk glass of lemonade, backed away and set off. A moment later, she found that Pete was hurrying to catch up.

'It's stupid, you walking.'

'That's what I want to do. I have a train to catch, and I can't risk missing it. It's no problem to go on my own.'

She smiled, not wanting to hurt his feelings. As she spoke, she tightened her grip on the shoulder bag and lengthened her stride. Pete was still keeping pace. They walked on in silence for more than a minute, while the sound of the scooters faded into the distance. Then, they came abreast a narrow alley, sandwiched between one of the warehouses and a little domestic terrace. He put his hand on her arm. Tegan shook him off.

'Don't do that.'

‘Don’t you tell me what to do, with your stuck-up ways!’ he shouted. ‘Oo d’yer think y’are?’ He grabbed her again and pushed her into the alleyway.

‘Get your hands off me,’ she said as she twisted her body, to make sure it was she who was closest to the road. He still had hold of her arm, and it was clear he wasn’t getting the message. Her heart was beating so fast, it was going to choke her, but she had to stay calm.

‘Hey, what’s the big deal?’

He pulled her closer. His face was very near, and a little ring of blackheads around the edges of his nostrils suddenly swung into focus. Beery breath and a sour smell from his coat. Nausea began to rise. It was time to stop this.

She pulled back with a jerk, but he was strong, and he wasn’t leaving room for manoeuvre. Okay, there was only one thing for it and first, she had to give the impression she was softening towards him.

‘Where do you want to go then?’ she said quietly. The corners of his mouth lifted in the beginnings of a smile.

‘Noo yer’d come round.’

When his muscles relaxed enough, she brought up her knee and caught him right between the legs. His mouth dropped open as she followed through with both hands, giving him a massive shove. A moment later, the boy was curled up on the ground among the rubbish.

‘Stroppy, stuck-up bitch!’ he screamed. ‘Jesus Christ!’ His face was bright red and there were tears in his eyes.

Tegan picked up her bag which had fallen in the struggle and hooked the strap over her head. Then she ran without looking back and didn’t stop until she reached the busy thoroughfare that intersected with the dock road. Its relative quiet behind her, she entered the stream of passers-by who were now hurrying home from work. This should be safe. He wouldn't attack her here in the town centre.

Her lungs were on fire, and she stopped to get her breath, people pushing around her as she blocked their path. The sky was clearing and for a moment, a few rays of weak sun penetrated the murk, as if she'd just walked straight out of a nightmare into the everyday scene on the high street. She was shaking, her legs numb. Feeling sick, she stumbled to the wall outside the Trustee Savings Bank and leant on it for support while she waited for the trembling in her legs to subside.

What a horrible person. He'd seen her as defenceless and decided to take advantage of the situation. Defenceless, and probably naïve. Tegan pulled back her shoulders and breathed deeply. Well, she obviously was naïve but at least she could take care of herself. Slowly, she calmed. She shouldn't let a stupid boy affect her like this, but it was a lesson learned. And she'd dealt with him. It was time to move on.

'You all right, Miss?'

The older man's voice penetrated her thoughts. She scanned him quickly, but didn't see a threat, and he seemed genuinely concerned.

'Yes. Yes, I'm fine now… thank you.'

She set off again and finally saw a sign on a street corner that pointed to the station. At last.

Chapter 20

'Do you have a public telephone?' Tegan asked the man who was clipping the tickets at the gate.

'You don't have enough time, miss. Your train's due in three minutes and you'll have to cross the bridge.'

'Oh, right … thanks.'

Damn, she'd come in on the wrong side. She hurried up the steps and raced over the footbridge, smoke billowing up around her as the train pulled in. It had only two carriages and a dark green steam engine. What a beautiful, exciting way to travel. This was something she'd only ever seen in pictures because Colombia had almost no rail network. And the idea they still used steam … she could hardly believe it. The last door slammed behind her, and the whistle blew.

She sank down in a corner of the carriage with relief, removing black dots of soot that the pale beige of her mac had picked up, and tried to compose herself. She touched her cheek which felt bruised. Her fingers were grimy, and face and hair were probably dirty as well.

Very soon, Abergavenny came into view – "Y Fenni", said a tiny plaque showing the name translated into Welsh.

It was almost dark when, moments later, she stepped down onto the platform, along with a dozen other passengers. Again, she looked for a telephone and found one just beyond the exit. Her heart sank as she read the instructions. She'd have to get the correct change from someone. She went to the little window of the ticket office.

'Could you change a half crown for me, please. I need money for the telephone.'

The man stared at her. Without thinking, she'd spoken in Welsh. Maybe he didn't speak the language – she'd forgotten that few people spoke it here, in the south of the country. She tried again in English, and soon, clutching the huge copper pennies, she was hurrying back to the red phone box. She shut herself inside.

The phone rang for a long time. Somewhat intimidated by a man waiting outside, she was about to give up, when her aunt answered.

'I'm at Abergavenny station, Aunt Mona. I'm sorry I couldn't ring from Newport.'

'It's late, Tegan. We were getting anxious.'

'A few things have happened, and I'd have missed the train if I'd tried to ring you, but I'm so sorry you worried. I'd really appreciate a lift.'

'That's not a problem, my dear. Just wait at the station.'

*

The journey from the farm would take a good half hour. Five minutes passed and she began to shiver, so she walked about a bit. The street was quite well lit around the station, but the heavy cloud had a more threatening look now, and a cold wind pursued her, whistling along the platform and through the entrance.

And her luck was out. She'd only covered a short distance when a heavy rain began to fall. She dragged her plastic hat out of her bag and rammed it down over her ears as she hurried back, but the rain pounded down, and in moments, she was drenched and cold. At the entrance, all she could do was stand under the archway and wait.

She paced up and down, trying to keep warm, wishing she'd brought a scarf with her. It wasn't yet truly dark, but the station had become very quiet, the dim yellow light giving the empty platform an eerie glow.

At last, the deluge was stopping. Now, rain pattered down, and the final few drops soon disappeared. With her arms wrapped about her, she cowered back inside the archway, trying to keep the warmth in. The wind picked up. She was wet, tired and miserable. Most of all, she hoped she would never have to see Angharad again. It was hard to imagine anyone more selfish and unpleasant. Tegan gave a heavy sigh. What a mess she'd made of things. Now she trembled with cold and sneezed several times.

Of course, a lot of what had happened during the day had been her own fault. She could see that now. She shouldn't have worried about being too pushy, should have been prepared to insist on what she wanted. There'd been lots of chances to walk away and she hadn't taken them. Of course, she could have refused to follow Angharad to places she hadn't liked the look of.

But being with someone and in some way obliged to them, it wasn't that easy to take a stand. And she hadn't wanted to look a fool. That was the problem with not knowing the place, particularly a country and its culture; she didn't know them, but she still cared about what people might think of her.

Another blast of wind caught her full on. She went to stand the other side of the entrance.

No sign of headlights on the road.

The events of that morning flitted through her mind and suddenly, a few things fell into place. That idea that Angharad was picking up a few things for a friend? That had sounded bogus when she'd said it, even more so now. Was it possible the girl was stealing some of the things she wore and had been carrying?

Maybe she'd been using her, Tegan, to cover her own activities in the store, allowing her to distract the shop assistant with her innocent purchases. That would also explain their hurried dash through the town centre to the Wimpy Bar and the strange way in which she'd kept looking behind, as if someone might be following.

A little desperate now, Tegan checked the road, but it remained obstinately empty. Yes, that was exactly what had happened. It was lucky the girl wasn't caught while they were together. It was easy to imagine how that might have gone, with her being a foreigner. How much more likely were the police to believe that Tegan was the thief, rather than the nice, local girl?

The girl had style – and confidence. She was plausible and cool-headed, so maybe she'd continue her successful career – as a thief.

A filthy farm truck appeared, the driver on the far side of the vehicle. It looked like Daffyd, and she wondered if Mona had asked him to pick her up, but he didn't even glance in her direction, and she couldn't be sure it was him. Anyway, he'd never choose to be in a vehicle like that.

She hadn't seen him since their visit to Swansea, though he'd phoned twice and she'd told him she was going to Newport today, that she wasn't free to meet. But she wondered if she wanted to go out with him again. He was nice, but she'd not felt any connection.

Chapter 21

Lights pierced the darkness, and they were high above the road, so it could be a Land Rover.

Wonderful. This was much earlier than she'd expected. The thought of the warm interior of Mona's vehicle was welcome, bringing with it a feeling of safety and the prospect of an end to this long and difficult day. Moments later, it drew up at the entrance to the station, and Tegan was already heading towards it, when a stranger in a long mackintosh and flat cap got out of the passenger door. Realising her mistake, she pulled back towards the wall. The man grabbed a suitcase and, hoisting another travel bag under his arm, he hurried towards the platform as he shouted good-bye.

The driver door opened, and a man with a beer belly and a disreputable pork-pie hat got out and approached.

'Want a lift, miss?'

'No thanks. I'm waiting for someone.'

Why was he offering her a lift? His vehicle didn't appear to be a taxi. And he was standing too close. She retreated and felt the stones of entrance arch at her back.

'Save them a journey. Where do you want to go?'

'No, I don't want a lift. They're already on their way, thank you,' she said, turning to go back into the station. A train was stopping and there'd be some people around, and the driver would go away. Maybe Angharad would get off this train, because even she would be preferable to what was happening. The man grabbed her arm and tugged her towards the vehicle.

Twice in one day. It was just too much.

'You don't mean that, miss. Come on, be nice.'

Be nice! Unbelievable. How many more unpleasant things were going to happen?

She tried to pull away, but he held on fast. She heard the engine of another vehicle arriving. Perhaps she could find someone to help her, if only they'd hurry up. By now, he was squeezing her arm painfully, almost dragging her towards his Land Rover. He wasn't going to let go but she screamed and began to struggle.

'Little whore,' he said, and tugged harder.

Tegan twisted around, about to mete out the treatment she'd given Pete, when a voice said quietly in Welsh, 'Let go of her.'

Immediately, the man's demeanour changed.

‘*Sori, syr!* Didn’t mean anything by it, but she was giving me the come-on. You can’t blame me,’ he said, dropping her arm.

‘I was NOT!’ said Tegan. How dared he tell such a lie?

‘Go, before I call the police.’

The man scrambled into his vehicle, grated the gears and roared off. Hywel turned towards Tegan. ‘I’m sorry that had to happen. It took me a bit longer to get here than I expected.’

She stared at Hywel, trying to deal with a mixture of surprise, shock and misery. He’d appeared from nowhere. It was all too much, and she burst into tears. Then, his arms went around her and held her close, and she was sobbing into his neck.

She was safe. No-one could get to her. She sniffed and caught his masculine scent and the faint, clean smell of soap, even as she fought to stop crying. She wanted to stay there in the comforting circle of his arms for a long time.

But suddenly, a large truck with its full lights on came careering down the road, and they pulled apart and stepped back. The passenger’s side was nearest to them, and a window was being wound down. Then the vehicle slowed, and a drunken voice called out, “All right, then, friend? Want to share? Ha, ha, ha!’

‘What … what was that about?’ Her voice was shaky.

‘A very drunk neighbour. Must have been out celebrating.’

‘What did he mean?’ she asked, momentarily forgetting her troubles.

‘Nothing much, I expect. People say a lot of stupid things when they’re drunk. Are you all right now?’

‘Yes, much better.’ She’d already forgotten the drunk. ‘That man with the hat – that was just one of horrible things to happen on this horrible day, and it really upset me.’ She smiled tremulously, trying to dig out her handkerchief to wipe her eyes.

‘Here.’ He handed her a large, dry one. ‘Let’s get you inside. You’re freezing.’

When she was seated and he’d slammed the door, he walked around the front and climbed in, turning up the heater. It began to emit a loud, bronchial wheezing. There didn’t seem to be any warm air coming from it, and she couldn’t still the trembling. He leaned over to the back seat, pulling out a travel blanket.

‘Wrap this around you. The heater is almost useless.’

He was so kind, was trying to make sure she was all right. A lump grew at the back of her throat, and tears gathered again in the corners of her eyes. What was wrong with her? This really wasn’t the Tegan she knew. She had to get herself together, and it was a moment before she could risk speaking.

‘I don’t understand – how come it’s you picking me up?’ she asked as he swung the vehicle onto the road. She leant forward to tuck the blanket more tightly around her, so that it covered her legs as well. Slowly, the frozen atmosphere was warming, and the trembling grew less. ‘I was expecting it to be Mona or George,’ she added.

He turned a moment to look at her. ‘Well, I could go away if you prefer.’

Of course, it was a joke – she could even see the half-smile on his face in the low light, but if she laughed, she'd burst into tears again. She swallowed. 'I didn't mean that. I just wondered. You do remember we've met?'

'How could I forget that?'

She looked at him, trying to understand his meaning, and then looked out of the side window. 'So, why you?'

'I've been in Chepstow most of the afternoon and I rang Mona from there to tell her I'd got the things she'd asked me to search out for her. Neighbours around here try to help each other like that. I wanted to know if it was all right to drop them off this late, really to save me a journey tomorrow. Things are rather busy at the moment.'

'Oh …and I'd just rung to ask for a lift?'

'That's right. George was getting ready to come for you. When Mona mentioned it, I thought I could save him the effort. Apparently, he's had a difficult few days. Politics is very draining.' Was he simply stating a fact or being gently sarcastic?

'It's very kind of you. Thank you.'

Still not in control of her emotions, she turned away and looked straight in front. Neither spoke for several minutes. He must think her such a baby. She had to explain.

'Look, I don't … er… usually cry like that. I'm sorry. It's just that I've had a terrible day. I'm very independent. Really, I am.'

'I can see that. But Mona said you were with another girl. Damn, I didn't even think to ask where she is. Is she OK? Do we need to go back?'

'No, she's part of the problem.'

Hywel gave her a quick glance, but it was now too dark to take his eyes off the road for long.

'So – why don't you tell me what happened.'

She was blushing again, from shame this time, as she began the story of her day in Newport.

She wished she could get out of the habit. He'd find her so childish if he knew, but hopefully he couldn't see the colour of her cheeks in the deepening dusk. She recounted what had happened, without any embellishments, not hiding how naïve she'd been, how feeble.

'I should have known better than to stay with her when she didn't want to go back to the station. I won't make a mistake like that again.'

Hywel made no comment, but when she described the scene in the alleyway, he winced. 'It seems you handled that situation effectively. He'll think twice before trying it on with anyone else. You're obviously very strong.'

'It's because of being a rider. You do become strong if you ride every day – and I come from a country where you have to know how to defend yourself – especially if you have my hair colour. It appeals to a lot of Colombian men.'

'And quite a few Welsh ones as well, by the looks of things at the station. I can see I shall have to be very careful with you. I wouldn't like to get on your wrong side.'

She looked at him as he drove, assessing what he'd just said. Did he mean he'd steer clear of her from now on? Or was it a sign that he intended to get to know her better? She hoped it was the latter, but her thoughts were all over the place. How could she know? Then she laughed and began to relax for the first time in several hours.

'It was good to hear that.' He smiled. 'It sounds as if you're feeling all right now.'

'Yes, I am.'

If only she could stay beside him. His profile was only just visible in the dimness, but she wanted to touch it, run her fingers over his lips, kiss … He was slowing as they passed a signpost, and she could see the turning to Court Farm ahead. What? Already? Where had the time gone? If she could stay close to this man, snuggle in the protective shell into which circumstances had thrown them, all would be well. That road sign was an unwelcome sight.

A triangle of grass divided the outgoing road from the farm into two, like a delta, so that a vehicle turning in could quickly leave the main route, even if something was on its way out through the gate.

'Just drop me here,' she said reluctantly as he began to turn right. 'I wouldn't like to hold you up.'

'Certainly not. It'll take me two minutes to get to the house and I want to make sure you're safely inside before I go. Besides, I mentioned I have a delivery to make.'

She'd forgotten, her mind occupied with other, more interesting thoughts.

Coming to a halt in front of the house a few moments later, he leapt from the vehicle, leaving the engine running, and hurried around to her side. He opened the door and helped her out.

'You need to have a hot bath and some food.'

‘Thank you, doctor. I’ll make sure that’s what I do.’

It was weak humour to hide the fact she didn’t really know how to leave things. Strange that now, as she stood in the dim starlight, she felt the need to be formal, almost ready to shake hands to say good-bye. But it wasn’t possible because his hands dropped onto her shoulders, pulling her close, and he was staring into her eyes.

‘They are green. I thought that’s what I remembered.’

‘I … I’m surprised you can see in this light.’

Tegan held his gaze for a moment and then looked down, feeling the red tide rise up her cheeks again. His eyes really were too intense. They made her shy and she wanted to look away. At the same time, she didn’t. Her eyes fixed on his lips; what would it feel like to be kissed by him. Maybe she was about to find out.

She’d forgotten the cold and the wet. She had other problems now, trying to control the violent beating of her heart, which was beginning to make her breathless and dizzy. Hywel took her chin in his fingers and a trembling ran right through her as he searched her face, a question in his eyes. She smiled in response. Then, very gently, he kissed her lips.

A moment later, a light came on and he drew back.

‘There’s Mona. I’ll have to get those things for her.’

Chapter 22

On Monday morning, Mona said she would be out for several hours. Tegan sat in the office on her own. She wrote three letters, answered the phone twice, started a type-writing exercise and, unusually, left it halfway through. Then, she tidied her desk, walked around the room, emptied the waste basket. There were other tasks she should work on, but her mind was wandering.

And today was no different from Sunday, half of which she'd spent in bed recovering from a mild cold, the result of getting soaked in Abergavenny, no doubt. After which, she'd mooched about the house and garden, not really talking to anyone. Every moment she could, she let herself drift into a dream, experiencing and re-experiencing the delicious feelings that suddenly inhabited her.

She was bewildered by her own reactions. It was not as if she had no experience. Daffyd had kissed her twice. She thought of it that way around because she had not invited him to do so. But it had been … pleasant. Yes, there was nothing unpleasant about being kissed by a personable young man. Yet this was different.

Most of the time, she was sitting, because moving around doing things distracted her, and she didn't want to be distracted. She preferred staring into space, mulling over the journey back to the farm with Hywel. What he'd said. What she'd said. How she'd felt. And that tiny little kiss and how it had sent a tingle of electricity as powerful as a bolt of lightning right through her. If Mona hadn't come to the door at that moment, would he have taken the matter further?

What might he have said? Or done?

She was impressed by his restraint. Luís would have been snatching up her hand, and kissing each fingertip with passion, dramatically begging her to allow him one real kiss. She had once given in to his entreaties for about half a minute and he'd seemed to think that gave him unlimited access to her body, so she'd brought matters to a swift close. In Colombia, decent girls simply didn't allow things to be taken further. And she certainly hadn't felt like this, had pretty much forgotten it until this morning. Whereas now, every time she allowed herself to reimagine the moment with Hywel, she felt again her shocking response.

There was a knock at the door, startling her out of her dream, and one of the farm hands, Dai, came in. 'Missus not here?'

'If she's back, she'll be up at the house. Shall I check for you?'

'We need her down in the rock head field – no rush.'

He left and she sank back onto her chair, his request already forgotten. She had no experience of British men, Welsh men in particular, except for her father, and that was no help in these circumstances. Was such restraint normal? The experience with the lout in Newport didn't give that impression. So, did it mean Hywel wasn't really that interested? Honestly, though – he didn't have to kiss her at all, did he? He didn't have to be so nice at the station. He must at least like her.

And what had he said about her eyes? That was flirtatious. But still, he'd treated her seriously, in spite of her silly crying. She liked that he'd done that because she didn't want anyone to believe she was weak. But she had to know what he thought and felt about her. So how was she going to bring that about?

Finally, it was one o' clock. Desperate to escape from the office, Tegan headed for the kitchen. As she sat enjoying the inevitable soup – pea this time – she asked Bethan, 'Do you know a girl called Angharad?'

'Would that be Angharad Jenkins from the village, by any chance?'

'I think so. She said her father's the baker.'

'That's her then. How did you meet her?'

'She walked into the office when you were away, and Mona was out. I wondered who it was because I'd not seen her before. She invited me to go to Newport with her.'

A frown appeared on Bethan's face but all she said was, 'Interesting that she waited until you were on your own before paying a visit. Have you said you'll go?'

'I should've come to talk to you because it sounds as if you don't approve, Bethan. I wish I'd known that before I accepted. We went on Saturday.'

The housekeeper came to the table, a cup of tea in her hand, and sat down opposite Tegan.

'You're right, I don't approve. She's a bit flighty, that one. So, what happened?'

'Quite a lot, and most of it not very pleasant.' She told the woman about Angharad's behaviour in the shop, and on the street afterwards. 'I've thought about this – do you think she might be stealing those smart clothes she wears?'

'Now you mention it, it's hard to see how else she gets them. Her father dotes on her but he's not a rich man, and no-one's left her any money that I know of. Unless she's got a sugar daddy, of course.'

'A sugar daddy?'

'Yes, an older man who supplies her with money in return for … favours.' She shuddered. 'It's a horrible idea but there are quite a few young women who will do that, especially the good-looking ones.'

'Oh, you mean sex?' It was no problem to Tegan to say the word that the older woman was so carefully avoiding. That could explain the fashionable getup. She frowned, calling up the scene in front of the pub – she'd seemed keen on the boys, though, and that didn't chime with what Bethan had said. 'I don't think it's likely. She hung out with a young crowd, mostly boys on motor scooters. There was a lot of drinking, and they were taking these little blue pills that seemed to make them quite wild.'

'I've heard of them – purple hearts, was it? There was an article in last week's "Post" about how more and more people are getting hold of them. It seems, these groups of youths break into chemist's shops and steal them. Thank the Lord you got back safely!'

‘I did in the end. And I never want to see her again. But I’m wondering if I should do something about it, tell someone. She’ll get into trouble if she goes on like that.’

Bethan was silent for a moment. ‘I tell you what, I’ll have a word with her father. He’s a decent man and it would break his heart if his only daughter ended up before the magistrates for thieving. Her mother died last year, and maybe that’s got something to do with it. Young girls can go off the rails when that happens.’

It was odd Angharad had allowed her to believe her mother was still alive, when she clearly wasn’t, so maybe Bethan was onto something. But it wasn’t really her business. She’d done what she could, even though the girl had treated her badly. She had better things to think about. And maybe she could work out how to see Hywel Davies again without seeming too obvious about it. That was much more interesting.

Chapter 23

Tegan pulled a thick, knitted jacket tight around her to keep the cold at bay while she worked. Two days of constant rain had gone by, during which everything felt damp to the touch. Mona had even lit a fire in the evening to bring some warmth and cheer to the house. But by midafternoon, everything was changing. A light wind was clearing away the clouds and the sun was out.

She gave a sigh of relief – at last! After days of gloom, it all looked fresh and clean, and she longed to go for a ride. She wanted to think, and she always did that best on the back of a horse. It was still a couple of hours to supper, and she'd been indoors most of the day. It would be wonderful to have a gallop.

The sun caressed the skin of her bare arms, though it wasn't hot enough to be uncomfortable, just a gentle warmth she'd missed of late. After a few minutes, she turned Thunder onto the track leading up the mountain and entered the shelter of the trees.

She was going over the col this time. There was that stretch of open moorland on the far side, where she could allow the horse his head. The big animal needed the exercise and there was little to match the exhilaration she felt whenever she swept along at full gallop with the wind in her hair. Thunder had already worked out where they were going and was pushing hard to get to the top.

Maybe they were moving just a little fast on the narrow road, but some instinct warned her. Or perhaps, despite the muffling effect of the trees and the drumming of the hooves, she'd caught the sound of the engine. She reined him in and pulled to one side, as a Land Rover came around the corner. It stopped dead.

Oh god, it was Hywel. There he was. This afternoon, for the first time in days, he'd been completely absent from her thoughts as the thought of that gallop chased everything else away, and suddenly he'd appeared in front of her. She had to get this right.

He was looking up at her. Totally conscious of his gaze, she slid gracefully to the ground and walked the horse over to the driver's side of the vehicle, a wide smile on her face. 'I just came to see –'

'I wanted to ask –'

'I –'

They both stopped, each glad to see the other.

'You first,' said Hywel, grinning.

'I wanted to try out the ride across the moor,' she said. She hadn't the courage to say she'd hoped to see him.

'I'm on my way down to a meeting. It wouldn't interest you – just local stuff – and it can go on for a long time, so that's my evening done for. But would you like to go for a drink and something to eat tomorrow evening?'

He was asking her out. Exactly what she'd hoped would happen. That meant …

'Oh, yes, I'd love to. Where would –?'

'There's a nice pub in a village down the valley. I know some of these places don't welcome women but it's a walkers' pub, and I know the people. Mixed company accepted – and they've a small restaurant next door.'

'That sounds lovely.'

'I'll pick you up at the farm, then, about six.'

She was standing right next to the open window. As they spoke, they leaned slightly in towards one another but suddenly, a large, bony, grey head thrust itself between them, and Thunder was blowing softly into their faces.

'Sorry!' said Tegan, laughing and stepping back. 'He likes to be part of what's going on. See you tomorrow.'

'Tomorrow at six.'

He was smiling as he let in the clutch. Tegan watched until the taillights had disappeared around the bend.

He liked her. He wanted to spend time with her. Her heart filled with joy, all her resolutions about not getting involved in another romantic relationship forgotten. She turned to Thunder. 'You don't know what you interrupted there, you bad boy.'

But she stroked him affectionately and then leapt onto his back, urging him up the slope. Suddenly, she was all excess energy and that gallop on the moor was the very thing to work it off.

*

Lower down the mountain, Hywel was driving without any real awareness of his surroundings. Her lovely eyes had lit up at the invitation. Exultation filled him, and he wanted to shout out, glad he'd risked getting a refusal. Because, after seeing her in Daffyd's arms, and in the car a few days later, he'd thought she might say no, and then he'd have looked a fool. She seemed confident, could have anyone, he was sure. The desire to get to know her had overridden his fears.

So did this mean she'd told Daffyd she wasn't interested in going out with him?

Daffyd was a much more suitable boyfriend for her. Even though he and Daffyd were more or less the same age, he'd told himself the man was smart and well-connected, and age wouldn't be an issue for Daffyd. Added to that was the little matter of money.

Damned horse, he thought, getting in the way like that, just when ... But it seemed she'd be happy to spend the evening with him, although … Whatever the reason, she'd said yes, and he was determined she wouldn't regret it.

Coming to the crossroads, before the village centre, he looked at his watch. Damn! He'd heard someone was going to address the meeting and that the information would be important for all the farmers in the area, so he'd wanted to get there a little early, to find out what was going on. But a lot of time seemed to have gone by and now, it looked as if he was going to be late.

Not that they were necessarily that punctual. He raced down the empty road. It was too narrow to park there, so he pulled into the village hall car park. He wasted further time trying to find a space, finally squeezing in beside an open truck, his passenger door pushed right up against the bushes. Listening to the scraping of the branches on the paintwork, he shrugged. Too late to worry about that.

Hywel closed the door quietly. It looked like he was the last to arrive. They used to hold the NFU meetings on the upper floor of the pub, until a teetotal member pointed out how little work was getting done because of the number of times drinks were being replenished. Now, the group would repair to 'The Ancient Briton' as soon as the meeting was finished. It was an improvement, although not welcomed by everyone. Items were now dealt with briskly by the participants who would already be thinking of the beer, and it had the advantage of shutting up those who wasted time.

'Sorry,' he muttered to a neighbour as he took the only empty chair. 'Got held up.'

The chairman was introducing Daffyd ap Llewelyn. So that's who was addressing the meeting. Most of the Young Farmers knew him, although they didn't socialize that much. His father, Sir John ap Llewelyn, had sent his son to Aberystwyth University to learn the business of farming.

It wasn't exactly common to do that in this part of the country. For many, there was no money for a college education, when a young man could already be paying his way by working on the farm.

Despite an ingrained respect for learning deep within the culture, more than a few of them would pour derision on the idea that you could improve your knowledge of farming at an academic institution. No substitute for experience, they said.

Daffyd launched into a spiel about changes in farming, and how they all needed to move with the times. Hywel was irritated by the man's arrogance and his tendency to shout people down. He had a long way to go if he hoped to convert this lot to his way of thinking.

But he was willing to listen. You got new ideas from all sorts of places – who knew? Maybe the man had learned a few things on the agriculture course. Besides, the need for new approaches to farming was something that had occupied his mind for some time now. His father's accident had underlined the need for change.

'So, I'm just saying that those in the know don't see us continuing the way things are at the moment – current practices don't produce enough money for a decent living.'

'And what do they think we're going to do about that?' asked Evan Wilson, whose forty years of hard work were written clear on his weather-beaten face.

'Make bigger farms. Join them together so that we can afford the resources and make the best use of them. I'm here to tell you that my father and I are willing to buy some of you out. There! – there's a deal on the table. If you're interested, just let me know.'

So that was it.

Waiting until the uproar had died down, Hywel said, 'He's right – but we could make better use of resources just by working together, club together to buy what we need. I've been thinking about this for a few months now myself. We don't have to give up our land. Not many of us want to lose our farms, but it's true we're all up against it.'

Daffyd cast a furious look in Hywel's direction. 'Do you believe this … this nonsense?' he said to the assembled farmers. 'It'd never happen that way, man. You'd never get people to co-operate. What if two people wanted a trailer or a tractor on the same day?'

‘You could book …’

‘Never works. There’ve been studies done. I tell you, all of you,’ he said, turning back to the meeting and slamming his fist down onto the table, thereby getting a momentary silence. ‘The way forward is in larger farms. Talk to us – we won’t turn anyone away.’

The hubbub broke out again and, in the ensuing row, Daffyd ap Llewelyn left, throwing a look full of rage at Hywel. He obviously hadn’t expected anyone to counter his takeover plan. Blind prejudice against change, yes, but not reasoned opposition and alternative suggestions.

When the chairman finally managed to bring the group back to order, the remaining business was dealt with in a few minutes, and the meeting broke up, thirsty members hurrying off in search of their pint.

‘That wasn’t such a bad idea of yours,’ said Colin Johnson, who farmed the land to the far side of Hywel’s. ‘Maybe we could talk, you and I, being next to each other?’

‘Yes, okay. Have you got time now?’

‘Sorry, but I can’t. My wife’s about to give birth. I don’t want to leave her on her own any longer than I have to.’

Hywel knew what that felt like. It was only just after nine, but he had no desire to prolong the evening anyway. And he was conscious of his father hobbling around the house, spending more time than was good for him on his own, and doing far too much for a man in his condition. He lived in a constant state of anxiety as to whether the old man would have another fall.

The two farmers exchanged good nights, promising to get together later in the week.

Chapter 24

Tegan arrived back at the farm just in time for supper. She changed quickly out of her riding clothes and washed her hands and face. She ate with hunger as she always did when she'd been for a long ride. Handling the big horse meant she had to be alert, and she'd expended a lot of energy.

She wanted to talk alone to Mona, but the dinner table wasn't the place. George was telling them about the coming elections, which apparently were usually held in early May. That had come and gone, but the local MP was unwell, and George's party had warned him the man was about to resign. It would trigger something called a by-election. George's plan to stand for parliament the following year would have to be brought forward. He was a methodical man, and it was clear that, temporarily, he was finding the idea of rushing things somewhat difficult.

'I am so sorry, my dear,' he said at one stage. 'This must be very boring for you.'

'Of course not, Uncle George,' she said, trying to pay attention. 'Besides, it's very important for you.'

'It is.'

Then, he turned to Mona and said, 'I'd like us to hold a dinner party in the next couple of weeks. It'll be a dozen or so people, those I think would support us. I need to know as soon as possible whom I can rely on.'

By "us", it seemed he meant the local Conservative Party, and more specifically, his candidature. Even if his fellow members were prepared to put him forward, it would be no easy win, he added, because South Wales was staunchly Labour. Glyn Griffiths had held the seat forever but, at the last elections, he'd had only a tiny majority, which was worrying to the Labour Party, who recognized it could swing the other way.

'So, you're trying to take the seat away from Labour,' Tegan said, having finally understood something.

'That's right, and it's time to concentrate on those who might not be Conservative Party members but who would support me anyway, and people who are unhappy with the way things are. You mentioned problems around the coal mines, Tegan. There are many things like that that need addressing, plenty of dissatisfied people on all sides, and if we work this properly, they might bring others in.'

Tegan heard the word, 'stronghold', as George explained what he hoped to achieve. It was getting technical again, and she concluded that preparing for an election was a bit like planning a military campaign – and the information was every bit as dull to her.

Mona tried to explain. George, she said, would be the face of New Conservatism if he could win the seat. Surrounded by a sea of Labour men, Liberals and pockets of Plaid Cymru supporters, he hoped to exploit the growing tension between Plaid and the Liberal Party. Whether that would work was anyone's guess, but maybe one or two of them would support George to keep Labour from hanging onto the seat.

'But why are you against Plaid Cymru? I don't understand,' asked Tegan. 'Aren't they very pro-Wales.'

'They are but they have a tendency to concentrate on what I personally think are the less important issues, like bringing the Welsh language back, rather than sound economic policies for the country.'

'But isn't the language important?'

'Of course, it is!' George was suddenly passionate. 'But it's more important to ensure we bring the country into the twentieth century and that people still have jobs. Speaking Welsh will not put food in their children's bellies.'

He picked up a glass of water and took a sip. Tegan thought he was probably practising the things he'd need to say over the next few weeks to win support. It would be a help that he was a fluent Welsh speaker. That removed the taint of the English invader, even if the majority no longer spoke the language.

'Wales is in an economic depression, except along the strip of coast between Port Talbot and Swansea. There, it's all shipbuilding and coalmining and, Labour or not, the agricultural communities are completely forgotten. We have to change that – *and* bring back the Welsh language.'

So, someone like Hywel must have difficulties, running his farm. It sounded as if George was the right man for the job. Would Hywel be supporting him?

Despite these thoughts, most of what was said floated over Tegan's head as she struggled to concentrate on anything other than the following evening. She still wanted Mona's advice. Maybe she could catch her after the meal.

But it became clear that George wanted to talk further and, when they left the table, Tegan realised the conversation would have to wait.

They went into the sitting room. It was gracious in a countrified sort of way, a pleasant place to end the day. Heavy pale-yellow curtains with an intentionally faded flower design reminiscent of tapestry hung at the floor-to-ceiling windows, all of which also had shutters.

'It gets very cold up here in winter, so we need them,' Mona had said.

Tegan had looked doubtfully at the sunlit valley and found it hard to imagine snow and ice and a temperature so low they had to keep the shutters closed all day.

'I'll get the coffee,' she said now, knowing it would all have been set out ready for them, the housekeeper having gone to her own quarters as soon as dinner was served.

*

A few minutes later, she set the coffee tray down on a large pie crust table and the aroma filled the room. It was great that her aunt and uncle liked real coffee. She'd heard most people in Britain drank the instant kind, and not a good variety, but when she'd arrived, she'd brought with her a large crate filled with packs of Colombian coffee beans.

'It's so expensive to buy coffee over here,' Mona had said with delight. 'This will last us several months.'

In the kitchen, there was a small cast iron machine for grinding the beans. When she turned the wheel, the ground coffee dropped into the little drawer beneath. Tegan quite often made it her business to carry out the process, because she could close her eyes and inhale the delicious smell, which took her straight back to her own home.

Now, she placed cups in front of George and Mona and selected a bottle of his preferred, single malt whisky from the tray of bottles on the sideboard, which she put beside him with a glass and a little jug of water. He favoured Scotch whisky, a brand called Glenmorangie, which he claimed was very mellow.

'Thank you, my dear. I've talked too much, and I could do with something to clear the brain. This should do it.'

Tegan smiled. George was a nice chap, but it was her aunt she felt closest to. After all, Mona was her father's sister and they seemed to have a lot in common.

She went to sit on a small two-seater sofa covered in a fabric that matched the curtains. In the large but relatively simple house, there was evidence everywhere of Mona's easy, relaxed taste.

'You'll help me with the party, won't you, Tegan?'

'Oh yes, I'd love to. I'd like to help in the kitchen.'

'Can you cook? I didn't know.'

'No, I don't think I know much about cooking, but Bethan makes such beautiful meals, I'd like to learn – if she can put up with me.'

'Good, we're going to need all the help we can get. It's no simple matter to cook for a dozen or more people and we'll have to make it special to get everyone on board.'

'Let's do it on the Wednesday evening,' said George. 'What do you think, Mona?'

Tegan spent five minutes thinking she'd have some fun learning to cook a few English recipes, but her thoughts were shooting off in all directions, and soon her mind went back to the outing the following evening. What should she wear? What exactly was a walkers' pub? It didn't sound like a dinner-jacket-and-bow-tie sort of place.

Suddenly wanting to be on her own, she got up. 'I'll leave you now.'

She said goodnight and went upstairs.

*

She went straight to her wardrobe, where she flung open the doors and stood staring at the contents. No, that long sea-green dress which she rather liked would be too sophisticated for a country pub. She pulled out skirts and tops, slacks and jackets and laid them on the bed.

Walkers? She'd need something practical and understated. But that wasn't right – she herself wasn't going walking anywhere. They'd be driving, so she could dress up a little. She went back for the third time to a mini dress that she'd bought in London. It was one of only two short dresses she possessed and had large orange flowers on green and gold. It wasn't understated, but the colours were muted.

She rummaged in a drawer and found a new packet of tights, white flowers on a white net. And those white, low-heeled pumps she hadn't had a chance to try. Yes, it would all look good together. The outfit would have to go under the mackintosh because she didn't have any other coat, and evenings were cool at this height. even in summer.

For a moment, Angharad's image flashed into her mind. She could never look that good. She sighed as she put things back in the wardrobe. Well, too bad. Looks were the surface; there were things more important than your appearance. But not that many, where the business of dating was concerned. In the morning, she'd ask Mona what she thought.

*

'Is it all right if I go out this evening, Aunt Mona?' They were having coffee in the small sitting room.

'Of course. Where are you going?'

'Hywel Davies invited me out for a drink and dinner.'

Even saying this pepped up her heartbeat and she felt the hot colour flood her cheeks. When was she going to learn not to do that? She turned away slightly, hoping Mona hadn't noticed, adding, 'He's coming to pick me up at six.'

'I am glad you're beginning to make friends, Tegan,' her aunt said warmly. 'I've rather worried about you being so far from other young people. Do you like him?'

'I do … more than like him,' she managed to say.

'He's a lovely man, but some bad things have happened to him. I'm sure he'll tell you, when he's ready to. He's a very good friend of ours, you know.'

What had happened to him? She wanted to know but didn't feel she could ask the question because, if Mona wished to tell her, she would do so.

What she'd said was a surprise. Tegan had been feeling vulnerable because she was not quite sure what the rules were over here. It had never occurred to her that Hywel, too, might have problems. Of course, there was his father, with the broken leg, but Mona seemed to be hinting at something else. He was older and probably had a lot of experience, but she'd grown up since Luís, and her natural confidence had reasserted itself.

She wasn't going to run away from getting involved or do anything other than what her heart dictated. She couldn't deny the tumult of feelings, but one important thing she had learned: those feelings must be controlled.

A wave of excitement swept through her, but she stayed calm. With Mona's words tucked away at the back of her mind, she invited her aunt to come to her room, to look over the clothes she'd chosen the previous evening.

'Do you think this would look overdressed?' she asked doubtfully a few moments later.

'I think it'll do very well. It's a nice place, not a rough pub, so you'll want to dress in something a little bit special, and those colours are perfect for you.'

'Thank you. I feel so ignorant about how things are done over here.'

'I'm always happy to help. But not having any daughters, I'm probably not that useful.' Mona's two sons, both engineers, were away working on projects in Africa. 'Now, I see it's already nearly twelve. We've taken a very long break. Let's get back to work.'

Back in the office, Mona placed a list of jobs on Tegan's desk, which made her smile; her aunt knew she needed to be occupied or she'd while away the morning, dreamily staring into space, while she thought of her dinner date.

It was soon lunch time, and they kept the conversation on the arrangements for the dinner party. Deep in thought, as she left the table to change for a ride, Tegan completely missed the pleased expression on her aunt's face.

Chapter 25

The clock said half past six, but that couldn't be true. Tegan's eyes followed the second hand around and she blinked. The evidence was there. Something had happened.

She carried on flicking through the pages of a recent copy of "Good Housekeeping Magazine" while she sat alone in the sitting room. The evening was warm, and the French windows stood open onto the garden. She would hear if a car arrived.

Why was he late?

Ugh, food packaging. She threw the magazine down onto the side table and began wandering around the room. Something was wrong. He wouldn't simply not turn up. He'd asked her to go out with him. You don't do that and then change your mind. She gave a deep sigh and swallowed, to crush the urge to burst into tears. She'd built this up in her mind to something so important that …

He'd been held up, that was all, and she should stop being so silly.

She sat down again. The house was still and quiet, with just a low murmur of sound issuing from the kitchen area where Bethan was preparing dinner, with Mona's help. George was shut in his study writing a speech. More time passed incredibly slowly. The sun was now low in the sky, and it filled the room with patches of light and dark. She sat motionless for long minutes as a shadow, which lined up exactly with the edge of a table, gradually moved until a quarter of the surface was in the shade. Something had happened at the last minute. That must be the reason.

She continued watching the shadow. When the whole table disappeared into darkness, she would know he wasn't coming. She smiled. Silly idea – it didn't mean anything.

Ten past seven. She heaved another big sigh, abandoned the creeping shadow, and picked up the magazine again, staring out into the garden without seeing anything.

The door opened. Another quarter of an hour had passed, but she'd been thinking so hard, she hadn't realised what the time was.

'You're still here, Tegan. I thought you'd have gone long ago.'

'Something's wrong, Aunt Mona. He's not come.' She was unable to hide the despair this had thrown her into, and the lump in her throat was threatening to choke her. 'I don't know why. I'm sure I got the time right.'

'Of course, you did.'

Her aunt came swiftly over to her and gave her a quick hug. 'I know him well enough to say there'll be a good reason why he hasn't come. You really mustn't take it personally. Something has happened to hold him up. Look, we're about to sit down to dinner. Why don't you come and eat with us? – you'll be too late for the restaurant by now, you know.'

'Oh, I don't feel like …'

Suddenly, there came a loud knocking at the front door. Her heart leapt, though Tegan knew it wasn't him because she hadn't heard a car. She slumped down on the settee by the fireplace, and the lifeless cinders could not have been colder than the feeling in her heart. She wanted to believe what Mona had said, but Hywel's absence might also mean something awful had happened. What about that morning when he'd gone down the mountain after the escaped sheep? What about the mudslide? Had something like that happened again?

'Here she is,' Mona was saying as the sitting room door opened again and she stood aside to allow Joe to enter, closing the door after him.

'There's been an accident, miss.'

Her worst imaginings were coming true. He'd been hurt. She was stunned, as if someone had hit her. Then, there was a loud buzzing in her head, and she fell back on the settee.

'Oh! Oh no! It can't be.'

'He asked me to tell you he couldn't come, miss,' said Joe, not looking at her and completely ignoring her words, 'because he's had to drive to the hospital. Dropped me off at the gate on the way down.'

'So … so it's not Hywel who …?'

The buzzing stopped, and her hearing was gradually coming back. She shook her head, trying to chase away the feeling of faintness.

'No, it's young Dan.'

The man of few words wasn't being any more forthcoming than usual, but she'd finally managed to understand the most important part of what he'd said: there was nothing wrong with Hywel. Relief was flooding through her heart. She got up.

'Tell me what happened?'

'Fell down into the quarry. Hit his head and there was a lot of blood, but he was still conscious when we got to him.'

'Oh, that's terrible! How …'

'He should be all right when they've patched him up, miss. Problem was getting him out. Hywel had to go down on the rope and I hauled the boy up and then Hywel.'

It was the most he'd ever said in her hearing.

Tegan was pulling herself together now, her heart soaring. He was all right. He was fine. He hadn't had an accident. She could breathe again.

'So, he'll be coming later to see you, but he doesn't know when. He said not to wait up, if it's after eleven.'

Completely unaware that his initial words had almost given her a heart attack, Joe waited to be told to go.

'Would you like some food?' she said, belatedly coming to her senses. 'Dinner's just been made, and you must be starving.' He was thin and wiry, but she was thinking of all the strength and energy required to pull two grown men up out of the quarry on a rope, after a full day's work. Especially when one of them was only half-conscious. He could have her share of the food. She couldn't eat a thing.

'I would, miss. I can go to the kitchen, can I? Wait there for Hywel to take me back up?'

She went through with him and asked Bethan to give him something to eat, explaining what had happened.

'You get some food into you as well, Tegan.'

'I don't really …'

'There's no case to sit moping around, now, is there?'

She was right, but although she went to sit at the table with her aunt and uncle, she barely ate anything.

'What's happening to Joe?' asked Mona, after Tegan had explained about Dan falling into the quarry.

'He's having supper. Hywel will pick him up when he gets back from the hospital.'

Chapter 26

Coffee in the garden seemed like a good idea because she'd be able to hear the engine of Hywel's vehicle as it climbed the road. There didn't seem to be much point in wearing the dress and delicate shoes any longer, so she changed into dark slacks and a white shirt. Although it was still warm, the temperature would soon drop, and now she slung a brown, suede jacket over her shoulders. She might have to wait a long time.

The rose arbour stood to one side of the large, circular lawn that fronted the house. Tall laurel hedges led her through an archway covered in a white climbing rose, and opened onto a round, paved area. During the day, birds splashed in the stone bird bath at its centre. She'd seen squirrels there, and other small mammals as well, but now all was quiet. The garden was charming, its shape and the planting lending it a feeling of intimacy.

With a number of roses just coming into bloom, a heavy scent accosted her as she entered. Too restless to sit at first, she placed her cup on a table and followed the bushes around, bending to catch the scents, but finally she sank onto the stone bench to drink her coffee. Of course, she would hear the engine of any vehicle from here, but she wouldn't allow herself to stay for long, so far from the front drive. She had to be there when Hywel arrived.

Tegan soon returned to the house with her empty cup and went in through the back door into the kitchen. Joe was snoring loudly on a large rocking chair and the kitchen cat, a huge grey Persian who didn't appear to have a name, had stretched itself luxuriously across his stomach. It twitched one ear in acknowledgement as she entered, but otherwise, neither of them stirred. The poor man was exhausted. She washed up and went to her room to find a scarf against the cooler night air.

It was ten o'clock when she heard it. She'd just done a circuit of the woods around the house, always keeping close, and got to the place where the long drive came out into the open, when the Land Rover drew up at the front door. The door clunked quietly shut, and Hywel hurried back across the lawn. She ran towards him, and he caught her in his arms.

'I'm so sorry –'

'I thought it was you who … I didn't understand –'

'You must have been so angry with me –'

'No, I –'

They both stopped talking, leaving their half-formed sentences hanging in the air, and smiled. Now that the emergency was past, they clung to one another, each still reacting to the shock they'd felt earlier in the day; he of seeing the boy fall and thinking the accident could be fatal, and she of believing he might have been hurt or even killed.

Now she took hold of his hand, and she led him across the grass and back into the rose arbour. They sat on the bench, pressed close to one another, taking comfort from each other's presence until, gradually, the tension of the day's events grew less.

*

She was beautiful. In the light cast by a tiny crescent moon, he could see a little pulse beating in her throat. He wanted to touch her, run his fingers over the delicate skin of her face, bury them in her glorious hair. He moved his left arm so that it was around her shoulders, holding her close, twisting the ringlets in his fingers.

Bending his head, he kissed her. Feather-light kisses, as if he feared chasing her away. He rained them down on her face and neck and then he moved inwards to her mouth, teasing at the edges, encouraging her to respond.

All the way down into Newport, worrying over the injured lad at his side, he'd held her image at the back of his mind, had wanted her, hoped she would understand why he hadn't come, wondered if she even felt the same way as he did. She was young, although in the valleys, nineteen was considered well into marriageable age, and many of the local girls bore children earlier than that. Nevertheless, she was a lot younger than him. He should be careful, not get too used to the idea of her as his girlfriend, not push her too hard. But now, her generous response to his kisses left him in no doubt of how she felt.

Tegan was transported. How could she not be, when every move he made stirred up feelings she had never before experienced, delighted her, left her gasping for more? He drew back a little.

'I'm sorry. I –'

'Please, please,' she whispered, hardly knowing what she was saying.

He came back and placed his lips on hers. The kiss deepened. She was lost.

A long time later – maybe it was only seconds – he pulled back. There were tears in her eyes which she did not shed, tears of joy. She'd been carried far away to a different land, a magical place.

'I have to go,' he said finally, his voice full of regret. 'Is Joe still here?'

She dragged herself back to the present. How strange this was. They were still sitting in the little garden, still leaning up against one another.

'Yes.' Even that one word was an effort. She took his hand and stood up, struggling to return to practical matters. 'When … when will I see you again?'

'I don't know, Tegan. I'm going to be very busy, with Dan away at the hospital. It will be as soon as I can make it. Could you do something for me?'

'Of course. Anything I can do to help.'

'I stopped by at Dan's mother's house on my way through the village but there was no answer when I knocked. WI meeting, I guess. We have to let her know about her son, so if Mona can spare you tomorrow morning, could you go down and tell her what's happened? And make sure she knows he's all right and not to worry.

She'll want to visit him. It's through the far side of the village but Mona knows where she lives. She'll tell you.'

They discussed further what she needed to say, and then they crossed over to the kitchen. When Tegan opened the door, Joe was still asleep, but the cat had gone.

Chapter 27

'Take the morning off, Tegan. There's nothing urgent here.'

'Thank you. I'll be as quick as I can.'

'No need to hurry. You've barely had a day off since you arrived, and this is important. It'll be a shock, so stay with her a while if you need to.'

Oblivious to everything around her, Tegan walked slowly to the village, hugging her new-found happiness to her, replaying the scenes of the previous evening.

Their relationship had changed, and what had been attraction and light flirtation had lurched into something altogether different. The passion in his kisses had rocked her, and it wasn't just knowing how much he wanted her. It was the fact she'd felt the same way about him. It was simple – she'd fallen in love. Could that really be true? So quickly? She wanted to indulge in the lovely feeling this idea gave her, but there was also fear and uncertainty.

She looked around suddenly, unsure for a moment where she was, and realised she'd walked half a mile without noticing her surroundings.

Maybe it was only infatuation, but it felt like something more serious. Could it be that he too had felt that way or was it perhaps a more physical thing for him? Growing up with the practical concerns of cattle and horse breeding, Tegan was not ignorant of relations between male and female. Men *were* different in some ways. She smiled a little, recalling that only days before, she'd been worried that he was showing too much restraint, and had thought this meant he didn't find her interesting enough.

But circumstances had heightened every moment of their time together the evening before. Where was it all leading? She took a deep breath, trying to calm the dizzying sense of heading towards a cliff-edge, with so much momentum, she wouldn't be able to stop the fall.

It was too intense, too soon. They had to have time to get to know one another. She could tell he was a dedicated farmer, but what else did she know about him? What did he like doing? – or was he so wedded to the farm that there was no room for other things in his life? Which might not be much fun in the long term. Luís had thought that about *her,* and it hadn't led to anything good.

Shouts and shrieks broke in on her thoughts. She rounded the bend and Mrs Evans at the cottage called across to her from the garden where she was pushing her little boy on a swing.

Tegan knew Mona had passed it on from a store of things left from the time her own children were small. Five weeks earlier, Mrs Evans's husband had suffered a heart attack and died, aged just twenty-four, and she needed as much support as she could get.

'More! More!' the child shouted.

‘Good morning, Miss Tegan. Heard about the accident, have you?’ said the woman who’d now left the swing and walked over to the fence. It looked like she was keen to have a gossip. It must be hard to adjust to living on your own and in such sad circumstances – and with only a three-year-old for company. Maybe she would offer to babysit. But not just now. First, she had to sort herself out.

‘Yes, I did. It could have been a tragedy. I hope he’s going to be all right.’

They talked for a few minutes, until the child shouted, ‘Mam, push me.’

‘Sorry. I’d better go.’

The woman turned away and Tegan went on towards the village.

Of course, there was a huge physical attraction between her and Hywel, but she needed more information to complete the picture. And what if she didn’t like what she learned? She tried to push this uncomfortable thought to the back of her mind, but it wouldn’t go away. Hywel seemed perfect to her, but people did feel like that about each other if they’d just met and they found each other attractive. They needed time to get to know one another. That was just common sense.

She heaved a sigh. This was going to be difficult. But they wouldn’t see each other for a few days, and when they did, she’d be calm and wouldn’t overreact. That was the plan, anyway. And maybe she could talk to Aunt Mona who was kind and sensible and had her well-being at heart.

The main road was coming into view at the bottom of the track. Apparently, Dan's mother lived in a cottage at the crossroads where the road climbed up into the hills again. The grey stone building with its slate roof was set back from the road, and her troubled heart calmed as she followed a path towards it, meandering from the gate through banks of sweet-smelling flowers. Those tall plants must be hollyhocks just coming into flower and they vied with creamy foxgloves for space along the walls. She bent to the dark red peonies, mixed in with lavender, stocks and pinks, and felt the smooth flesh of their petals. The heavy heads were her favourites.

Here and there, a rose was just beginning to open, and dotted about were clumps of daisies. All along the path, someone had planted catmint which glowed like cushions of deepest purple. Ah, and there was a small, black cat strolling along, ready to get drunk on the scent from the flowers. Even as she thought this, it flopped down into one of the clumps and rolled over onto its side.

Entranced, she tried to take it all in. Except for the roses, she'd never actually seen those plants growing, but she remembered the names of every one of them. Back home, her darling grandmother had eagerly awaited the books and magazines she received from Foyle's in London and then together, they would pore over them. The plants here were so startling, so colourful in comparison with the washed-out images on paper.

This was a plants-woman's domain, and it took her straight back to the small garden she and her grandmother had cultivated together, a lovely, sheltered oasis of green and bright colours on the edge of the desert. The same profusion of plants pushed out in front of one another, as if they were vying for space, but they were different varieties. In her native country, the flowers were bigger, smelled stronger and were more vibrant but they also only grew naturally where there was sufficient shade or in certain places where the land was frequently irrigated.

Most good gardens in Colombia were in the cities, hidden behind high walls that sheltered them and created the right conditions. They were the province of the rich, and outsiders rarely saw them. This cottage garden delighted her as it opened up, and with it came a longing for the elderly woman who had died three years earlier, well before her time.

With huge reluctance, she dragged her gaze away from the gorgeous array of plants. She'd been putting off the difficult moment. Now, she steeled herself to deliver the news, wondering how the mother would react. But still she waited another moment before tugging at an old brass bell.

The woman who came to the door had pale-blonde hair pulled into a tight bun and was younger than Tegan had expected, probably only in her late thirties. She took one look at her visitor and said, 'It's about Dan, isn't it?'

'Yes, but he's all right. Please don't worry.'

Her expression tense, the woman invited her in and sank down onto a small settee by a fire which had been made up but not lit.

Tegan took time to explain what had happened and said there appeared to be nothing serious, despite the height from which the boy had fallen. 'They wanted to keep him in hospital overnight, just to be sure, but said you can probably bring him home today.'

'Thank you. Thank you for coming to tell me.'

‘Hywel did call round last evening but he wasn’t able to make you hear when he knocked. I’m afraid he couldn’t come himself today, so he asked me to do it instead.’

‘I was at the WI.’ She pressed her hands to her face as she looked at Tegan. ‘I’ve feared this for some time.’

The woman slumped back on the settee, her face now very pale. Perhaps she was going to faint. Tegan hurried into the kitchen visible through the open doorway, found a cup on the draining board and filled it with tap water.

‘Here, drink this. He really is all right.’

‘This is the way Dan is, you see.’ She drank deeply from the cup. ‘He’s a good lad and I love him dearly, but he’s … well, a bit slow to pick things up, doesn’t always recognize the danger to himself until it’s too late.’

She was quiet for a moment, visibly pulling herself together, and Tegan waited quietly. Finally, she said, ‘I’ll catch the bus to the hospital at two. There’s plenty of time. Would you like a cup of tea?’

Tegan accepted. It was obvious the woman had had a shock, and it gave a reason to stay with her a while. They both needed that drink.

‘Shall I light the fire?’

‘Please. I won’t be a minute.’

*

She closed the garden gate half an hour later, her mind on the conversation with Dan’s mother, Emma. A woman on horseback appeared around a bend in the road, called out good morning and brought her horse to a halt. She was riding an elderly roan mare, and looked about sixty, dressed in jodhpurs, a brown, close-fitting, tweed jacket and proper leather riding boots. She sat very upright in the saddle, but as the horse stopped, she leant down, holding out her hand.

'Henrietta Glyn Price. I think you must be Mona's niece, Tegan.'

'That's right, Tegan Lewis. I'm staying at Court Farm.'

'Thought so. That means it was you I saw riding the other day. You looked like a natural, even though that was a big horse you were on.'

'Oh, yes, Thunder. He is big but he's good-natured. You just have to know how to handle him.'

Henrietta's smile broadened. 'Well now, that remark tells me quite a lot about you. I'm glad I've met you. I was going to pay a call on Mona because I had a thought when I saw you. It's the Children's Gymkhana next Saturday but one, and I wondered if you'd like to join the panel of judges. It would be good to have a young person help us.'

'Oh, I'd love to. That's so kind of you.'

'Not at all. You'll be doing us the favour. We work quite hard to encourage the children and they're usually well-behaved and delightful. It's the parents who can be difficult, especially if they disagree with the judges, which I am sorry to say happens quite frequently. I'll be able to introduce you to a few people. You're a bit out of the way up at Court Farm.'

They continued to talk about the event until they heard a car engine in the distance.

‘So, I’ll see you on the Saturday about half past ten. Come to my place,’ said Henrietta. ‘Good-bye.’

Before the car had rounded the bed, the woman had ridden away. It was only then that Tegan realised she had no idea where Henrietta Glyn Price lived. But no doubt, someone would know.

She’d never done anything like that before, but she decided she could handle it and began to look forward to the event. And for the next few minutes at least, she wasn’t thinking about Hywel.

Chapter 28

He'd come for her. Of course, she'd known he would, but she'd hardly dared believe it. He kissed her on the lips, so lightly she felt she'd almost imagined it. But that couldn't be true because that tiny brief caress had left her aflame, and she wanted to fling herself into his arms, but she had to behave herself. There was a whole evening to get through and she was resolved to take things slowly as they got to know each other.

He took her hand as she got out of the car, and they walked together up the road. Her heart was beating hard, leaving her a little short of breath. They were about to meet others, and this was the first time anyone would see them out together. In a place like this, it would be known everywhere by the next morning. It was exciting and terrifying at the same time.

First, they went into the pub. It was almost empty, so they stood at the bar and talked to Hywel's friend, Tim. His eyes swivelled from her to Hywel and back again. He made no comment but had a wide smile.

‘Good to meet you, Tegan. You enjoying life up at Court Farm?’

Did everyone know everything about her? It was such a close-knit community. She hadn’t thought too much about it in the wide-open spaces of Colombia, but probably things were much the same there.

‘Yes, I am. I really enjoy working for my aunt and I love this part of the country.’

The door opened and a group of hikers came in, crowding around the bar. Tim was already moving over to speak to them. ‘Catch up with you later.’

‘Not this evening,’ said Hywel. ‘We’ll be next door.’

*

‘I’m going to be very busy over the next few days with the farm. We’re shearing and it takes up a lot of time.’

‘I do understand how that works on a farm. Some things you have to do at a particular time, and you can’t avoid it.’

They were sitting in the tiny restaurant alongside The Duke of Wellington pub.

Hywel still had his pint of bitter, which he’d brought out with him. He wasn’t even halfway through it, but Tegan had drunk a dark red sherry rather fast, not realizing its potency. The delicious glow it had left was great, but she refused a second, especially as he’d already ordered her a glass of wine to go with the food.

It looked as if the pub and the restaurant were part of the same original house, since all they’d had to do was walk out of the one door, onto the road, and into the other. There were eight tables in here and five were already occupied by other couples. She sat back, looking around.

'It's really nice in here.'

The lighting was discreet and the décor simple. She had never before seen anything like the exposed beams that crossed the ceiling. They did look good with the plastered walls which were painted in a pale peach colour. The effect was stylish and not at all what she'd expected, so deep in the Welsh countryside.

'This is different, Hywel. Is this typical of rural Wales?'

'Well, it's only one side of it – don't forget the slag heaps and the tiny miners' cottages. There aren't many people who live in buildings as good looking as this. You should see some of the land worker's cottages.'

'Like Olive's?'

'Yes, although that had work done to it before she moved in. You wouldn't have been impressed if you'd seen it a couple of years ago.'

There was a basket of logs in the fireplace just by their table. How charming it would be in the winter when the fire was lit. Someone with very good taste had distributed a few pictures here and there, all landscapes with buildings in them. Noticing Tegan's interest, Hywel said, 'The artist is the owner's wife. Do you like them?'

'They are well done. I love this one of the farmhouse on the moor,' she said, pointing to a large unframed canvas that'd been hung close to their table. 'She's talented. Look at those clever brush strokes – it makes you imagine more than is actually there.'

'You sound as if you know something about this.'

Tegan reddened, wondering if she'd sounded pretentious. 'I don't really, but I am interested. My parents gave me a landscape last year for my eighteenth birthday. It's by a well-known Colombian artist, and it was a big present. It set me off, looking at different types of art. What about you? Do you like art?'

'I like looking at it, but I don't know much about it. Music is more my thing. And I've been able to indulge in it much more since we got the electricity up to the house. That's made a big difference to my life.'

'You mean, you couldn't even listen to music before?' She was horrified. 'That's really sad.'

'Oh, there was always the radio, with batteries, and we had a generator, but it's expensive and noisy so we didn't run it if we could avoid it. Somehow, music seemed something of an indulgence and when the generator was on, there was always that low rumble in the background. It makes a difference.'

'What kind of music do you like? Beatles, Rolling Stones?'

'The Rolling Stones are okay, yeah, when I'm in the mood, but I prefer jazz. I love the saxophone.'

'Do you play?'

'I used to when I was at school, but not for a long time now. Maybe I could start again.'

'Oh, you must,' she said with passion. 'Things like that are so important.'

He looked at her curiously, as if her words had revealed something he hadn't expected.

She hardly noticed the food as they ate, enjoying instead the delicious exploration that now began, as each filled out their knowledge of the other. The slow process of discovery was fascinating.

It was getting late when Hywel said, 'So, can you be patient for a little while? Once the shearing's over, I'll have some time.'

'Of course.' She took a deep breath. 'Hywel, I think that might be good – that we take our time. Tonight has been wonderful, but things have been moving so fast that I've found it a little difficult.'

'I'm sorry. I wouldn't dream of pushing you –'

'No, it's not that. I … I just have to get used to this. To the idea of us. I need time. You do understand?'

'Of course I do.'

She looked at him, trying to fathom the effect her words were having on him.

'I'm beginning to care rather a lot about you, Tegan. We'll do things exactly as you want.'

He was quiet for a moment and then said, 'What if you ride up to the farm one afternoon during the week? You can see the shearing for yourself.'

'That's a great idea.'

Yes, it would be good, she thought. She wanted to know about the shearing, about the other things in his life.

What a fantastic evening it had been, with the simple, local food, so well cooked, and the long-drawn-out conversation. So many tastes and ideas they shared. She couldn't believe how easy they were together, the talk flowing gently along, sometimes with gaps when they said little of consequence. If only she could drink it all in and keep this moment within her forever.

But that was silly – it would become a treasured memory, yes, but things would move on. 'Thank you for bringing me here,' she said, as they waited for the bill.

Was it very expensive? Even so, maybe he'd find it demeaning if she offered to pay her share. She held back. Next time, she could offer to pay.

He opened the door for her and took her hand as they headed for the Land Rover which they'd left in a spot where the road widened. When she felt his touch, it set off an effervescence in her veins that left her weak and trembling. A sideways glance at him was enough to show he wasn't unaffected, but now he let go her hand and stepping back, he opened the door of the vehicle and bowed. 'Your chariot awaits, my lady. I do wish I could offer you something better than an old farm vehicle.'

'It feels like a chariot to me.' She leaned forward and dropped a kiss on his mouth, moving back before he had time to respond. 'Thank you.'

Then she climbed in, and he slammed the door. It was obvious it wouldn't close otherwise. Everything was perfect, and she wanted to spin out the journey back to Court Farm, enjoy his nearness, but it took no time at all. Already they were coming through the gates, and now he was parking on the grass, just inside the grounds.

'Let's walk,' he said as he opened the door for her.

So he, too, was unwilling to end the beautiful evening. Placing his hands around her waist, he swung her down, a process which was helpful for her modesty, given her short dress. But the length of her skirt was the last thing she was thinking about. Instead, her mind was thrilling to his strength and how much she loved the feeling of his hands on her body. The moment was far too short.

It was a fine night, balmy, the sort that makes sleep difficult, but they were outside in the fragrant air and not a leaf stirred, and it felt good. Local people were saying this was a heatwave, according to Bethan. Well, maybe that's what it was called here, but in fact, it just felt pleasantly comfortable to Tegan, a return to a normal temperature after weeks of shivering. It had taken her a long while to acclimatize.

Although the gates were about a quarter of a mile from the house, the walk was over all too soon. Standing by the front door, Hywel took both her hands in his.

'This has been a wonderful evening. Perfect food and perfect company.'

'It's been lovely. Thank you.'

Polite words, when all she wanted was for him to envelop her in his arms and kiss her the way he'd started to the other night. And she'd just told him to hold back, to take things more slowly. Was she mad to say such a thing? How could she have been so stupid?

Then he pulled her towards him, and he did kiss her. It was sweet and gentle, but not lingering at all. A stab of desire shot through her, and she clung for a moment. When he let her go, she felt cheated that it had ended so quickly. He'd heeded her concerns. And she didn't like it at all.

Now, he walked her towards the door. 'I'll wait until you've gone in.'

It was late and Tegan used her key. 'Good night, Hywel.'

'Breuddwydion melys, fy nghariad,' he said softly.

Oh, yes, her dreams would be so sweet.

Chapter 29

Tegan had never been so busy, and when she sat down to supper on Monday, she was exhausted. Preparations were well in hand for the formal dinner and now, as she passed George the vegetables, Mona was already onto the next thing, talking about the agricultural show.

'This year, the show will be held from Friday to Sunday, 20th to 22nd of August. That's less than six weeks away and there's a lot to do. It's a big event for the area.'

'Where does it happen?' asked Tegan. She had no idea how such things were organised.

'It'll be held through the fields down from the house, and the animal pens will be in our meadows between the village and the river, you know, beyond the bridge.'

Tegan had some vague idea of where she meant. It was the only flat ground in the area.

'What happens? Does everyone get involved?'

'Pretty much,' said George. 'I can say there's a bit of everything agriculture-related and everything linked to village life. It's a good show. We get contributors from a fifty-mile radius, from Chepstow and Monmouth to the east, Brecon of course, and even as far away as Aberystwyth on the coast.'

'Yes,' said Mona. 'Lots of animals competing for "best of" – cattle, prize bulls, horses, goats, sheep, pigs. Then there are the smaller animals like rabbits. There's a dog show and a mini horse race. And lots of stalls selling home-made items – cakes, jams, farm produce and plants. Maybe even some farm machinery. And finally, there are the games for the children.'

'It sounds like a lot of work,' said Tegan feeling a little overwhelmed.

'It is. We're not like the big shows but it's great fun, as well as being good for our area. It brings in quite a few visitors. Can I rely on you for help in putting it all together?'

'Yes, I'd love to do that.'

'I've been handling enquiries for a while but now it's time to step up the pace. In fact, why don't you take a couple of days off before it all gets started? You might like to visit a couple of places … I don't know, that's not such fun on your own, and we can't spend time away from the farm to take you anywhere. You could visit the Monmouth cousins for a few days. I could get in touch for you.'

There were cousins all over the place, and the Morgans lived close, just over the border in England. Her father's cousin, Victoria, was a writer and had been thrilled at hearing about life in South America at first hand. Apparently, she'd decided to set her next novel there.

‘Could I think about it. I’m not sure I want to go away anywhere just now.’

This was the simple truth. She had plenty to keep her occupied and interested – and she really did not want to let go any possibility of seeing Hywel.

‘We’ll be working longer hours in the run-up to the show, and later on, you may not get the opportunity. Let me know if you decide to do that. I can tell you, if you’re feeling tired already, it’s going to get a lot worse.’

When she gave it some thought, she decided a small amount of time off would be welcome. She hadn’t gone away since her parents had left, except for the visit to Swansea with Daffyd, and that had only been a few hours.

‘Are you sure you can spare me?’

‘This weekend would be a good time and then you’ll come back refreshed to help us with the dinner.’

Maybe she would go. The cousin nearest in age was Susan, just a couple of years older than Tegan. She’d stayed there for a few days with her parents so many weeks ago, and the young women had got on well. In fact, she felt a traitor to her Colombian friend, Mari-Dolores – Susan and she had a lot more in common and she’d enjoyed their conversations. She’d have to think about it.

Despite the increasing work, some part of her afternoons remained free and the following day, as soon as lunch was over, she changed her clothes and saddled Thunder, who showed his usual enthusiasm for a ride. She headed up the mountain towards the Davies farm, but having promised Mona to call on Olive first, she stopped for a quick cup of tea, and it was after three by the time she rode in through the farm gate.

Everything was interesting. Basking in the summer sun, the farm bore no resemblance to the bleak place where she'd delivered Joe on that rainy morning in April. There was a distant sound of sheep bleating. No doubt there'd be a few penned up, awaiting their turn to be shorn. Hywel had said they'd be shearing all this week and she hoped she'd chosen a good day to see how it was done. She longed to see him, but she resolved to keep things cool.

It was a hot, damp afternoon and her horse was sweating. She hitched the reins over a post by a stone trough filled with water, knowing the animal would take the opportunity to drink if he felt the need.

It was easy to tell where the shearing was taking place. As she approached, a low buzzing was coming from the barn, and she could hear the baaing of the sheep as she went in. Joe was working by the far doors. He was bending forward and had his knees clamped around a large ram, his left hand holding firmly onto the animal's neck.

While she walked towards him, he cut away a large section of fleece, so it fell to one side still attached, and then he flipped the animal over, making it effectively powerless to protest. Now, he began shaving the stomach area. She watched, entranced, as the wool dropped away in one single piece.

Dan came up behind her.

'Hello, Miss Tegan. Mam said you came to our house to tell her what happened to me.'

'I did. Are you better now?' she asked, looking at the gash on his forehead with its dark scab.

'Yes, thank you,' he said politely.

He nodded to her and used his broom to pull the wool towards him, away from the sheep. Gradually, Joe turned the animal, continuing until it was completely shorn. Finally, he stood it on its four feet again and tidied it up, removing a few stray pieces of wool, but in truth, there was practically nothing left.

'That was amazing, Joe.' He almost managed a smile.

'Had a lot of practice, miss.'

He released the animal, and it scampered away.

'You'll be looking for Hywel, I suppose.'

'Well, I was, yes.'

She knew she was blushing.

'Just gone to have a rest. We must've done fifty of these this morning. He's up at the house.'

Tegan watched as the two men shooed the sheep into a pen and latched the gate, before going to another to let out the next victim. Seeing Joe start work again, she walked past him and out through the back doors of the barn, which faced the side of the house.

While watching the shearing, she'd heard a car had arrive. It was standing close to the front door with the driver door open, as if the driver had skidded to a halt and jumped straight out, without taking the time to park it properly. It was a nifty, little, blue Mini, new looking, very smart. She wondered idly whom it might belong to and then, as she moved forward, she saw Hywel, his arms around a rather beautiful girl with deep gold hair who was kissing him with abandon. Hywel had his back to Tegan, and the girl's eyes were closed.

She felt sick, and all confidence seeped away. How could she interrupt this?

In spite of herself, she stayed in the shelter of the barn, unable to drag her gaze from the scene unfolding before her. What was going on? Who was this? Then Hywel appeared to move in towards the girl and, placing an arm about her shoulders, he led her into the house, shutting the door behind them.

She looked at the closed door and almost staggered from the wound this sight had dealt her. How dared he? It wasn't just a peck on the cheek. She'd seen the way the girl had fitted herself against him, clung. And he hadn't pushed her away … or what had she just seen? Was this some old girlfriend, come to claim him back?

She was an idiot. If she'd been a bit more mature, she'd have walked towards them and said hello, made some comment, but she hadn't been able to. Instead, she'd gawped and then run away to hide, and now she couldn't do anything about it.

But they'd spent all those hours together and it hadn't felt as if there was a problem. In fact, it had seemed so right, so there must be something she'd not understood. Suddenly, she was really angry, and wasn't sure whether it was with him or with herself.

She stared at the front door, willing herself to go over and knock but she couldn't. She turned away. It was too late to do anything about it. A cloud travelled over the sun, and, for a moment, it was darker. Everything felt darker, not just the day. How could this be? She hurried back through the barn, unhitched Thunder from the post and leapt into the saddle, not seeing the bewildered stares of Joe and Dan, not seeing anything at all except what was in her head.

'Come on, boy!' she said, urging the horse out of the farmyard at a fast clip.

She didn't know what the scene between her lover and the unknown beauty meant but she knew she didn't want to meet that girl or hear any lame explanations.

Chapter 30

Tegan went straight to her room after the ride, saying she felt unwell. She'd be sick if she had to eat anything, and she couldn't face the evening hours with her aunt and uncle. She ripped off her riding clothes, casting them around her, forgetting that nowadays, she'd be the one picking everything up. How could things have gone so spectacularly wrong? And more important, what on earth was she going to do about it?

A bath would make her feel better. Since everyone was involved with dinner, the main bathroom would be empty. She locked the door and turned on the hot tap over the bathtub. With its huge, bronze clawed feet, it must be the original Victorian tub of the house, and she thought it looked as if it was about to get up and walk out of the room. Today, she scarcely paid it any attention.

Sitting on the side of the bath, she opened a new box of six cubes: rose, gardenia and lily. It really didn't matter which. She threw a gardenia cube into the swirling water and then followed it with the second. As the cubes broke down, a deep fragrance rose into the air on the steam. Water gushed into the bath, adding a percussive quality to the headache that was developing. Suddenly, she remembered other people might want to bathe, and turned it off, before the tank emptied. She opened the cold tap for a few seconds before stepping into the water.

Leaving only her head above the surface, Tegan lay back, allowing the hot, fragrant liquid to wash away a few of the cares of the day. But she couldn't wash away the fact that she'd been monumentally stupid? Naïve? Innocent? She'd allowed herself to believe she was in love, had accepted the whole romantic story. Thought that love conquered all.

Ha! Ha! The bitter truth was that he was a man like any other and she'd seriously changed the way he thought of her, with her foolish words about slowing things down. He'd seen Daffyd kiss her and probably thought she was fickle, didn't care that much. She took her flannel and wiped her face, trying to wash away the memory of Daffyd's kiss, wishing it had never happened.

He hadn't said anything about that incident, though.

She knew what the average man was like – but Hywel wasn't average. He was something much better, or so she'd believed. She almost wailed at how stupid she'd been.

But it *had* been reasonable for her to say she wanted time to adjust, and if he was so offended, so put off, then he just wasn't worth her love, whatever Mona might say about him. Mona was partial of course, but then, she wasn't his girlfriend.

'Would you like a hot drink, Tegan? It'll help if you have stomach pains.' The question had followed a discreet knock at the door.

‘Not just now, Bethan, thank you. I’ll come down to the kitchen for something later.’

Tegan had even thought that he agreed with her about the need to take it a little more slowly. But somehow, she’d got things confused, misread the signs.

Tears now poured down her face. The idea that she would lose him, might already have lost him, broke her heart. She stared absently into the clouds of steam, feeling as if her head would explode in the heat. Swirls of vapor drifted to the mirror and blotted out the reflection. It didn’t matter; she didn’t want to see her eyes reddened by crying.

Gradually, she calmed down. She was stronger than this, and if she had to lose him, then so be it. She’d behave in the way that was right for her. Recognising that made her feel better.

His fierce blue eyes, flashed before her. Eyes that only had to glance her way to spark into life some hidden pool of desire. She heard his caressing tones again, with the melting Welsh sounds, the words like a poem to her ears. And what had he called her? – *fy ‘ngariad?* – my darling?

She roused herself and began to wash, aware of the cooling water. Something was wrong here. It wasn’t credible that they’d had such a wonderful time together – *enjoyed* each other’s company – and now, he was being passionately kissed by another, very beautiful, woman. She squeezed out the cloth and dabbed at her sore eyes, while her mind wandered over the scene for the hundredth time at least, and once again she felt the indignation and anger rise in her breast.

God, she was an idiot! It had been the girl kissing him with what she’d thought of as hungry passion, and not the other way around? Wasn’t that point important? Had she seen Hywel kiss her back? She took a deep breath and pressed the flannel again to her swollen eyes, trying now to remove the evidence of her tears.

Why hadn't she just continued walking towards them? Why had she not spoken? This shyness was unusual for her, but falling in love had made her vulnerable, and she hated having to admit that. Most of all, she hated not knowing where she stood with him.

She dipped her head under the water and then soaped her hair with angry, jerky movements. Then she activated the rubber hose that was attached to the tap and rinsed out the lather.

She needed to get away. If Susan's family would have her, she'd go this Friday afternoon as Mona had suggested.

Having finally come to a decision, Tegan quickly felt better. She was winding a towel around her head when someone knocked at the door.

'Are you feeling all right, Tegan?'

'I'm fine, thanks, much better. The bath was just what I needed. Sorry – I'll only be a few minutes.'

The water was nearly cold. Quickly, she finished washing, stepped onto the mat and pulled the plug. Picking up a cloth, she began to clean down the sides of the bath as the water drained away, her mind now clearer.

She'd concentrate on getting things right this time.

Chapter 31

Daffyd had rung, asking her out on Friday and now she was glad she'd said she couldn't come. Monmouth looked utterly charming, casting other towns she'd seen into the shade. It had been a thrill when Mona had said she could drive the old green Morris Traveller shooting break.

She couldn't believe that the vehicle had a wooden frame, but seeing at least two more similar cars here in town, she felt like a real local as she drove past the white stucco and stone houses and onto a bridge with a huge stone arch. All this was such a contrast to the coal heaps and mean terraces further west.

The change would do her good. The ache in her heart hadn't gone away but at least there was a chance she could talk it through with Susan, and that might bring some relief. Seeing it from someone else's point of view did help.

Mrs Morgan took one look at Tegan and enfolded her in her arms like a long-lost daughter. 'Come in, my dear, and I'll get you a cup of tea. Afterwards, I'm sorry, I'm going to have to abandon you – I have the cows to milk. I'm so glad you arrived on time, or I might not have heard you.'

'I'll go and unpack my things shall I?'

'Yes, it's the same room as last time. Susan's at work but she'll soon be back. She couldn't wait to see you.'

Tegan took her tea and headed up to the room.

*

'Come on then, tell all?'

Tegan was tucked up on a small sofa in Susan's room while her friend sat on a chair in front of the dressing table, painting her toe nails a lurid shade of purple.

'What do you mean? There's nothing –'

'Tegan, I can see something's not right. Is it a new boyfriend?'

Tegan blushed. 'No, well, I … yes … Actually, I think I've been a bit of a fool. A big fool.' Susan's face was bright with curiosity, her eyes wide. 'Tell me,' she said in hushed tones. 'Just tell me.'

'You really don't want to hear this.'

'Really I do. Of course, I do. Who is it?'

She began telling her cousin about that first time she'd seen him coming up the slope with the lamb under his arm. Two minutes in, Susan had stopped painting her nails and was so enthralled, she didn't speak although she wasn't the type to hold back. Finally, she said, 'Oh that's just so romantic. He sounds dreamy.'

Tegan hadn't thought of him quite like that; the link she felt between her and Hywel seemed more visceral than mere romance, but she supposed it was romantic. 'He is dreamy, romantic, all of that. But what if he's got back with some old girlfriend? She looked really fab, Susan, with the gorgeous blonde hair and the tan. You know.'

'What? You think it all changed in four days? After what sounds to me like a declaration of love? – even if not in so many words. You've got it wrong somehow.' She looked down at her toes. 'Damn, it's dried off all rough. I'm going to have to redo this.'

'Sorry, I distracted you.'

'As if that matters. He cares about you, Tegan. And he's being sweet, thinking about what you want. What more could you ask?'

'I do think I may have got it wrong, but what am I going to do about it?'

'Do you really like him?'

'Yes. I realise I've fallen in love. Nothing else could explain the way I feel.'

Susan took a long look at her. 'I think you have. Which means you have to get him back. When are you going to see him next?'

'I don't know. Oh, there's a dinner party Mona and George are giving. He'll be there.'

'Great, if he doesn't bring her, no problem. You can easily talk to him – and just ask who she was. Honestly, Tegan, it's what you should have done anyway.'

'I know. I don't know what happened to me. I'm ashamed of myself because I'm not usually such an idiot.'

‘It matters, that’s what. And look, if she is a guest at the party, just try to work out if there’s anything between them. It’ll be easy to see – and he won’t want to look you in the eye if he’s got something going with her.’

Tegan giggled – it sounded very dramatic.

‘And if that’s the case, you’ll have to decide what you’re going to do about it. Are you ready to fight for him?’

‘Yes. Yes, I am.’

‘Good, because you may have to, and if you don’t show you care, what’s he to think? You’ll have to forget your pride and really try to work this out.’

Tegan jumped up from her seat and threw her arms around Susan. ‘Thank you so much. You’ve made me feel so much better.’

‘Hey, watch out, you’re knocking over my nail polish!’ But she returned the hug. ‘I’d really like to meet him.’

‘Then why don’t you come and stay the weekend after the party. I can’t take much time off, but it would be lovely to see you. Please say you will.’

Chapter 32

Helping Bethan and the girl who'd been hired from the village for the evening, Tegan had missed the pre-dinner gathering with the guests and didn't leave the kitchen until they were about to serve the first course. She slipped quietly into the only empty chair at the table. It was a bit of surprise to see the person to her left was Daffyd, now talking animatedly to Mona at his other side. She hadn't realised he was invited.

Looking up, she saw Hywel diagonally opposite her, at the far end of the table near to George. Seated right next to him was the gorgeous girl, and she was even more lovely than she'd looked from a distance. Her deep gold hair and tanned complexion made her the focus of all the men's eyes. Only Hywel seemed oblivious to the very attractive, sexy effect she was having on everyone.

That was easy for him – the girl was *with* him. He had turned slightly away from her and was listening to the woman sitting to his right. Tegan stared at her. It was Henrietta, out of her riding clothes, dressed for the evening. How elegant she looked. She was clearly enjoying the conversation with him.

As if aware of her gaze, Hywel lifted his head and smiled at Tegan. Everything else dropped away, and for a moment, there were just the two of them. She smiled back, trying to ignore the wild acceleration of her heartbeat and forgetting altogether about holding him at arm's length. It was as if the last week had been instantly wiped away.

Although nothing had changed, and they still had to talk. But there would be no chance of that for a while yet.

As she dipped her spoon into the chilled watercress soup, she took another, surreptitious look at her rival. It was obvious now that she was a little older than Tegan had at first thought. Uncle George, at the far end of the table, said something to her, and she laughed, blinking her eyelashes flirtatiously as she replied. There was no doubt that George was greatly charmed, and Tegan wondered if it bothered Mona, but if it did, she was showing no sign of it, devoting herself completely to the woman seated to her left. The table was lopsided, seating-wise, because one of the guests had fallen ill that afternoon. Hywel was still deep in conversation with Henrietta and continued to pay no attention at all to his stunning guest. She was getting more than enough attention without his help.

'So, aren't you going to speak to me?'

'Oh, I'm so sorry. How rude of me!'

'You were miles away.'

'Actually,' she said, recovering quickly, 'I was trying to fix the scene in my mind, so I can describe it in my letter to my parents, and I was thinking that we rarely do anything as magnificent as this at home. We live quite a simple life.'

'Cattle ranch, isn't it?'

‘Yes, but we’re deep in the interior of the country and we don’t have that many neighbours, so something like this feels very different.’

It was similar at Court farm. Tegan had been astonished at how their everyday life here had suddenly been transformed this evening, into this rather grand occasion. The house looked beautiful with light shining on polished surfaces and twinkling on silver and glass. There were so many people around, and a lively buzz to the atmosphere.

‘Tell me something about your home, Tegan. I’ve never visited South America.’

They talked throughout the soup course, getting on quite well. Then Tegan said, ‘How come you’re here this evening? I thought it was your father who was invited.’

‘Yes, it was, but he’s been called away and he wanted to lend his support to George, so he asked me to replace him. He believes in what George is trying to do. And I was very happy to come. More than happy.’ He stopped, waiting until she turned to look at him, and then added, ‘See how my filial behaviour has been rewarded: I’ve been placed next to the most beautiful woman in the room.’

‘Thank you, but I really don’t think that’s true.’

She grinned at him, her eyes returning to the blonde amazon, and he looked in the same direction. ‘I do agree she’s quite something, but you’re wrong. She’s a little too strident for my taste, you know.’ He paused for a moment, watching. ‘I have to say, I didn’t think Hywel had it in him.’

So, he too had concluded that this was Hywel’s girlfriend. Tegan made no comment, and the next minute Mona was asking Daffyd to tell her about the idea of joining the smaller farms together, leaving Tegan to herself for the moment.

When the girl from the village came to clear the plates and then the salmon en croute was being brought in, Tegan took the opportunity to introduce herself to the man sitting to her right, who turned out to be Henrietta's husband, Peter Glyn Price. She'd hardly realised who would be at the dinner, all the organisation having been done by her aunt.

'A little more wine?' he asked, holding up a bottle of Chenin Blanc.

'Please.'

She took a sip, enjoying the crisp flavour of the cold white wine, delicious on this warm evening, and as Mr Glyn Price told her, it was the perfect accompaniment to the salmon. He was an entertaining conversationist and, for a short while, she forgot all about Hywel and his glamorous companion and instead, enjoyed listening to Peter talking about Henrietta's children's gymkhana of the previous year. His account was filled with amusing anecdotes, and she laughed out loud at times. He was doing a good job of preparing her for the event on Saturday.

They finally got to the dessert and individual dishes were placed before each person.

'Ah,' said Peter appreciatively. 'Peach Melba. Do you know there's a story to this dessert?'

'I didn't. Please tell me.'

'Well, during the opera season in the early 1890s – it was 1892, I think – there was a famous chef at the Savoy Hotel in London called Escoffier. He created this dish for Dame Nellie Melba, the famous Australian opera singer.

Originally, it was made up of just peaches and vanilla ice cream, but I see there's a raspberry purée to go with it this evening. An excellent choice.'

'How do you know this? You sound very knowledgeable.' Tegan didn't think she knew any other men who had the slightest idea about cooking.

'That's because I'm interested in food. I like to think of myself as a gourmet.'

'Doesn't that just mean a greedy person? I'm sure you're not that,' she added quickly, with a smile.

'No. that's a gourmand. A gourmet is someone who understands and appreciates good food. I like to cook.'

'You actually do the cooking yourself?'

'I do. Henrietta won't take umbrage if I say she's useless in the kitchen because she is. But she's a heroine in so many other ways that I'm happy to take over the cooking, especially now I've retired. You'll see what I mean about Henrietta on Saturday.' He paused for a moment and then added, 'I'll have to remember to tell the story to the young Australian over there.'

'Australian?'

'Yes, Hywel's guest. I can hear the accent from here.'

So, the girl was Australian. She hadn't picked up on that. Of course, she didn't have the British hypersensitivity to accents and their meanings. Her ears simply weren't attuned to the nuances, and she was some distance away.

What was getting through to her, however, were the ways in which she might have jumped to all sorts of wrong conclusions.

Chapter 33

As people got up from the table and began moving across the hall to the sitting room, Daffyd placed his hand under Tegan's elbow and steered her the opposite way, towards the French windows.

'Daffyd, we can't leave the others.'

'Just give me a few minutes, Tegan. Please.'

She shouldn't have allowed him to corner her like this. It was exactly the moment when she'd hoped to speak to Hywel. And she really didn't want to talk to Daffyd.

He was holding tightly onto her arm as they stepped through the French windows that ran along one wall of the dining room. It would be private, the sitting room being on the opposite side of the house. They were on the terrace now and already the level of noise had fallen away. This was so isolating, just the two of them here, away from everyone else. She tried to return to the house, but he hurried her along, a firm hand on her arm. It was almost dark, with the faintest trace of pink lingering on the horizon.

A low murmur of voices travelled into the quiet garden, over from the gathering on the sitting room terrace, as people mingled with friends, looking for a place to sit, and she noticed that no-one else had followed them out to this side of the house. The evening was beautiful, but she was blind to it because she was sharing it with the wrong man. There had to be a way to make him go away without being rude. She did like him. She just didn't want to be with him.

They walked on, stepping down onto the damp grass at the back of the house. Light spilled out onto the lawn in squares and triangles, leaving everything else in deepest black. He was intent on heading for the shadows of a big oak tree. Finally, he stopped.

'You've been avoiding me, Tegan. I haven't seen you since Swansea.'

'I'm sorry. That wasn't my intention, but I –'

'I'd really like to get to know you better, to take you out again. We could have some fun together.'

'Daffyd, I don't think –'

'Tomorrow, for instance, I have to go to Cardiff. Why don't you come with me? My business will be finished by lunch time, and we could –'

'I'm sorry, Daffyd, I really appreciate the invitation, but the answer is no.'

'Why? Where's the harm? We can get to know one another.'

He was quiet for a moment but, when she didn't answer, he said roughly, 'There's someone else, isn't there?'

'Yes, there is. Daffyd, I don't know what else to say but it means there can't be anything between us. Please let me go. I can't do this just now.'

'Who is it?'

She said nothing. He stared at her, as if trying to read the answer in her face. Then he went on, 'Well, whoever it is, it's clear there are problems, or you'd be with him. He'd be here with you now and I wouldn't have got a look in.'

He was still holding on to her arm and she tried to twist away but he pulled her closer. 'Look, why don't you ditch him?' He gave this a moment's thought, and added, 'Oh, wait a moment. Maybe he is here. It's Hywel, isn't it?'

She shrugged him off, not wanting to answer the question. Seeing her reaction, he gave a harsh laugh. 'God, not again. I can't believe this. Well, you can see you've no chance there, with the blonde bombshell hanging on his arm. Cut your losses, Tegan, and go out with me. I really fancy you. Maybe –'

He grabbed her arm and swung her around to face him. The kiss came with a force that surprised her, aggressive and demanding. She pushed him away.

'Please do not do that again, Daffyd. I don't want this.'

She waited a beat and, trying not to sound unkind, she added, 'I'm sorry, it's never going to go anywhere for me.'

She wrenched her arm away and fled back the way they'd come, desperate to get away. She really didn't want anything to develop with Daffyd. Even if Hywel didn't care for her, she couldn't just drop into a relationship with Daffyd as if it didn't matter which man it was. Rounding the corner in the gloom, she ran full tilt into someone coming in the opposite direction.

'Sorry, so sorry!' she said breathlessly and then couldn't say anything else because she was being crushed in strong arms and her face was buried against Hywel's broad chest, so she could scarcely breathe.

'Don't tell me I've managed to save you again,' he said. She pulled back and looked up, giving a shaky laugh.

'I'm all right. I didn't need saving. It was just Daffyd.'

'Ap Llewelyn? Now why doesn't that surprise me? That man is really beginning to annoy me.'

They were standing in the faint light that emanated from the dining room. Now, he took out a clean handkerchief, saying, 'Before we go in, you might like me to remove that spot of lipstick which seems to have lodged itself on your cheek while you were kissing him.'

She blushed a fiery red and said indignantly, 'It wasn't me kissing him. He took advantage!'

'And it's so easy for me to understand why he gave into the temptation. I'd do exactly the same right now if it wasn't that I want to introduce you to my cousin, Helen.'

He wanted to kiss her but … what was that? … cousin, he'd said.

'Cousin?' Her voice came out in a squeak. 'The girl with the blonde hair?'

Still thrilling from the lazy caress of his words, she pulled herself together and focussed instead on the piece of information.

'She doesn't look a bit like you, Hywel. How could you expect me to know she was your cousin?'

Damn! Her snappy tone must reveal everything about her state of mind, so she added quickly, 'Peter Glyn Price says she's Australian.'

'Yes, she left for Australia with her parents nearly twenty years ago. She was about nine at the time. I have to say she's changed quite a lot – amazing. And she looks just like her mum, not my uncle. Which,' he added, smiling innocently, 'is why you can't tell we're related. We were good friends when she lived around here, even though she was a bit older.'

'So, she's just ... er … just visiting?'

'She's visiting.'

They were standing very close together, and she was finding it difficult to breathe, but she didn't want him to move. On the contrary.

'She's going on to North Wales to see her mother's relatives tomorrow.' He waited, allowing her time to absorb the information. His arm was around her shoulders, and he gave her a little squeeze. 'You couldn't possibly be jealous, Tegan? Surely that couldn't be true?'

'Of course not! That's ridiculous. I just wondered … er … who she was, you know. You never said anything about her coming to visit.'

'I would have done, if I'd known – but she turned up without any warning, which is very much Helen's style.' He was quiet, watching her. 'So, am I forgiven?'

He was onto her. Joe or Dan must have said something about her hurried away the other day. But she didn't care.

'There's nothing to forgive.'

And there really wasn't. An immense wave of happiness washed over her as he took her hand. He placed a tiny kiss on the inside of her wrist and led her back through the dining room.

Chapter 34

Hywel had so much work she couldn't see him for several days. It would be nice if he could spare the time to come to the gymkhana. He'd said he'd try, but it had to be low on his list of priorities at this busy time of year. After all, she wasn't riding, or anything, just helping out. She didn't need his support, but she wanted it.

Saturday dawned a little overcast and cool, which would be good for riders and horses. She was going to start the day by riding down to Henrietta's. Maybe she and Hywel could spend a little time together in the afternoon, but this morning was for the gymkhana.

Tegan was expecting Henrietta's home to be like her aunt's place, but they didn't live on a farm. She rode up to a relatively small house of exquisite proportions and scrutinised it, pleased when she was able to identify it as Georgian. With its stables and paddocks behind, it was very attractive. She didn't know how they did these horse events in Wales, so she looked around with curiosity.

Behind the house and off to one side, a large field stretched away to a distant road. The setting up had already begun, with busy figures running back and forth. A magnificent mountain, which rose steeply from just beyond the arena they were creating, dominated everything, the stern grey rock more impressive for appearing bald, as no trees grew on the slopes.

The summit was wreathed in cloud, and it looked as if someone had taken a knife and sliced off the top. It was easy to pick out the public footpath, which skirted the whole property and went over a stile, before winding its way upwards into the mist. Splashes of red and blue halfway up the slope suddenly moved, probably a group of hikers heading towards the top. She fished a pair of binoculars out of her bag and raised them to her eyes. There they were, sitting on a rock now, consuming drinks from a thermos flask as they watched the activity below. They'd be put off by the low cloud but would have ringside seats for the show.

In the field, Tegan dismounted, walking over to where someone had linked together a couple of long trestle tables and placed chairs behind. A few of the older children were setting out poles in preparation for the first event. Piles of brightly-coloured cones, tin cans, flags and other objects stood ready for later.

The gate of a small paddock at the front of the property had been opened and the area was rapidly filling up with an assortment of horse boxes, Land Rovers and general farm vehicles. People encouraged horses out of their boxes, secured their dogs and calmed the excited young riders. It was, as Peter had said, a very British scene. She had never attended anything quite like it.

In contrast to competitions at home, it was all very low-key whilst at the same time, she was aware of a certain formality and adherence to rules. For a start, a lot of the riders were wearing hard hats. When had she seen anyone do that at home? Never.

Tegan tied Thunder to the fence close to the table. They'd walked sedately down the road from Court Farm, and he seemed calm, watching the activity with interest.

The children were hard at work. Obviously well-versed in how things were done, they were leaving a broad track, eight or nine yards wide, free of obstacles around the entire field. She wandered down to where they were working.

'What are you doing?' she said. 'I'm curious.' There was no lack of volunteers to pass on this important information: the children crowded around her and told her it was to allow for a walk-trot-canter session which would serve as a warmup for all the riders. It meant they could get to know the field.

'We have to do it because some of the other riders don't have their own horse,' said one small girl in full riding regalia, who didn't look old enough to participate. 'Are you going to help us?'

'Just tell me what to do.'

A diminutive nine-year-old with pigtails, who already had the authority of an old hand, began to give her orders as to how she should place certain obstacles. This was so entertaining. Tegan worked alongside them, doing what she was told and enjoying herself. She returned to the table when she realised a large number of people had arrived.

Henrietta passed over a cup of tea. 'Thank you for coming in early to help, Tegan. There's nothing else you need do now, so I'll just show you how the system works.' She indicated a pile of cards with large numbers printed on them and proceeded to explain. 'We'll be starting around half past, as soon as everything's been checked. I should sit down and watch what's going on, get a feel for things.'

A few moments later, as Henrietta whisked away to catch up with someone else, a blonde woman in her thirties, slightly overweight and wearing a broad smile, bounced up to Tegan.

'Just wanted to introduce myself, since I haven't seen you before: Sheila Pleydell from the Lloyd George Children's Home.'

They shook hands. 'Tegan Lewis. Have you brought some of the children with you to watch?'

'I've brought them to take part. We're so lucky to have Henrietta to help us. She has them out here once a week and she's taught them all to ride. It transforms them – gives them confidence and goals, and I'm so proud of them. Maybe we'll meet at one of her sessions.'

At that, she took off again, heading for a shabby-looking minibus of an indeterminate blue colour. A couple of children were hauling equipment out of the back.

The competitors seemed to divide roughly into three groups: first, the smartly dressed little riders with their mummies and daddies in tow; then, these city children who wore an assortment of riding kit and other clothes, clearly hand-me-downs; and finally, the children from local farms, mostly in jeans and rough shirts. But an air of excitement and expectation was shared by all the children shared.

Henrietta appeared by the bus with a large cardboard box from which she withdrew riding hats, insisting that each child put one on. Tegan saw her checking that the other participants were similarly equipped.

‘She’s very strict about it.’ The judge next to Tegan had noticed her interest. ‘People don’t think it matters until someone has an accident.’

It was the woman who worked in the post office. This really was a local affair.

A farm hand led a group of ponies into the field behind where Thunder stood. These would be the mounts for the children from the city. Still keeping an eye on what was going on, Tegan went across to her horse, but he showed no sign of needing reassurance. Instead, his head was up, and he was watching what was happening around him.

‘Lovely boy,’ she said, holding out a piece of carrot. ‘Just you wait here quietly and maybe we’ll get a good ride this afternoon.’ She hadn’t seen him interact with children or with large groups of people before, but there wouldn’t be a problem. She went back to her place at the table.

The judges sat down, and they got started. After the warm-up, the first event began. This was a bending race. Poles had been set in the ground and the riders had to wend their way between the poles without touching them, as fast as they possibly could. Tegan watched carefully. How good some of the riders from the children’s home were, especially that small boy with the black curls and dark brown skin. She awarded him an eight and realised hers was the highest only when the scores were read out. Had she given too much? She thought not. She’d based it on his excellent control of his mount. He deserved it.

But not everyone agreed. At the end of the round, one of the mothers hurried up and complained about the boy being awarded a total score greater than her daughter’s.

‘It’s clear,’ she said, ‘that he’s nowhere near as experienced.’

‘Mummy!’ said an exasperated voice behind her. ‘Please don’t.’

Ignoring her daughter, the woman glowered at Tegan, but Henrietta smoothed things over.

‘We abide by the decisions of the judges,’ she said, ‘but Alice will score highly later on. She’s very good, one of the best.’ Visibly mollified by this praise of her daughter, the woman walked away.

‘Told you.’ Henrietta wasn’t herself involved in the judging, merely keeping an eye on how things were going. ‘Now, don’t be tempted to change a thing. We’re not giving in to bullying. And as it happens, I agree with your score. Just because these young riders are from the children’s home doesn’t mean they shouldn’t be judged in the same way as the others. Some of these parents have a hard time understanding that.’

‘He’s very good.’

‘One of our biggest successes. You know, it’s so important for them to take part. Why don’t you come down one Saturday? You might enjoy it.’

‘I’d like that.’

She would. It was encouraging when someone suddenly got the hang of things, and she could see why Henrietta was so keen to do this.

When the last round came to an end and the children were engaged in a trot around the track, there came a series of loud explosions. Everyone looked around, trying to work out the source of the noise, and the trot was quickly abandoned. There was a kerfuffle, and some of the young riders let go the reigns but the animals were quickly recaptured. Parents were urging their children to dismount. Then, someone began screaming. Out of the corner of her eye, Tegan thought she caught sight of Hywel but there was no time to check because one of the horses was bolting.

It came almost from behind her, from level with the table at least, and one of the older boys was clinging to its back. As Tegan leapt from her chair, she flashed back to her own recent experience of a bolting horse. It had been terrifying for her. How would a child cope? She had to help. Now, the horse streaked across the field, scattering riders and people on foot to right and left. Someone else began to scream and a distraught mother ran to the table.

'What are we going to do? It's my Philip,' she wailed.

'What're we going to do?'

But Tegan was already running toward Thunder.

Chapter 35

Hywel led his horse along the fence, a dozen yards behind where Tegan sat with her fellow judges at the table. He knew she'd be surprised when she saw he'd come on horseback because he'd somehow omitted to tell her he could ride. On their approach, her big horse, Thunder, blew through his nose, acknowledging his stable mate. Hywel looked around, enjoying the familiar Saturday morning scene – one he'd left far behind in his childhood.

These days, Saturdays were filled with other activities that came strictly into the category of work. But, for once, he was taking time off. His father was on the mend and had told him in no uncertain terms to get down to Henrietta's, and he hadn't needed much persuading. Maybe if he was lucky, Tegan would ride out with him in the afternoon.

Things were winding down, and he was leaning lazily against the fence. It would be a few more minutes before she was free to ride away, but it was quite nice to be doing nothing for a change.

Three loud booms sounded, and suddenly the whole scene changed. People shouted and children screamed as riders held onto terrified horses and attempted to calm them. But the boy on the bay horse had been taken by surprise and now the animal was bolting, heading towards the gate to the field beyond. It had to be stopped. At the far side of that field was a busy road.

There was only one way to avert disaster. He saw Tegan spring to her feet and begin to turn toward her horse, but he was right beside his. There was no time. Hywel loosened the rein, leapt up onto Midnight and set off in pursuit.

The bolting horse jumped the boundary at the bottom of the field that had been used for the gymkhana, his hooves ploughing through the top of the hedge, scattering broken twigs and leaves everywhere.

A much bigger animal, Midnight was stronger and faster. Three seconds after the runaway, they too cleared the hedge and soon began to gain ground. Hywel's heart was pounding, seeming to keep pace with the drumming of the hooves. It was one thing walking the animal quietly down the road and quite another, this mad, purposeful gallop with so much at stake. And there'd been no time to prepare himself after such a long time without riding. He hoped his muscles remembered the routines.

As the distance quickly shortened, knowing about that road concentrated his mind. The message got through to the horse and seemed to lend him wings. From the corner of his eye, he saw someone had set off in a Land Rover, ready to halt traffic and now, he caught sight of it again, hugging the far distant edge of the field, but it wouldn't get there in time. He had to stop this happening.

He decided what to do. His strategy was simple: head off the horse by getting slightly in front of it and force it around to the left, and into circling the field. He had to stay on its outside, but at the same time, he mustn't get too close at the speed they were moving, in case the boy fell. As he finally came alongside, they were approaching the bottom boundary fast. The child had moved a long way forward and was almost out of the saddle and onto the horse's neck.

That wouldn't help to slow the animal.

Midnight was responding well. Hywel had borrowed the horse from Mona, and he didn't know the animal, but it seemed to understand exactly what he wanted it to do. Now, the young rider looked over his right shoulder. Their eyes met but Hywel couldn't tell him yet what moves to make, not knowing what the boy had been taught. There was so much noise, he might misunderstand, and the wrong move could end in disaster.

He increased his efforts and heaved a sigh of relief as, gradually, the boy's mount was deflected from its intended jump, one which could have taken him right into the path of an oncoming car or crashing into the hedge on the far side of the road. The young rider was now racing around the field in relative safely, with Midnight between him and the hedge.

Hywel moved further towards him and could see the lad was trying to take back control, pushing himself upright, pulling hard on the reins. This was counterproductive too.

'Hey,' he called, trying to get his attention. The boy turned his head again. Hywel mimed pulling the reins first to the left and then to the right.

'Gently,' he shouted, 'and sit in the saddle.'

It needed to be a light touch. He wouldn't want him to apply too much pressure, or he'd be on the ground. The boy caught on quickly and their speed began to slacken. Hywel continued to press in from the boy's right, forcing the other horse into making smaller and smaller circles. Gradually, they dropped down to walking speed and finally came to a halt, right in the centre of the field.

Furious, the boy threw down the reins and swung out of the saddle. Hywel understood exactly what was going through his mind. He leant over and grabbed the reins, in case the terrified animal took off again.

'I hate him,' the boy screamed. 'I hate him.'

'Why do you say that?' Hywel asked calmly, anxious to lessen the boy's shock.

'He's made me look stupid in front of all those people, even that little black face from the Home. I can't ever come to anything like this again.'

A bit surprised by this odd reference to the boy with the dark skin, Hywel ignored it and said, 'No, you don't hate him, lad. It wasn't his fault. And now he needs you. See how frightened he is? Look, he's shaking. Stroke him. Go on! Tell him what a good boy he is.'

'He's not a good boy!'

'Yes, he is because he didn't throw you and he didn't jump into the road.'

The boy looked at him as if he'd said something completely insane, but then he put out an uncertain hand and stroked the horse's neck.

'That's right. Don't get in front of him for the moment but go closer, lean against him, let him feel you're there. Talk to him. Calm him down.'

Hywel had dismounted and was treating Midnight in much the same way as he'd told the boy. Still, he kept his hand on the other horse's reins. The boy now had his arms around the animal's neck and was sobbing into its sweat-streaked coat. Hywel heaved a sigh of relief, knowing he'd got through to him. He'd be all right in a minute.

Across the field, someone opened the gate from the arena and a group of people stood there, anxiously awaiting their return. Hywel raised a hand to show that all was well, but he wasn't going to rush. He knew enough about twelve-year-old boys to realise it would be better if Philip had a chance to wipe away the tears before they went back. He hadn't forgotten what it felt like to be that age when confidence is so fragile. The boy mustn't be allowed to lose his dignity in front of all those people.

'Right, up you get! Want a leg up?'

'Course not!' When they were both in the saddle, Hywel said, 'You've been brave and everyone's going to be admiring you now. You need to be ready for that.'

'What? What do you mean? They'll think I'm an idiot.'

'No, they won't. You stayed in the saddle until you stopped your horse. How many of them could have done that? It took guts and they all understand that because they're all riders.'

'You think so?'

'I know it. Now, calm down. You're both shocked, you and your mount. If you really want to impress people, take it slowly and show concern for your horse. *Tell* them how concerned you are. What's his name?'

'Ringo.'

'Well, when you get over there, make sure Ringo gets a proper rub down and something to drink before you do anything else. Before you do anything for yourself. He has to come first. He's sweating and he's probably dehydrated.'

Any effort the lad made to help his horse would lessen the shock for him, too.

When they'd gone half the distance back to the gate, the boy turned to him. 'I'm sorry about … well, back there. Just … thank you.'

'I was glad to help, and you did really well.'

He'd had time to internalize the comment the boy had made earlier and said, 'Would you do something for me?'

'What?'

'Don't call the children from the Home "black faces". It's very unpleasant and it doesn't make you look good. They're just like you – it's only the colour of their skin that's different.'

This time, the boy didn't say anything, although a flush of red rose on his cheeks. As they approached the gate, Hywel reined in Midnight and allowed Philip to go through first. The crowd was dense and immediately swirled around him. Hywel dropped to the ground, thinking he'd try to work his way around it while the attention was elsewhere.

Chapter 36

Hywel couldn't make his way through, as people offered thanks and congratulations. Suddenly, he'd had enough and wanted to leave, but was hemmed in by the young riders and many of the parents.

Philip's mother almost dragged her son from the saddle and hugged him tightly. Clearly embarrassed, he escaped from her embrace as soon as he could. 'It's all right Mum, I'm okay. I have to look after Ringo now. He was so frightened. He needs me.'

He was a quick learner.

'I'll help you. One of the older girls was looking at the boy with admiration, and Hywel smiled; it didn't take much for people to form an opinion – favourable or otherwise.

It was another ten minutes before he could work free of the crowd, but all the time, behind the milling people and horses, he could see Tegan waiting, with a broad smile on her face, and that made everything feel right. She waved and turned away, heading back to her horse. Finally breaking free, Hywel led Midnight slowly across the field. At that moment, the Land Rover came around the side of the house and Peter jumped out and waved him over, but he was hardly aware because Tegan was there in front of him. Peter could wait.

Her eyes were shining. She threw her arms around him and hugged tight. 'That was fantastic. As soon as we could see there was no danger that he'd jump the hedge, we all just stood there watching you. It was masterly.'

'Tegan, you're embarrassing me.'

'I didn't realise you could ride, that's all,' she said, a note of reproach in her voice. 'You never said.'

'Rough and ready, and I'm sure I'm not as good as you, from what people have been saying. I've never seen you ride, you know – apart from that day I nearly drove into you, and that didn't give me much idea of your riding skills. I was distracted by other things.'

'And what were those things?' she asked, smiling up at him innocently.

He laughed. 'Do I need to tell you?'

'Not if you don't want to, but it would probably make me feel good.'

He paused for a moment, composing his reply, and then said, 'Well, to begin with, there was this stunning vision in front of me. I was blinded by its brilliance and terrified it would vanish at any moment and then I'd have to accept I'd just been dreaming.'

'That's a pretty good start, Hywel, but you do exaggerate. The way I remember it, it wasn't like that at all.' She looked up at him a little shyly and then added, 'There was my heart's desire, sitting in an old farm truck, looking as if he wished I'd get out of the way.'

They were leaning against the fence by now, his arm around her shoulders, and it felt as if that was where it should always be.

'I was in a hurry,' he protested. But he was smiling at what she'd said.

People were beginning to drift back. He tightened his grip, but Tegan straightened up.

'I should help clear away but I'm so tired.'

'It's the adrenaline. You were all fired up to go, but I just happened to get there first. You'll feel better in a few minutes.'

Henrietta came up and congratulated him. 'I was always sorry when you stopped coming to our Saturdays,' she said.

'It was a long time ago, Henrietta.'

'I know there was a good reason, but it was a pity to lose my star rider.'

Hywel reddened, embarrassed, but Henrietta wasn't to be put off. 'Seriously, what you just did was magnificent, and you probably prevented an accident on the road. I can't bear to think of how horrible it could've been. Thank you.'

'Do we know what the explosions were?' he asked, anxious to change the subject.

'No, but Peter's looking into it. I have my suspicions.'

'Can you do without Tegan's help, Henrietta? I want to take her away now.'

'You do that.' She gave them a look that said she was drawing her own conclusions. 'I've plenty of helpers here.'

As the woman walked away, Hywel said to Tegan, 'Wait just a moment.'

The black horse had scarcely broken sweat, but Hywel led him over to the trough, and the animal slurped noisily at the water and then threw up his head, covering them in a fine, cool spray.

'Come on, then.' He climbed back into the saddle. 'We've lost half the day already.'

*

They rode slowly, side by side, down the narrow lane. The sun came out and the whole afternoon stretched out before them, full of promise.

'I didn't know you could ride,' she said again, breaking a long silence. She looked at his horse, a little smaller than Thunder but easily strong enough to bear his weight, and added, 'Wait – that's Midnight, isn't it?'

'Yes, I borrowed him from Mona. I don't have a horse of my own.'

'So when … when did you learn?'

'I rode pretty much every day of my life until I was twelve. Stopped when my mother died. She was the rider, you see. Afterwards, things were difficult for Dad and me. There wasn't time and there was no money. It's expensive to keep a horse. So we sold him, along with Mum's.'

'What was he called?' she asked softly.

'Toby.' He smiled. 'It's all right – I've got over it.'

'Well, I guess – it was a long time ago.'

But she was thinking how hard it would have been if she'd been forced to give up Bonita's predecessor at the age of twelve. She'd have been heartbroken. And then to have no animal at all to ride! It was unthinkable. He'd lost his mum as well.

They rode sedately through the village and over the river, and then hacked across a few empty meadows until the terrain began to climb up the other side of the valley. She was linked to him now in a way she recognized and yet had never before experienced. Every tiny movement he made brought a reaction deep within her, every separate thought gave rise to a spurt of desire.

And her mind was functioning on two levels – while she responded normally to what was going on around her, to comments he made and things she saw, another part of her was busy encompassing what it meant, just being with him. Something was building, something was binding them together, tying them so tightly, they'd soon be indivisible.

Now they found themselves on a steep bridleway which slowed their progress. Often having to fall into single file to get through, they passed under interlaced branches in woodland and around rocky outcrops, always rising. How beautiful these delicate greens were. In the woods, the sun broke through in patches and spilled golden light across the ground before dappling again into deep shade. This countryside was so different from home.

Enjoying the warm afternoon and the activity, they scarcely spoke until she said, 'You know this track?'

'Often came here as a child. There's a cave a bit higher up. I was usually with my friend, Tim. You know – he was the one in the bar the other night. And sometimes, my cousin Helen would come along with us. We'd build a campfire, cook sausages and invent all sorts of stories.'

'It sounds very "Famous Five".'

'I suppose it was, in a way but there's not much for children to do out in the country except explore and have adventures, so as soon as we were allowed to get away from the farm jobs, that's what we did.'

They picked their way up a steep slope and then he said, 'You used to read books like that?' 'Of course. I have a huge collection of books in English and a few in Welsh. My parents have always kept up with the old country. I could speak Welsh, English and Spanish from the very start.'

Suddenly, they emerged above the tree line. Tegan looked back and saw the whole valley had opened up. Far below, she could make out Henrietta's house where tiny, brightly-coloured figures scurried about, probably still clearing away after the morning's activities. She lifted her head. The morning cloud had gone and straight opposite them was the peak.

'We're looking towards Llantony and Hay Bluff, on the English border. We can do the whole thing one day if you'd like to. It's a good trail, quite demanding.'

'Oh, I'd love to!'

What a great idea. She caught his eye and smiled. Here was something very important to her, that they could share. Maybe he didn't have an equal love of horses, but it didn't matter. He was a great rider, and after what he had done this morning, she was so proud of him.

'Just a bit further. There's a good place for lunch.'

Chapter 37

The trees were now thinning out, and only a little way above them, they ceased to grow altogether. They secured the horses in the last of the shade, on long reins so that they could move about. Then they started to climb, Hywel with a knapsack slung over his shoulder. The terrain became rocky, and several times, he scrambled to the next level and then reached down to grasp Tegan's hand and pull her up.

'This is quite hard going,' she said, 'I'll be aching all over tomorrow.'

'You're not used to rock climbing but today is the first ride I've done in years, and I'll be a lot more sore than you after this.'

She laughed. 'I wasn't suggesting we swap pains.'

Finally, they were up on the bluff. It was a grassy plain with spectacular views to distant peaks.

'See that purple smudge on the horizon? Those are the Malvern Hills.'

She stared her fill of the beautiful landscape, and then turned her gaze in the other direction, where the land undulated for many miles to the West, and she narrowed her eyes, straining to make something out.

'I can see Aberystwyth, and the sea glinting beyond.'

'You must have better eyesight than I have, then,' he said, disbelieving. She grinned. 'I can see it, really.'

There was a cave, and she went to have a look, while he spread a blanket on the ground in the sun. She wandered in, wanting to pick up on what his childhood had been like, learn more about him, but it was disappointing, just a cave.

To children, it would have seemed enormous but was no bigger than a small room with a very low ceiling. A ten-year-old might be able to stand upright but she had to bend her head. The stale smell inside soon drove her back into the open air. He'd unpacked their lunch, and she sat down.

'Don't get your hopes up. It's very simple.'

He handed her a thick piece of ham, sandwiched between two slices of white bread that looked as if they'd been carved, rather than cut, from the loaf. But the bread was fresh and spread amply with butter. There were small, home-grown tomatoes and apples with fragrant skins that were slightly wrinkled. Amazing. They must be from the previous season.

'A cattleman's lunch.' she said.

'A sheep farmer's lunch, more like.'

She bit eagerly into the ham, only now aware of how hungry she was, while he extracted a couple of bottles of beer wrapped in a towel.

'Should still be cool,' he said.

‘I’m not sure about beer. I’m not used to it.’

But she tried it anyway and voted it good for her thirst. A lot better than the rough cider, she thought. But remembering his expression as he looked at her and Daffyd the evening of the dance, she stopped herself from sharing the fact that that’s what she’d drunk. Better not to remind him about that.

‘Be careful, then. The thirst-quenching effect doesn’t last. And put this on,’ he added, handing her a cotton hat, ‘or the sun may get to you and then you’ll regret the beer.’

She loved these small exchanges which showed the growing ease they felt in one another’s company. But all the time, she felt a separate tension in him, as if he had something important to say but didn’t quite know how to. Several times, she met his gaze.

‘What?’ she said at last. ‘What is it?’

‘Nothing. I’m just fixing every single moment of this wonderful day in my mind.’

That might be good or bad. It could almost be a farewell. What was really on his mind? But she didn’t know how to respond, and so she kept quiet. Then, the beer began to take effect. Feeling drowsy, she lay back on the grass. Just as she was drifting off to sleep, she felt him place the hat gently over her face.

*

The sun had moved around the rocks and now, they were lying in full shade. As she stirred, Hywel lifted up the hat. She knew at once he hadn’t been sleeping. He was propped up on one elbow, looking down on her. She returned the look, and he leant over to kiss her. It was a long kiss that deepened as time went on. His heart was beating fast and strong against her chest, and she felt hers respond, falling into the same rhythm. She wished he'd stay close, but he pulled away and lay back, looking up at the sky, saying nothing for a long time. Then, he turned again to her.

'I think it's time we talked about some difficult things.'

'Difficult? How?'

'I need to tell you about … me. You may change your mind about me afterwards, but it's only fair to tell you.'

This had to be what Mona had hinted at.

'That sounds very dramatic, Hywel. I can't imagine that anything you say might change my opinion of you.'

'Sshh,' he said. 'You can't be sure of that.'

He was quiet again for a while, and she let him take his time. Then he sat up, encircling his knees with his arms, looking away from her down the valley.

'Three years ago, Caitlin and I got married. She was a girl from the village. I'd known her all my life. Daffyd and I both loved her, and both courted her. But she chose me, and I was the happiest man alive.'

He glanced at her, but she remained silent, her face giving nothing away.

'Ten months after our wedding, our child was due to be born. It was all going well, and we were overjoyed at the thought. But there was a complication, and he was born dead, the cord wound several times around his neck. Two hours later, Caitlin died, with a massive haemorrhage. There was blood everywhere..' He stopped as if he couldn't find the words to continue. After a long pause, he said, 'I do remember that. And then, there was Dad, trying to comfort me, and everyone afraid to say anything to me for months afterwards.'

Seeing his distress, Tegan laid her hand on his arm and gave it a squeeze. 'Hywel, you don't need to …'

'I do. I need to say this. It's important for you to you understand. I was a wreck. I couldn't believe what had happened. I could only remember the bad things, the blood, the purple face of the baby. I wished then with all my heart that I'd let Daffyd take her. With him, she might still be alive. I wished I could die.'

His voice was cracking, and it sounded as if he couldn't quite get his breath.

'They say a funeral helps people get over the loss, gives permission to the survivors to go on living. Maybe that's true if it's your grandma who's died. But not when it's your young wife and baby.'

Her heart went out to him. She wanted to gather him in her arms and heal his pain, but she knew it didn't work like that. She mustn't interrupt.

'People kept saying it would get better but, a year later, I was still grieving. I buried myself in farm business and gradually taught myself to appear normal, but there was nothing left on the inside. All I really remember of that time is how good Dad was and how much I owe to Mona's friendship. Without them, I'm not sure what would have happened to me. I'm not sure I could have been strong enough on my own.'

He was silent a long time, staring at the peaks opposite.

‘And then at the beginning of this year, I suddenly saw how selfish I was being. I don’t know what changed. Maybe it’s true that time eventually heals you. Maybe. But you don’t forget, and I wouldn’t want to. Anyway, I knew I had to snap out of it. I forced myself to see old friends, to go to social things. But nothing really touched me.’ Now he turned to her.

‘Then, one day in April, I saw you, Tegan, and my whole life changed. Of course, I still think about her. I still love her, and I always will, but that was in another life, and I was a different person.’

Once again, the silence stretched out.

‘And now?’ she said, after an interval.

‘Now? Now, I think I’ve fallen in love with you.’

Tegan was sitting upright. She’d let go his arm and tears ran freely down her face. What could she say to help?

‘I’m so sorry for the pain you’ve suffered,’ she whispered, and putting her arms around him, she pulled him close. ‘How can you think this will make me not care for you? It just helps me understand.’

‘You’re young. You deserve something better.’

‘Hywel, I’m not that young. Not so selfish and demanding that I can’t understand what’s happened to you. I know I don’t have much life experience and have always been indulged, and that has made me selfish – but only out of ignorance. It doesn’t mean I can’t change. What I don’t know, I can learn.’

It was her turn to stop and think about what she was going to say next.

'And you see, it's not so simple.' She moved so that she could look into his face. 'It's not simple at all, because I've fallen in love with you too, and I can't undo that.'

She saw the fierce joy her words had given rise to and this time, it was she who initiated the kiss. They fell back then and lay entwined in each other's arms, unmoving, until the air cooled, and the sun began its descent to the horizon.

Chapter 38

Mona and George left for London early on Friday morning. They expected George to be nominated by his party as the candidate for their area, that he'd simply been summoned for talks. But though there'd been no mention of other potential candidates, he was nervous.

Mona also had reservations. 'I'm in two minds about his entering parliament, but he's set his heart on doing this so I'm going to help him in any way I can.'

If Tegan had married Luís, she'd have had to do the same, spend time in the capital, make an effort to ingratiate herself with others on the political scene. She'd been lucky to have her eyes opened in time, though she believed George was sincere in his desire to help others. And maybe Luís's father was too.

'What can I do to help while you're away?'

'You're going to be in charge, Tegan. If there's anything you're doubtful about, put them off and say you'll get an answer from me next week.'

And that was it. Tegan began the morning with trepidation but the first couple of hours were quiet, bar a few routine telephone calls, and she dealt with the jobs she'd been asked to do. She decided to keep to their usual timetable and, at eleven o'clock, she locked the estate office and headed for the kitchen. Bethan poured coffee and they sat either side of the big table with its scrubbed planks. Tegan had scarcely taken a sip when there was a ring at the door.

'I'll get it,' she said, thinking the older woman worked hard and deserved time to rest. 'You have your coffee.'

When Tegan opened the door, there was a uniformed police constable on the step, helmet in hand and perspiring. He'd propped a black bicycle against a stone garden urn and must have cycled up the steep track from the village.

'Miss Tegan Lewis?'

Her heart sank. 'Yes. I'm Tegan Lewis.'

'We'd like you to come down to the police station in Crickhowell to answer a few questions, miss.'

'Oh? Why? What do you want me for?' Then her heart gave a great thud, and the terror of what might have happened seized her. 'It's … it's not my parents, is it? Has something –?'

'I don't know the details, miss but it's nothing to do with your parents. I'm sorry if I frightened you.'

With her anxiety reduced a little, Tegan said, 'I'm the only one in the office here, so I can't leave until lunchtime. I could drive over some time this afternoon.'

'That'll be all right, miss. Shall we say half past two.'

Tegan returned to the kitchen. 'I don't know what they want of me, but I've just had a thought – did you ever speak to Angharad's father?'

'I did, but it was only a few days ago, when he made a delivery here, because I was too busy. He was very put out by what I told him, angry really, but then he said he hadn't seen his daughter for nearly a week because she was staying with a cousin in Newport, so he wouldn't be able to talk to her until she got back.'

She went back to the office but couldn't concentrate. This summons had to be about Angharad. She couldn't imagine any other reason why the police might wish to see her. Instead of working, she thought through what had happened between them that day in Newport, and the suspicions she'd had later about Angharad's odd behaviour.

After lunch, she tucked her passport into her bag, in case she needed to prove her identity, and headed into Crickhowell over the far side of the mountain. Having forgotten to ask where the police station was, she drove slowly around the central part of the small town, wondering if they still had a little blue lamp these days to show which was their building. She'd gone right past the station before she spotted the sign and then had to turn around and find a parking space in the lea of the castle wall.

She'd done absolutely nothing wrong, but she was nervous, frightened even. What a pity this had happened when her aunt and uncle were away. She didn't know how the Welsh police might behave. In Colombia, they were very high-handed, and an interview would not be a pleasant matter, even if you were completely innocent of the crime they were investigating. But when she thought about Constable Morgan's pink, sweaty face and earnest manner, she was somehow reassured that they wouldn't be clapping her in irons.

Besides, George was an important man in the neighbourhood, and he would be able to rescue her if things went badly wrong. They wouldn't be back until the following afternoon, but the police wouldn't detain her, would they? She imagined herself behind bars in the picturesque little town. Anyway, she should sort this out herself. It was her fault she'd accepted Angharad's invitation to go to Newport.

*

The inspector, a balding man in his fifties, introduced himself politely and thanked her for coming in, while showing her into a small office, where he invited her to sit down. He didn't look like an inquisitor, any more than Constable Morgan did.

'Would you like a cup of tea, miss?'

'No. No, thank you,' said Tegan. She wanted to hurry the interview along, but it was reassuring to be offered the courtesy, making her feel they would treat her fairly.

He sat down. 'I've been handed this investigation because the people involved are local to this area. Do you know a Miss Angharad Jenkins?'

'Yes, I do. She's … not a friend, exactly but, when I first arrived here, she invited me out for the day, and we went to Newport. I thought it was nice of her to do that. But I haven't seen her since.'

'When would that be?'

'The Saturday at the beginning of June. I don't remember the date.'

'Would you mind telling me what you did? Just run through your day, as things happened.'

It took Tegan a good quarter of an hour to do this. Then the inspector said, 'You wouldn't have a receipt from the department store, would you. I know that shop usually gives receipts.'

She'd stuffed it into her large handbag and never looked at it again, and today was probably the first time that she'd used the bag since the visit. She opened it up and pulled out her purse, compact, comb and handkerchief and there, at the bottom, was the receipt for the silk scarf. She handed it over and said, 'I have another here, for some things I bought for an old lady, in the haberdasher's across the road. I did it while I was waiting. I noticed the shop and I didn't think Angharad would be very patient with things like that, so I took the opportunity.'

The latter was a hand-written receipt in an almost illegible scrawl, but she noticed it was indeed dated the second of June.

'That's very useful, miss. Miss Jenkins said she was the one who bought the item in the department store, while you were looking around.'

'Well, as you can see, it was me. I don't know how I'd have got hold of the receipt if it had been hers. And I'm sure the assistant would remember me because she made a comment about how my friend seemed to be in a big hurry. There's also Olive Jones, the lady I bought the silks for. She would confirm that she'd asked me to do that.'

What a cynical, unpleasant person Angharad was turning out to be. How could she have behaved like this to someone she'd only just met and who had done her no wrong? Tegan hadn't wanted to get the girl into trouble, despite her feelings that she was up to something not quite right. But it was a different matter now that she was attempting to cast blame.

‘And you say you haven’t seen her since? Not met her anywhere? Maybe talked on the phone?’

‘No, I haven’t. I went away for a weekend to Monmouth but otherwise, I’ve not left the farm except to go into the village. Oh, and one evening, I went out with a friend. I didn’t see her any of those times.’ While the inspector studied the notes he’d been making. Tegan said, ‘Would you mind telling me what this is about and how you think I’m involved?’

He frowned, gathering his thoughts. ‘At the moment, it’s a double enquiry. We were following a trail of stolen goods, and we asked the young lady to help us with our enquiries just as we have with you, but now she has become a missing person. When we tried to get her to come in to talk to us for a second time, her father said she was staying with a cousin in Newport, but they hadn’t heard from her in months. We have no idea where she may be.’

This sounded serious – and might mean something had happened to her, particularly if she was mixing with people prepared to receive stolen goods.

‘How can I help?’

‘If you don’t mind, miss, I’d like you to go over everything again, everything that happened after you came out of the cinema, anything at all you can think of, even if it doesn’t seem very important to you.’

Maybe he had now dismissed her as a possible suspect and was hoping to get as much information from her as he could. She thought for a moment; there were quite a few things she hadn’t been particularly clear about, had rejected as not worth mentioning. Now, she began to talk about the meeting at “The Bunch of Grapes” and the behaviour of some of Angharad’s friends.

She’d been at the police station for hours and a pain hovered behind her eyes. There wasn’t anything more she could tell him, and now, she wanted to go home. Obviously, the inspector had come to the same conclusion.

‘That’s very helpful, miss. If you remember anything further, just telephone the station.’

‘I don’t think there is anything.’

‘You’ve told us a lot we didn’t know. Just one more thing – and it’s definitely a long shot.’ The inspector was looking hopefully at her. ‘Can you remember any of the number plates on those motor scooters? Some people have a good memory for things like that.’

Tegan hadn’t, not particularly. She thought for a moment, seeing the parked scooters in her mind’s eye. Now, she recalled Brian’s extraordinary machine. She had noticed that part of the registration plate was a collection of letters: HBN. It had stayed in her mind because the same letters were on the registration plate of one of the farm cars. She explained this and the inspector looked jubilant.

‘You don’t remember the numbers as well, do you?’

‘I’m afraid I don’t.’

Finally, the inspector said he’d finished. As she left, she took gulps of fresh air and waited for her head to clear, before climbing into the car. It’d been an unnerving experience, and all she wanted now was to get home.

Chapter 39

'He said they may need to speak to me again.' Tegan passed the marmalade to Mona at breakfast on Monday morning. Unsettled by what had happened, she'd wanted to talk to her aunt about Angharad's strange behaviour and her experience at the police station. 'They don't know what's happened to her, so they'll have to keep on searching.'

'She'll have gone into hiding with friends,' said George.

'Into hiding?' Tegan had been thinking more of her safety than a need to keep out of the way of the police. 'You make it sound like the plot of a spy novel.'

'Well, I think that's the correct term. They were obviously catching up with her, so she had to leave. It's all very unpleasant but I shouldn't worry about it, my dear. It has nothing to do with you.'

George smiled. He was looking very cheerful. Having now been confirmed as the chosen candidate for his party, he would have to work hard, as the upcoming by-election would take place in a little less than six weeks. Of course, they could lose to another party, but it was unlikely. He looked as if he relished the prospect of the battle to come.

Mona yawned and poured a second cup of tea.

‘I do love going to London but all that socializing tires me out. By lunch time on the second day, I was ready to come home.’

George patted her hand. ‘But thank you for staying, my dear,’ he said. ‘It made all the difference to me.’

*

Tegan had finished her breakfast and was walking through the hall when she heard the post drop onto the door mat. She gathered it up and sifted through the letters, taking her own and placing the others on the hall table. Three for her today. One was from a friend in Cape Cod in America. She opened it straightaway, seeing it was a long strip of postcards folded together.

Her friend was on holiday. The others were from Colombia, one addressed in her mother’s neat handwriting, while the second was emblazoned with Mari-Dolores’s undisciplined scribble. How on earth had that letter even got to her? The address was all but indecipherable.

She glanced at her watch. There was time enough to spare before work, and she hurried upstairs, eager to read her mail. Letters had become precious, to be read, re-read and savoured.

As she opened her mother’s letter and began to read, the feeling of home slowly wrapped itself around her, bringing her up to date on what was happening around the ranch and locality, with news about Dad, and the ongoing adventures of Miguelito, Julio’s ten-year-old son. She couldn’t help laughing at his latest mad escapade. She loved being transported back home, seeing the people and scenes as her mother filled her in on the various activities.

Then, she opened Mari-Dolores's letter.

"My dearest little Tegan," she began, assuming the role of older, wiser friend, as usual. Her friend did have superior experience of the ways of the world, or rather the ways of men and courtship. Why should she be offended? She looked over the loops and whorls that raced across the four thin sheets of blue airmail paper. How much they reminded her of the warm, emotional character of the writer.

"Querida amiga mia," she continued in Spanish, *"you are suffering badly - but a delicious suffering, I hope. Sofia and I had such a delightful time over your description of this beautiful man - and a real man, not a mere boy. Very good! You have done well. How we wish we could meet him. (Luis, by the way, has already strayed and has been seen twice at the paseo with Carmencita Hinojos.)"*

Aha! Well, that didn't surprise her. It was good that she felt not the slightest hint of hurt or jealousy. And she'd been right about who had attracted his eye.

"I hope you haven't waited for an answer to your letter to get to know your farmer, because if so, he'll be long gone. Do you know your letter took three weeks to get here? And I expect this will take another three weeks to get back to you.

"Just a word of caution, my sweet. Don't let on too much how passionately you feel about him."

Yes, right, good advice – but she'd probably already told him everything that mattered. Maybe it would have been better if the postal system were just a little faster, while she'd still had the chance to do something about it. But it wouldn't have changed anything.

Tegan sighed as the letter slipped from her fingers. Things simply weren't like that – not any longer, anyway. Her friends were still playing the flirting game, and she'd moved on to some other plane. The way in which girls were so closely guarded back home really did hold them back, so that the possible depths of a real relationship could scarcely be glimpsed. Until she'd come to Wales, she too had operated on the level of a schoolgirl, her emotional life full of melodrama. What she had with Hywel was real. Or maybe she'd been different from her friends all along, and she was finally discovering her true self.

When she looked again at the time, only five minutes remained before work. She scooped up Mari-Dolores's pages and thrust them into her pocket, brushed her teeth and ran down to the estate office.

She and Mona worked quietly once Tegan had passed on the various messages from Saturday. Towards the middle of the second hour, there was a knock at the door and Hywel came in.

'Good morning, Mona. Good morning, Tegan.'

He gave Tegan a smile that made her heart leap. She wanted to hurry over and throw her arms around him, but he hadn't come to see her. She worked quietly while he asked Mona if he could talk to her about Joe and one or two other farm matters.

'Pull up a chair, Hywel. You're going to ask me if you can keep Joe, aren't you?'

'I am.'

They were soon deep in conversation and Tegan had turned her attention to the work she had in front of her. But she didn't get much of it done, her eyes straying constantly across the room to the two figures huddled in a serious discussion. Just the fact that Hywel was sitting there, almost within arm's reach, disturbed her concentration. She was restless and had to force herself to sit still.

After a while, Mona stood up. 'Right, Hywel, I think we've agreed all that. I'm going over to the house now, Tegan. I'll see you over there in a few minutes.'

She left the room. Tegan stayed where she was, looking at him. He picked up his chair and brought it across to her. Then he leaned across the desk to kiss her, before saying, 'I wondered if you'd like to ride up to the farm this afternoon. I'm selecting lambs to take to market. Maybe you can help me.'

'I'd like that. I'll see you after lunch.'

He stood up but still clutched her hands in his, pulling her to her feet.

'And now, I have to go. I wish I could stay longer.'

With a peck on the cheek, he released her and was gone.

Tegan wandered over to the main house in a daze. Every time they had any physical contact, it interfered with her perceptions. How had she allowed him to walk away like that? She joined Mona in her little sitting room and drank a cup of coffee. After a time, she worried that she wasn't very good company and she tried to start a conversation, but Mona said little and was content to sit quietly, no doubt recovering from her busy visit to the capital.

Chapter 40

'I'll give you a tour. You've only ever been in the yard and the barn, haven't you?'

Hywel took her hand and they set off, skirting the barn instead of walking through it. At first, they followed along the borders of the farm, and Tegan saw the fresh wood and wire where he and Dan had been at work.

'Was this where Dan fell?' she asked when they came to the part of the fence that bordered the edge of the quarry.

'It's a bit further along. He wouldn't have survived if he'd fallen here.'

Tegan looked carefully down and drew a sharp breath at the shear drop. Hywel came to stand beside her.

'Poor Emma, she'd have been devastated if anything had happened to him. Her husband died five years ago, and she's had to work hard to support Dan. I think she believed he was launched, when Dad said we could give him a job. He's a good, hard worker but a bit slow and naïve about things. You can't leave him to take important decisions.'

'What does Emma do?' Tegan asked.

'She's the district nurse. You've probably noticed her on her bicycle. We'll be seeing a lot of her in the next few weeks, now that Dad's had the cast off. She has to persuade him it's in his own best interests to do the exercises he's been prescribed, and at the moment, they're at the learning stage.' He laughed. 'I don't envy her the job. He's not going to be a good pupil.'

They walked on around a stand of trees. There were fields dotted with sheep. Beyond that, the moor stretched out, the peak rising at the far side, about half a mile away.

'What is that building?'

She pointed to a low, white house that was now coming into view beyond the trees, over on the right. Even at this distance, you could see it was a relatively new building that had been constructed on the footprint of an older one. Some of the original, rough stone had been retained and rising from the rest of the foundations were simple, white-rendered walls and then a slate roof. 'I didn't even realise it was here. You can't see it from the main farm.'

'Dad and I built it gradually over several years. It's standing on the foundations of the original farmhouse. The one we now live in is only two hundred years old or so.' They continued towards the structure and the details became clearer. 'That was where Caitlyn and I lived. Now Dad's talking about taking it over.'

She wondered about it. She'd love to see inside but her instincts were telling her he wouldn't want to show her.

'It's lovely, and I see why your dad might want to live there. It's probably more convenient than the main house.'

'Well, we'll have to extend the electricity, of course, but that shouldn't be too difficult between the two houses.'

They returned to the barn and spent an hour helping Joe isolate the lambs that Hywel would take to market in Brecon the following day.

'The farm truck arrives at six, so we have to be ready, and I'll travel with it. It belongs to Owen Evans from the village. If I were driving myself, I'd invite you.'

'Oh, what a pity! Is there really no space for me?'

'No space I'd want to subject you to. The lorry's dirty and uncomfortable. And Owen would be put out. He enjoys these trips with someone he knows. He's very shy and would find it difficult with you there. I'm sorry but I wouldn't like to annoy such a useful person. Now, come and see Dad.'

*

In the kitchen, Hywel's father greeted them with a beaming smile. He was presiding over a pot of stew, and looked much better than on her last visit, a different person altogether. He soon demonstrated that he was able to get around.

'Hello, Mr Davies.' She glanced down. 'I see the cast has gone. Are you feeling better?'

'I am. It still aches a bit, but I'm told that will gradually go away. In the meantime, I'm being well looked after.' He turned to his son. 'I have to tell you, Hywel, that Emma Matthias is a hard woman. I wouldn't let on to her, but some of things she makes me do bring tears to the eyes.' He was smiling, though, obviously not too upset by the district nurse's hard-line approach to physiotherapy. 'Would you like to stay to supper, Tegan?'

'Dad!'

‘I’m the cook today so I can hand out the invitations. It’s not often we have such a beautiful guest.’

Tegan blushed at the compliment. ‘Well, I’d love to, Mr Davies, but Mona might worry if I don’t get back.’

‘Actually, if you want to stay, that won’t be a problem. I told her this morning Dad would probably try to get you to eat with us,’ said Hywel. ‘I know him – he’s been desperate to get back to normal life, so I thought I’d leave it up to him to decide whether or not he could face visitors.’

‘Well, that would be wonderful, thank you.’

While Tegan went off to wash her hands, Hywel and his father set the table. The simple meal was entirely to her taste: beef stew, mashed potatoes and vegetables. This was followed by tinned peaches and a thick local cream. Mr Davies had planned this all along – the beef for a start. They certainly didn’t produce that on the farm.

Conversation covered a wide range of topics.

‘I get nearly all my information from the radio,’ the farmer said, ‘particularly since I’ve been confined to the house. I wouldn’t know what’s going on, but for the Home Service. So, it’s nice to talk to a real human being.’

Hmm, so Joe and I don’t count?’ said Hywel. He turned to Tegan, with a grin. ‘Do you realise the weight of responsibility resting on your shoulders this evening?’

They continued to talk, and it was after eight when they finished eating.

‘I’m going to walk Tegan home,’ said Hywel. ‘I’ll wash up when I get back, Dad.’

‘Take your time. I can do it.’

‘That was a wonderful meal, Mr Davies. Thank you.’

Hywel steered her out of the door.

‘I can ride, Hywel. We can say good-bye here. You have to be up early tomorrow.’

‘No, I’ll walk back with you. Let’s get Thunder.’

*

At first, it was quite dark under the trees, although there were nearly two hours of daylight left.

Tegan and Hywel held hands and they walked slowly along the track, leading the horse.

‘I do like your father.’

‘That’s good. He can be a bit obsessive. More than a bit, especially since he’s been cooped up at home all this time. It was a bad break, but he seems to be healing properly now. At the moment, his focus is on charming you, so I suppose it’s a good thing – if you like him, that is.’

‘Charming me? He doesn’t have to try.’ She thought about the way in which father and son interacted with each other. ‘He really cares a lot for you, doesn’t he?’

‘Yes, and I care for him. We’re very close. That comes of there just being the two of us for a good part of my life. I did wonder how he’d react to change.’

‘What do you mean, Hywel?’

They’d come to the bend in the road, where Tegan and Hywel had first met, all those weeks ago as he drove the sheep up the mountain. Golden sunlight filtered through the branches and a gentle breeze stirred the air and fanned their warm skin. It seemed a different place this evening.

'Things are changing, *fy 'nghariad*, since you've come on the scene. Dad knows how things are between us – he's not blind. It's funny. I thought he'd be a bit put out, worried he might be left on his own. But actually, it's the opposite way around. It's you who's charmed him!'

'That's a nice idea. But maybe he's just feeling better since the cast came off, in less pain. I'm sure that will have cheered him up.'

They walked on, and where the road began to open up, they stopped by a gap in the trees to look down on the whole valley. Houses were scattered here and there, far below them, a church spire, a bridge over the river. The white dots of sheep were everywhere. It looked as if someone had spread out tiny toys on a vast green mat.

Hywel pulled her into his arms and kissed her. It was different this time – urgent, demanding. He left her lips bruised. She loved what he was doing, loved him, and returned his kisses with enthusiasm.

'Come away with me for the weekend, Tegan, will you? I love you. I want you so much.'

She took a deep breath and tried to calm the wild beating of her heart. It had all been heading to this. Back home, no well-brought-up young woman would sleep with a man before marriage – at least, if they did, they didn't admit it – and many of the older families still closely chaperoned their girls. Her parents not so much. But they trusted her, and she had no wish to betray their trust.

That knowledge took away her confidence and made her not entirely sure what was the right way to behave but, suddenly, she knew it was what she wanted. Maybe she'd regret the decision later, but for the moment, it was the right thing. Her heart filled with a surge of happiness.

'I will,' she said. 'I love you too, Hywel, and I want to be with you.'

His lips crushed hers now, and his eyes were filled with longing. 'I'll look for somewhere to stay,' he said a little while later. 'What about going to the sea?' And then he added with a little smile, 'So you can really see Aberystwyth?'

'That would be perfect.'

Chapter 41

The weekend before the agricultural show was the last opportunity for anyone to take time off. The following week would be all hard work.

'I'm going away with Hywel,' said Tegan to her aunt.

She'd agonized over this decision for a long time. She'd met up with Hywel several times and they'd kissed and had long conversations since he'd asked her to go away with him, but they'd not grown more intimate, and she knew he was giving her the opportunity to back out if she wanted to. She didn't want to, but it was still a big step.

And she'd braced herself for protests and warnings. Now her aunt came across and placed her hands on Tegan's arms, looking seriously at her.

'Are you sure about this, Tegan? I am afraid for both of you if you rush things. And I'm not sure how your parents would react if they knew what you were proposing to do.'

'I've thought it over again and again – and we've talked about it. I love him, Aunt Mona, and I believe he loves me, too. I know … I know what you want to say to me, but this is important for both of us.'

But her aunt looked at her and said, 'I am concerned, but I think you've made up your mind. It's a big decision for a couple, and you must be responsible, or others get hurt. You have your whole life in front of you. Be sure it's the right step and take care, both of you.'

Tegan hugged the woman. 'Thank you,' she said. 'Thank you for being who you are. And for caring for me.'

'You're very dear to me, Tegan.'

'I know we have a lot of work coming up. We'll be back on Sunday afternoon, I promise.'

*

On Friday, Tegan was packed and ready to go, well in advance of the agreed departure time. She'd left herself too much time with nothing specific to occupy her mind, and now she paced the sitting room, thinking over her decision. Was it really the right thing to do? Things were changing in society and many young women were prepared to sleep with a man they cared about these days.

But was it right? Fear of unwanted pregnancy and society's condemnation ran deep. She'd heard there was a pill available, but that was only to married women, which sounded as if the medical profession had got things the wrong way around. And then, what if she'd misjudged him? Would she regret it? No, she truly loved him and recognized his honesty and goodness.

They'd talked about so many things. She was a very different person from the young woman who had run away from the farm when his cousin had come visiting so many weeks before. She wasn't mistaken. Her decision wasn't based on hope but on what she knew about him and her feelings for him.

Still … she could just tell him she wasn't ready. Maybe that would be best. He wouldn't make it difficult for her. She looked at her watch, willing him to come before she changed her mind.

But then he arrived and, on seeing him, she forgot all about what she'd been going to say and somehow, here they were, on the road to Aberystwyth. She settled back into her seat and talked about plans for the show and the letter she'd received from her parents.

Eventually, they fell silent. But it was a good silence, and she didn't feel she needed to break it. He glanced across at her once or twice and smiled. Probably, he wanted to reassure her. This was a big thing for her, and he surely knew that. She'd said she'd never slept with anyone before.

They were on the high mountain road and suddenly, he was having to concentrate. At places, the road narrowed to single track. On the rare occasions they met an oncoming vehicle, they had to squeeze up against the mountain or perch over the dizzying heights to allow it to pass. Facing into the sun as it moved slowly into the west, their eyes were filled with the peachy, golden light.

'Not far now,' he said, letting his breath out as they came down onto a wider stretch of road. It was more than an hour since they'd seen another vehicle. 'We'll be staying at a small hotel, not far from the sea. I hope you like it.'

*

'*Croeso*! Welcome! Come in! Come in!'

The landlady seemed to be entirely round. The black, shiny material of her dress stretched across her ample, corseted stomach and pulled tightly at the shoulders. Despite her bulk, she led them quickly up a polished wooden staircase, on which was a dark red, flowered carpet fixed down with shining brass rods. At the end of a wide passage, she opened a door onto a large room.

'The Blue Room.' The curtains and quilt were a pale blue flower design, the chairs upholstered in royal blue moquette, and grey-blue swirly-patterned carpet covered the floor. The blueness was overwhelming, but the room was clean and pleasant. Tegan scarcely paid attention.

The woman walked further into the room, flung back a door in the right-hand wall and said proudly, 'And your own bathroom, with a shower, as well. We had it put in last year.' She waited for their exclamations of appreciation, which they duly provided, and then added, 'You didn't order dinner, did you, sir?'

'Not for tonight, thank you.' He turned to Tegan and said, 'I thought we'd go out and have a look at the town. What do you think?'

'Oh, yes, I'd like that.'

She tried to inject some enthusiasm into her reply, to sound like her usual self, but could not quite control the quiver in her voice. Finally, the woman was gone. Hywel closed and locked the door and then wrapped his arms around her.

'It's all right,' he said, holding her for a long moment. 'Look, why don't you freshen up and then we'll look for a nice restaurant.'

*

They wandered up and down wide streets, narrow lanes and flights of steps, past shops, houses and chapels and even one or two restaurants. Then they walked on the promenade, taking their time to appreciate the sun, now low over the water. Finally, as it began to grow dark, they found a hotel with a dining room that was willing to serve non-residents. In the deepening twilight, the place looked attractive and inviting.

The waiter seated them and handed over the menu. Tegan laid it down almost immediately and said, 'I don't think I'm very hungry.'

'Neither am I. Let's just have the fishcakes.'

The waiter looked thoroughly unimpressed as he took their order.

'Wine, sir?' he asked.

'No,' said Tegan.

'Yes,' said Hywel. 'A glass of white wine for the lady. And I'll have a small glass of bitter.'

The waiter's face acquired another half-degree of sourness to show his disapproval of patrons who thought it was acceptable to drink beer with their dinner.

'I'm sorry,' she said when he'd gone. 'You're right of course. I'll enjoy the wine. I'm just terribly nervous.'

His hand covered hers and he looked into her eyes. 'Trust me, Tegan. I would never hurt you.'

The fish cakes, which were served with vegetables and fried potatoes, were surprisingly good and they both found they were able to finish their meal.

'Anything else? I think they have a fruit pie and custard.'

'No, that's all I can manage.'

Chapter 42

It was nearly ten when they arrived back at the hotel. Most of the street was now in darkness, except for the bar attached to the hotel. With its huge plate-glass windows, it stood out like a beacon. Tegan's heart was beating fast. She swallowed a couple of times to moisten her dry throat as they drew level.

Inside, two couples sat at tables with cups of coffee or tea in front of them, and several men occupied the bar area. As they walked into the dimly lit hallway alongside, laughter drifted out and Tegan's heartbeat went up a notch. She must calm down. Every woman in the world went through this process, the first time. She was lucky to be doing it with a man she loved instead of on her wedding night, with some "suitable" person chosen by her parents. Wasn't this exactly what she'd wanted when she'd said she would not allow them to choose a husband for her?

In their room, he kissed her gently and ran his fingers down the bare skin of her arms. It was just a light caress, but it sent ripples of heat through to the very inner part of her being. 'You use the bathroom first.'

He hadn't turned on the light. The evening sky provided just enough light to see by. Now, he opened the big, old-fashioned sash window and leaned out.

Tegan went into the bathroom, washed quickly and cleaned her teeth. Then, she stared into the mirror. She looked much more confident than she felt. Pulling her dressing gown around her, she came out and joined Hywel at the window.

'I've finished,' she said. 'Your turn.'

He smiled at her and dropped a kiss on her cheek.

'Don't go away, will you?'

Could he even guess how much she wanted to do just that? She stared out the window.

When he came back, she said, 'I don't know how to do this. You'll have to show me.'

'I will.'

First, he held her and then, he began to nuzzle gently into her neck. She put her arms around him and drew him towards her, but he pulled back a little. His eyes on hers, he slowly loosened her dressing gown, shaking the ties loose until the front panels fell apart.

Embarrassed, she made to close the gown again, but he said, 'No. No, let me see.'

He looked then, drinking in the small, rounded breasts and narrow waist, the womanly curves behind the expensive silk.

Her unruly curls, set loose from the pony tail she'd worn earlier, had fallen to the front, just long enough to cover her nipples. He reached out, carefully lifted the hair away and laid it gently behind her shoulders, kissing each breast as he did so. Then, his tongue was licking, rasping, its roughness making her nipples stand proud. Her swift intake of breath made him increase his efforts. A burning sensation began low in her abdomen. That humming sound – it was coming from her. She pushed herself up against him and felt his hardness.

'Dewch i'r gwely,' he whispered. 'Come to bed.'

*

'Darling, darling, I'm so sorry. I just can't.'

'It's all right. I'm really tired, too. Tomorrow will be much better.'

On her shoulder, she felt the dampness from his silent tears, and then he lay back with his arm tight around her.

A little while later, he got up and dressed. She hadn't fallen asleep, but she'd lain still, knowing he didn't want to talk. He closed the door quietly behind him as he left.

What had gone wrong? Was it something to do with her? Was there something she should have done? It was a dark moment. She cried a little and then sat up and wiped her eyes. Turning the light on, she looked at her watch: only just after eleven. She wouldn't be able to sleep now.

She got out of bed. The cool air touched her warm skin and she shivered. Quickly, she put on the clothes she'd worn during the day and then slipped on a jacket and picked up her handbag. She couldn't lock the door because Hywel had taken the key with him, but she didn't care.

The bar was still open although the crowd was now reduced to two men on the high stools. A waitress was wiping newly washed glasses, hanging them from a rack overhead, exchanging the odd word with her customers.

She'd just sit in the corner, as far from them as possible. She didn't really want anything, but she couldn't stay on her own in the room, surrounded by the blue phantoms of her hopes.

Eventually, the waitress spotted her and came over. 'What can I get for you, love. A Dubonnet, maybe?'

The thought of alcohol made her feel sick.

'Coffee, please. Black, with sugar. Or tea.'

While the coffee was being prepared, the men left. Relieved of her responsibilities, the waitress came across to Tegan's table with two cups.

'Mind if I join you? I've nearly finished me shift.'

Tegan nodded and the woman sat down, angling her chair so she could keep an eye on the door. A notice at the bar stated that no alcohol would be served after half past ten but maybe she thought there'd be other late-night coffee-drinkers.

A large tear rolled down Tegan's cheek. She swiftly brushed it away, but not before the woman had noticed.

'There's no need to cry, love. He's just trying to work something out.'

Tegan looked up in surprise, about to tell the woman to keep to her own business but, instead, she found herself saying, 'What? What do you mean?'

'I saw him go out alone earlier – nice-looking bloke with black hair, right?'

Tegan nodded, unable to say a word.

'Something's wrong, I thought, and right away, I remembered you. Saw the two of you arrive, see? After dinner? Saw the way you looked at each other, like there was no-one else in the world. Then he comes rushing through just now, in a right state, and I thought, she's young. She's going to blame herself.'

Still, Tegan said nothing, wishing something would happen to take away the woman's interest in her, but no customers were arriving. The waitress relaxed and said, 'I'm Janet, by the way.'

She took out a packet of Player's No. 6, slid a cigarette one-handed into her mouth and offered the pack to Tegan.

'Smoke, do you?'

'No. No, thanks.'

She struck a match, lit up and then inhaled deeply, as if her life depended on it. When she blew out, her eyes followed the smoke as it curled up towards the ceiling and the scent of burning tobacco filled the room.

'It wasn't because of you," she said finally. 'See, you're beautiful. And you didn't turn him away, did you?'

'No. I …'

Tegan suddenly realised she was on the point of telling this stranger about the most intimate moments of her life. She closed her mouth. Why didn't the woman go away? But she herself made no move to leave.

'I know you don't want to talk to me, but you need to listen, girl. No man would turn you down. I guarantee that. So, *he's* the one with the problem, see. Something's happened to him. Am I right?' She looked up at Tegan. 'Or maybe you don't know?'

‘I think … yes, maybe you’re right. His wife and child died in childbirth. It wasn’t his fault – how could it be? But he feels guilty about it. Is that the sort of thing you mean?’

‘Sounds about right. You’ll just have to be patient. Men aren’t the simple beings they like us to think they are, and he looks like a deep one to me.’

They sat side by side for a while, drinking the dreadful coffee and saying nothing.

‘Your first time?’

Tegan blushed. ‘Yes.’

‘Did you come prepared?’

‘I … no … We talked about the risks. I thought he’d –’

I wouldn’t rely on that. Even the nicest men can forget these things. Or think they don’t matter. If I were you, I’d find a barber’s tomorrow and make him go in. Make sure your man gets something there.’

‘Yes, that’s a good idea.’

Tegan swallowed the last of her coffee, suddenly struck by the surreal nature of this meeting: in a bar, at midnight, with this blousy woman giving her contraceptive advice. She laughed.

‘Thank you, Janet,’ she said. ‘I didn’t expect this when I ordered the coffee, but you’ve made me feel a lot better. Thank you.’

She stood up and leaving the money for the drinks on the table, she walked out.

Chapter 43

The water glinted at the bottom of the street. It was madness to come out here at this hour in a strange town, but she couldn't not do so. She jumped as a blacker shadow detached itself from a dark corner. What was that sound? Could someone be walking behind her? The hairs rose on the back of her neck and a cat leapt across the narrow street in front of her. As her heartbeat returned to normal, she focused on what she had to do and hurried along, hoping it would be lighter and more open by the water's edge.

She must find him.

The whole place seemed to have shut down in the short time since they'd been out together. She heard only the sound of her footsteps on the flagstones. She reached the sea and struck off to the right, and there was the promenade, covered in a thin layer of sand and little shells. Her feet made a crunching sound as she strode along.

The tide was coming in fast, and it brought with it a strong smell of seaweed. Branches of brown kelp floated in and were deposited high on the beach. She followed the curve of the bay until the walkway narrowed and then came to an end. She didn't stop until she found herself about to step down onto wet sand. The water was well up the beach at this point and ahead, there were rocks, a steep climb in the dark. She stared up at the jutting headland but there was no movement. He wouldn't be here.

Her anxiety increasing, she turned back in the other direction. The water was higher now and swishing against the stones, and it was hard to avoid the spray where the incoming waves hit the curve of the promenade. There was no sign of Hywel, or of anyone else.

Worry gnawed at her. Maybe she'd got it wrong, and he hadn't come down to the sea. It could be better to return to the hotel. But first, she'd check this other end of the promenade. It would only take a minute or two.

The pier loomed ahead. She scanned it as she approached. It looked scruffy, and there was some kind of Fun Palace at the point where it left the shore, but nothing moved. Darkness shrouded everything, leaving indistinct outlines, and the water slapped against the pilings, echoing eerily. She went closer. Now she heard the undertow beneath the structure.

The gate to the right side was open and there was a turnstile. Maybe he'd gone up onto the pier itself, even though everything indicated there was no-one there. She edged her way around the spokes and began to walk along the boards. That bulky mass ahead was probably a kiosk or a viewing post. When she was no more than a few yards from the end, she saw a figure in its shadow, leaning on the rail, staring ahead. Hywel. Thank Goodness. She went to stand next to him.

'I couldn't sleep either.'

He said nothing for a long while. Then: ‘I hate what I’ve done to you, Tegan. After I said I would never hurt you. I don’t know how to apologise. Can you ever forgive me?’

‘There’s nothing to forgive.’

She took a deep breath. She had to have an answer to her question. ‘Do you want me, Hywel? Really want me?’

‘God, yes! How can you ask me that? Of course, I do.’

‘Then there is no problem.’

‘I don’t know what happened, why it happened. I want you but, what if I … can’t? Again?’

‘We’ll make it work. I was so worried about you when you left like that.’

She waited a while beside him, looking out to sea, thinking. This was how it had to be, both facing in the same direction, aiming for the same thing. They had to take the next steps together and if they couldn’t, then there was no future for their relationship.

He’d always seemed strong and, so far, she’d been content to be pulled along. That had been the right thing then, in the early stages of getting to know each other, when she’d been sorting out her own jumbled feelings, trying to distinguish between attraction and love, to find her way.

But there were layers to him that she was only just beginning to sense. It was difficult because she didn’t know enough about male sensitivities; she might hurt him, damage what they had, although she could tell he thought he’d already done that, without any help from her.

‘I’ve thought about the things you told me when we went riding,’ she said. ‘Maybe this is about your wife.’

He frowned at her. So he didn’t want to talk about it. But now she understood that was the problem – it needed to be talked about. She pushed on, still looking at the incoming waves.

‘I knew you were upset when you told me about her. I think maybe you’ve been feeling guilty about a situation you could do nothing about.’

‘No. That’s what I’m finding so difficult: I could have done something about it. It was a duel, see, Daffyd and me, ever since we first saw each other at infant school. Five years old on our first day, and we had a fight. With Caitlyn, it was no different. We both fought hard, and I won.

‘If she’d gone to him, with all his money, he’d have had her in an expensive nursing home when she was going to give birth, people on hand to pick up the signs there was something wrong. Not on a remote farm in the mountains, and the doctor held up by a snowfall.

She could have lived. Maybe they both would have – his child and her. But I was determined to have what I wanted.’ He turned to look at her. ‘This … today has brought it all back. I can’t do that again, Tegan.’

Her heart was melting at the pain she saw in his face. She wanted to throw her arms around him and comfort him, but she could not let this go.

‘Don’t you think she – Caitlyn – had a choice in all of this, Hywel? She chose you. Unless of course, you dragged her off by the hair, like some sort of caveman.’

He gave a short, bitter laugh. ‘No, I didn’t do that. But I might as well have done.’

‘Do you really, truly, imagine, if *we* get together, that it’s all going to go the same way again? Of course, it won’t. You said it yourself – you’re not the same person. And I’m sure I’m not like your wife. Who’s to say it would have been different if she had chosen Daffyd? It wasn’t anything you did, Hywel. You have to stop thinking like that.’

When he remained silent, she feared she’d handled it wrongly by being so forthright and added, ‘You said your dad’s obsessive, Hywel. Maybe it’s a Davies trait. Maybe that’s something you have to consider.’

She stopped then because there was nothing else to say. She forced herself to stay still although her heart was beating so fast, it was almost choking her. She couldn’t bear it if he shut down now and tried to break off the relationship with her. If he did that, she’d sacrifice her pride, cry and beg. She couldn’t lose him.

‘You are so young and so wise.’ He spoke softly, and she had to strain her ears to hear him. ‘How do know me so well?’

A tentative smile played about his lips now, teasing a little. She shrugged and smiled back with more confidence.

‘Age doesn’t come into it.’

She would never, ever reveal the conversation with the waitress. In fact, it seemed so strange to her now, she was beginning to wonder if it had really taken place.

‘So,’ he said, taking her hand. ‘Do you want to walk?’

They did walk, miles it seemed, ending somewhere up on that bleak headland she’d contemplated earlier. There, they lay in each other’s arms among the stiff, prickly marram grass, buffeted by the cold wind which began to blow at around two o' clock in the morning. When they finally got back to the hotel, the sun was coming up. They climbed into bed and fell into an exhausted sleep.

Chapter 44

Aberystwyth was like no town she'd ever been in. Shoppers and visitors strained at its seams this Saturday. It was the height of the summer season and families strolled with push chairs and pulled small children along by the hand. Toddlers in cotton rompers, with ice cream covered faces, screeched and shouted and tried to escape their leading reins. Kiosks were selling brightly coloured buckets and spades and yellow rubber rings. Grouped in front of each were stands of naughty post cards that displayed very fat women in skimpy, white-spotted dresses and men with extremely red faces, up to no good.

'I've never seen anything like this. It's so different.' Tegan was fascinated by everything around her. It would be impossible to find something like this in Colombia.

'It's very British, I suppose. The side we don't usually show to the rest of the world. I've never really thought about it.' He was gazing at a poster on the front of one of the kiosks. 'Would you like one?'

'What? – one of these? I couldn't send it to anyone.'

'Not a post card, silly. An ice cream, a 99. You won't have had one of those.'

‘Oh … I’d love one.’

He bought two cones, and they found a bench, where they sat enjoying the carefree afternoon crowd. Hywel pulled the chocolate stick out of his cone and demolished it in a couple of bites. The tide was quite a way out and fathers were busy digging holes in the wet sand and building sandcastles with their sons and daughters, allowing their womenfolk to stretch out on the beach and absorb the hot sun. The shouts of the children and the cries of the gulls carried along on the breeze were all around, but as if veiled, so they seemed very far away.

‘I remember doing that at their age,’ Hywel said, watching as a small boy carefully upturned his turret-shaped bucket onto a mound of sand. ‘Two or three times, when my mother would take time off from the farm. It wasn’t often she could. I suppose it was different for you.’

‘Our home is quite a long way from the sea, out in the country, so horses were always the thing for me,’ said Tegan. ‘And the traditions of the countries are different, I think. There was none of this.

We used to go to Cartagena on the coast from time to time, but it wasn’t this simple type of holiday, just a day spent by the sea enjoying the sun. We’d be in a hotel, and it was all a lot smarter. The hotel, not the city – that’s still quite run down. I hope you’re not insulted. I love this. It feels more … genuine, somehow.’

Later, they strolled hand in hand along the streets, peering into shop windows with no wish to buy, but suddenly, Tegan stopped, and using the phrase Janet had employed the evening before, she said, ‘Have you come prepared, Hywel? I didn’t even notice last night.’

For a moment, he looked completely bewildered. Then, through a window, he took in the sight of a man getting his hair cut. He gave a bark of laughter, and she saw a return of the old Hywel in his eyes.

'Of course, I have,' he said. 'I love you and I want to cherish you and protect you, not expose you to pregnancy and the problems that could bring.' He caught her up in the middle of the pavement, and gave her a long kiss, ignoring the affronted stares of passers-by. 'I'm pleased to see your mind is on the same track as mine.'

'People are looking,' Tegan said, as she extricated herself from his embrace. But she felt an ache begin in her loins, a flaring desire, from which she needed release.

He gripped her hand. 'Come on. Shall we go back?'

*

There was a deep hush in the hotel entrance hall. Even the reception desk was empty. The other guests must be out enjoying the sun on the beach, because they didn't see a single person as they crept up the shadowy stairs, not wanting to meet anyone because this could not be delayed.

When he'd secured the lock, they began to pull off each other's clothes, punctuating the process with kisses and caresses. This time, there was no half-light, no dressing gown. All modesty was gone. She saw him naked for the first time and when he pulled her into his arms, she felt him harden against her, and wondered at the thought that she was the cause.

But he knew better than to force the pace.

‘You’re so beautiful,’ he said. ‘Is it any wonder that I’ve set my heart on you?’

His voice was breaking as he spoke. He gathered her up in his arms and laid her gently on the bed.

*

It had grown dark once again. They’d probably missed dinner, but Tegan didn’t care. She wasn’t hungry. This was bliss, lying here, luxuriating in the feelings, both remembered and still lingering, euphoric waves of sensation, brought back to life if she made the slightest movement. She ached in all sorts of good places but wasn’t aware of any real pain this first time; they said that riding was often a good preparation.

She could hear him in the bathroom. The shower was running, but she thought maybe she’d have a bath, only not right now – perhaps at some distant time, in some undetermined future. Just for the moment, she didn’t want to move. The deep longing was gone, temporarily satisfied, and she floated, feather-light, on a sea of ecstasy.

He’d known how to bring her right to the brink. She’d tottered on the edge and then, somehow, he’d pulled her back, and started to build again – and again – until she could stand it no more and had cried out, begging him to carry her over, push her over, drag her over – whatever it might take to bring the release she craved.

The door clicked and he came back into the room, wrapped in a bathrobe, and sat on the bed. He leaned across and kissed her with a sweet intensity.

‘Thank you, *fy nghariad*,’ he whispered. ‘I’ve started to run the bath for you.’

It pleased her that he'd read her mind even in this small matter. She stretched languorously and pulled him down towards her. 'I love you, Hywel.'

'And I love you, Tegan.'

Chapter 45

On Wednesday morning, Tegan sat at the table with the feeling that this was likely to be the last calm moment before the opening of the show. They'd done so much in the last weeks and time to themselves for the family was reduced to the half-hour over breakfast. Sir George was reading, while she and Mona concentrated on eating. Suddenly, George said, 'Well, well, we have a hero in our midst, Mona. Listen to this.' He began to read from "The Post."

"**LOCAL FARMER SAVES YOUNG RIDER.**

Young equestrian saved in dramatic rescue in rural Wales.

Mr Hywel Davies, 26, who farms over the col on the back road to Crickhowell, dropped into Saturday morning's gymkhana, an annual event in which he used to participate regularly until the age of twelve. When a startled horse bolted with its young rider, he threw himself onto the back of an animal he'd borrowed from a friend and took off in hot pursuit. They jumped the first fence only seconds apart. He quickly caught up and begun pushing the runaway, Ringo, into circling the field.

Mr Davies used his considerable skill to stave off the headlong flight which could have resulted in the horse jumping into the path of an on-coming car.

We have it on good authority that Mr Davies was there to meet Miss Tegan Lewis, 19, from Colombia in South America, who is the guest of Sir George and Lady Mona Ffrench at Court Farm. Miss Lewis, no mean equestrian herself, had just spent the morning helping to judge the children's efforts at the gymkhana."

'Oh no,' said Tegan. 'Where did they get it from? I didn't tell anyone.'

'Not even us,' said Mona. She smiled because she'd heard the story, which had spread over the whole district in a matter of hours, and realised Tegan must have been so pre-occupied that she'd forgotten to say anything. 'I expect the reporter was the father of one of the children. Read some more, George.'

"Interviewed later, Master Philip Brown, 12, the rider of the runaway, Ringo, said, 'Mr Davies was jolly good. He probably saved my life. I really admire him.'

Asked if he had suffered any ill-effects, he said he didn't think so but that he'd been so taken up with Ringo's welfare that he hadn't really noticed.

'I am eternally grateful to Mr Davies,' Philip's mother, Mrs Iona Brown, 34, said. 'I wish I'd had the opportunity to thank him in person.'

Mr Glyn Price, on whose land the incident took place, said a bad accident had been averted and police were now investigating the series of explosions which frightened the horse. Police gave no comment, but it is believed the these were the work of a local gang of boys.

Neither Mr Davies nor Miss Lewis was available for comment. Miss Lewis is said to be staying with her aunt and uncle for the rest of the year."

'That was well done!' said George, getting up from the table. 'Now, I have to leave you. I'm sorry but I have some work to do.'

He handed the newspaper to Tegan so that she could read it again for herself. The article was on the fourth page. She glanced quickly at it but then noticed a report at the bottom of the facing page: "**Local Girl arrested in Swansea**."

'Aunt Mona, look at this.'

The article was clearly about Angharad who had finally been traced by police to an address in the big port. There was very little information, but it was obvious that they now had enough evidence to bring the case up before magistrates.

'I feel really sad about it,' said Tegan, 'and stupid that I fell for her stories.'

'You didn't have the experience to judge. And I'm sorry to say I was too busy to pay attention and give you advice. But as George said the other day, there's nothing you can do. Please don't think that's normal behaviour for around here. People can go wrong in any society.'

Chapter 46

It was the Thursday before the show. Tom Davies finished his late supper, got up from the table and headed towards the door.

'Coming?'

'Where're you going, Dad?'

Usually, they cleared up in the kitchen after eating.

'Just going out to have a look at the sheep. Come with me. I want your opinion while it's still light enough to see.'

He was talking about his tiny flock of rare sheep. They were Balwens, a breed that had almost died out twenty years earlier, but they were tough mountain animals and flocks were gradually being built up again by farmers like him. He'd been convinced they would do well on their farm and so far had been proved right.

He'd bought the first ram and ewe two years earlier. They were black, unlike the main flock, small, with a white blaze from the top of the head to the nose, white socks, and white tail tip. Tegan had fallen in love with them and said she could spot them a mile away.

At the moment he had a dozen, including the new lambs. There was only one ram, a magnificent specimen with curved, almost black horns, who had sired the lambs that were now going to the show.

'They look good, Dad. Think they'll sell?'

'Yeah, they've turned out well. Just wanted you to take a look at things.'

Dad had a lot of experience. It was a compliment to be asked to contribute something. They talked through various issues and logistics, given they'd be moving them down to the showground the next day. Both men, relaxed before the activity of the next few days, leaned on the wooden fence, watching the animals in their pen. Hywel said, 'Did you think any more about the house, Dad? Are you still determined to move in?'

'Yes, now more than ever.'

'More than ever? What do you mean by that?'

'What I mean by that is that I will be moving in. Along with Emma Williams. I took advantage of you being away in Aberystwyth to talk it through with her.' Hywel stared at his father, mouth agape.

'With … with Emma? What's going on, Dad?'

'What I've just said. We've been getting on really well. I've asked her to marry me.'

'Marry you!'

Hywel shut his mouth. He was repeating everything his father said and beginning to sound stupid. The older man smiled. 'Don't be so surprised, lad.'

'But you've only known her a few weeks, since the … the physiotherapy started. Isn't this a bit rushed?'

'You're being very dense, my boy – if not completely blind. I've known Emma for nearly three years. I might have done something about it sooner, but she was getting over her husband's death. And I had the strange notion that you still needed me.'

Hywel felt completely floored by this news. First, that his dad and Emma … well, never mind. His dad! And now, the fact that he was about to get married again. It had been just the two of them for so many years, before and after Caitlyn. This was going to take some getting used to.

'I like her, Dad,' he said, finally gathering his wits. 'She's a very nice woman. I'm glad for you.'

They lapsed into silence again, the only sound the occasional bleating from the little lambs. It was true – he really did like Emma. Then his father said, 'We'll sort out a date, once we know what you're doing. But I'm not trying to rush you, Hywel. You take your time. Ask her when you think she's ready.'

'Dad, I …'

'She's young, Tegan is. Maybe she won't want to bury herself out here in the country. You have to consider that. Maybe you'll have to look at other possibilities.'

Chapter 47

Friday, the first day of the show, dawned misty and cool although the weather forecast was promising sun and higher temperatures by mid-morning. The official opening for visitors was at one in the afternoon but, soon after seven, the first farm vehicle arrived, and a farmer, Sean Talbot, attempted to get his prize bull off and into its allocated pen. It was reddish-brown in colour, had big, vicious horns and was belligerent.

'He's a difficult one,' Talbot said to the farmhand who was helping the new arrivals, 'so I came early.'

The pens had been arranged so that the vehicles could drive up alongside to unload their animal cargoes, their feed and other baggage. Once this was done, vehicles from the immediate locality would go home and not return until pick-up time on Sunday evening.

The bull had a thick leading rope and Sean Talbot was a very experienced handler but, somehow, he slipped and let go of the rope as he landed on his back. The bull, already angry at the way it'd been confined in the truck, let out a great bellow, swerved through the narrow opening between the van and the pen and took off, over the meadow and up the hill in the direction of the house, scattering people to left and right. Suddenly, it stopped, head raised, diverted by the sight of the huge marquee, which had been erected the previous afternoon.

When the bull charged in through the only opening, a quick-thinking farmhand grabbed the flap and tied it closed before running off, not sure that the thin canvas would keep the animal contained. Mr Talbot arrived, red in the face. 'We can't go in yet, not while he's behaving like that.'

The bull could still be heard snorting and moving around inside, but for some reason, it was not attempting to break through the canvas walls.

'Got to be something that's stopped him,' said the farmer. 'Not someone in there, was there?'

The farmhand looked baffled. 'Didn't see no-one.'

All other work came to a halt, while the problem was being addressed.

'We'll have to coral him,' the farmer added. 'He's wily. Escaped a few times.'

'So, how are we going to do it?' asked Mona, who could see all their carefully made plans being ruined. She looked around. 'And where's Tegan?'

*

Inside the marquee, Tegan was considering her options, which were limited. The bull had come to an abrupt stop in the middle of the huge space. It was mostly still empty, but some display staging had been erected along the wall facing the main entrance flap and a small number of tables and chairs were stacked in a mound, ready to be set out, the job she'd been about to tackle. She stood mid-way between the staging and the tables and was the same distance from where the bull had come to a halt, still snorting. Very exposed. Oh God, that threatening, pawing movement. She knew what that meant, and it didn't bode well.

Very slowly, she bent down and picked up the hammer she'd dropped in her shock. She'd use it as a weapon if she had to, but it was a very large animal. Just how useful would it be against the ton of aggression in front of her? Her heart was banging against her ribs, threatening to choke her, and beads of perspiration had gathered on her forehead. What was she going to do?

Standing still wasn't an option because he'd move eventually and there'd be no warning. The answer was to stay calm but get out of the way – and make it soon. No sudden movements until she knew where she was going, unless it moved first, of course. She took a careful step backwards, wishing all those years of living on a cattle farm would produce some clever insight into dealing with rampaging bulls at close quarters, but no obvious simple solution came into her mind.

The animal was still immobile, but he'd caught her movement, and had his eye on her. The tables and chairs were rickety things, no help at all, but she could see the staging slightly behind her to her right, and it looked solid. Maybe … she took another step back. He still didn't move, and she was able to confirm what she'd hoped was the case: at the side, below the shelves, there was a hollow opening, and she was slim enough to worm her way in. The structure was built of heavy wood and might protect her from the furious animal. If she could get there in time.

Although the bull was standing calmly, staring at her, sooner or later, he was going to be angry because that was the way with every bull she'd ever come across. As she had this thought, the animal began the pawing movement again. Bulls worked up a head of steam and then they liked to toss and gore whoever was in front of them, and this one was well on the way to doing just that.

Then outside, Monda was calling, "Tegan! Tegan!"

The bull turned its head. She didn't dare reply but, instead, took advantage of the distraction, sprinted for the opening below the staging and threw herself in, scraping her forehead and arms on the rough, splintery wood. The space was narrow, and she had to use her elbows to pull herself further in, so that her legs would not be exposed.

The bull was already on the move. The ground shook under the hooves of the galloping fury and then it collided with the staging, half-lifting the structure into the air. As it came tumbling down again. Tegan covered her head as best she could, and then everything went dark.

Outside, Mona was beside herself with anxiety.

'Tegan's in there. We have to get her out. I'm going in – maybe we can distract it.'

She was running toward the tent as she spoke, but Farmer Talbot grabbed her arm and said, 'You don't know she's there and you can't go in. I know him – you'd not survive. Leave us to sort it out.'

Things had gone quiet again, but word was out now that Tegan was in the tent. Men ran back and forth collecting some of the heftier pen fencing. They brought it up to the flap and, working as fast as they could, they erected an enclosure, tying the panels together with baler twine. A fourth panel, held by two of the men, stood ready to be slotted into place behind the bull, once he exited the marquee – if they could get that to happen.

'We can't drive him,' said Talbot. 'It'll only get him moving too fast and he'll knock the whole thing down.'

At this point, a Land Rover drove up to where Mona was standing. It was Hywel. When he saw the grey look of her face, he knew immediately something terrible had happened. 'Mona, what is it?'

'The bull went on the rampage and Tegan's in there.' The tears spilled over. 'They won't let me get near.'

Hywel had already taken in what the men were doing. That fencing looked far too delicate to contain an angry bull but maybe, they could reinforce it. He got back into his vehicle and drove it over to the improvised pen. As he parked alongside one section of fence, he was shouting to the farm hands to bring up more vehicles. Finally, a couple of trucks and a tractor arrived and fitted themselves nose to tail behind his vehicle. Even if the bull succeeded in barging through the barriers, this would stop him. Now they'd be able to force the animal out of the marquee.

Once everything was in place, Talbot re-opened the tent flap. As it dropped away, everyone anticipated chaos but instead, there was complete silence. The man cautiously peered in and finally located the animal lying down in one corner of the dimly lit structure. It didn't look as if it had any intention of moving. Instead, they would have to annoy it enough to get it to stand up and run towards the opening.

Hywel had followed the man in. He could see the tumbled staging and hear a groaning sound. Tegan had to be underneath. While others attended to the animal, he hurried over to the heap of splintered wood. A foot was poking out from beneath and a feeling of complete terror washed over him. Please, please, he was thinking, not knowing to whom he was addressing his prayers. 'Over here! Help me!' he shouted to one of the men.

Together they began to lift the heavy structure. Unable to banish the terrifying image of those powerful horns getting to Tegan, he thought he was going to be sick. They worked carefully in case they did more damage, but finally, he was able to reach her, just as she was beginning to regain consciousness. He knelt and held her in his arms. 'Darling, darling, tell me you're all right.' He stroked her head. 'Where does it hurt? What can I do to help you?'

'Hywel?' she said. 'What's happened?' Suddenly her expression cleared. 'Oh – the bull. Has it gone?'

'They're dealing with it now. Can you stand? I want to get you out of here before it decides to move again.'

Leaning on him, she pulled herself upright and he picked her up and carried her out of the tent. He strode over to where Mona waited in a fever of anxiety, and deposited Tegan on a chair.

It was obvious she was still dizzy. Something must have hit her head so hard that she'd lost consciousness. Blood trickled down her forehead and she was covered in cuts and scrapes. But very quickly, she was sitting up properly and making sense when she spoke. The local doctor took a look and said she'd had a lucky escape.

'Healthy young woman,' he added. 'Just watch out for concussion.'

Hywel was sitting on one side of her and her aunt on the other. Now Mona said, 'I have to go – there's so much to do. Can you get Tegan back to the house?'

Meanwhile the men had got behind the animal and goaded it into getting up. Once it was on its feet, it walked sedately into the makeshift pen, and they closed it up behind him. By this time everyone's nerves were on edge, and it wasn't over yet.

*

Tegan watched what was going on, still holding Hywel's hand. An older woman came across with a cup of tea.

'Hot and sweet, that's what you need for shock.' she said, as Tegan took it from her and drank greedily.

'I feel much better,' Tegan said a while later, fingering the bloody patch on her head. 'And you need to move that vehicle. It's okay to leave me here. The tea really works.'

'Come on, I'll take you up to the house.'

'No, I want to watch. I really do feel better.'

Looking unconvinced, Hywel hesitated, saying, 'but you might have a concussion or something. If you feel unwell, you must –'

'Hywel, there are dozens of people around. There won't be a problem.'

She kissed him. 'Go on. Really – you can leave me now.' She turned back to the drama unfolding before her.

Mr Talbot had managed to get hold of the leading rope, and now he attached it to the back of the tractor – in case the bull decided he didn't want to be led after all. The men moved the vehicles and began to untie the pieces of metal fencing. A few minutes later, the bull with his aggression level reduced to something they felt they could handle, was in his pen in the meadow and no damage had been done.

There was a collective sigh of relief and a renewed flurry of activity as people went back to setting up the stalls and activities.

*

They'd had to work fast, but they were still ready by half past twelve on that first day.

Tegan watched the brass band from a nearby colliery as it patrolled through the meadow and played a medley of tunes. The musicians wended their way slowly up the slope until they arrived at the empty green area in front of the marquee. There they formed up and waited.

The guest of honour about to open the show was Dai Evans, a poet who was beginning to gain a little local fame. As he was making his way towards the lectern, the band struck up with 'Guide me, O thou great Redeemer,' a hymn, so well-known in that part of the country that everyone began to sing.

As the last notes died away on the summer air, the poet stepped forward and read one of his poems about the gifts of nature, before talking about how important the show was to the district. He didn't take too long, and finally, he declared it open. There was a smattering of applause before everyone got down to work.

'That was extraordinary,' said Tegan, bemused by the juxtaposition of poetry and agriculture. 'I've never seen anything like that before.'

'*Dim ond yng Nghymru,*' said Sir George proudly, his arms around his wife and niece. 'Only in Wales would you find a poet opening an agricultural show.

Chapter 48

The show was a huge success. By late on Monday afternoon, all the animals were gone and most of the structures had been taken down. Only the marquee, empty once again, still filled the lawn in front of the house, and further down the slope were the portable toilets. Lorries would arrive the next day to deal with them.

It would be lovely to see more of Hywel. Tegan thought about him every time she had a moment to herself, but she had been so busy during the show that they didn't meet alone until later that evening. He'd driven down to Court Farm to snatch a couple of hours together.

'I know it's late,' he said after kissing her as if he hadn't seen her for weeks, 'but can you manage a real walk? How's your leg now?'

'It was just a scratch.'

'And your head? Let me see.'

'Nothing to be seen. I really am better.'

'Unless you're too tired, of course?'

'I love that you are so worried about me, *querido*, but no, I'm not tired, and yes, I can walk. I really am all right, Hywel, and I'd like some fresh air, too. Let me get a jacket.'

It was growing dark already although it was only a little after eight o'clock. Unbelievably summer looked as if it was coming to an end, but at least it was still relatively warm outside. 'It's great that the weather held until after the show. Everyone put so much work into it.' Tegan had gradually come to realise how much sway the unpredictable weather held over people's lives in this region of high hills and small mountains.

They talked about the various things that had happened, eventually coming to a stile on the eastern boundary of the farm, the gateway to the mountain track. He went over first and helped her down, as if afraid she might break. Tegan relished these moments, these opportunities for intimacy, when his touch sent her pulse soaring.

Tonight, there was an added excitement which came from a tension she sensed in him. It was wonderful to have become so sensitive to his changes in mood, to feel that they were beginning to mesh together, and two people were becoming one. Wasn't that what love was?

They began to climb and, half an hour later, they reached a point at which the trees grew fewer, and the rocks started to show through the short-cropped grass. That long-horned sheep, white against the darkness of the rock, must belong to Court Farm. It had the characteristic smit mark, the pink double cross and dot, on its rump. It backed behind the stump of a tree and stared at them, but suddenly, as they got too close, the animal ran off, baaing.

They sat down on a boulder, facing back towards the farm. Over to the west, a few orange and lilac streaks, like lines on a child's drawing, illuminated the sky, but where they sat was already in darkness.

Hywel drew her into his arms, and they kissed. Then, he pulled back a little.

'Please don't stop.'

'I love you very much. You know that, Tegan. Will you marry me?'

She'd guessed his intent. 'Yes,' she said simply. 'I will.'

A little time passed before he said, 'I would like to give you a ring. It was my grandmother's and then my mother's. It may not fit, but we can get it altered if necessary.'

He took a leather box from his pocket and opened it. Inside was a small emerald, set in a cluster of tiny diamonds, on a gold hoop. 'It's Welsh gold. That's rare because there's so little of it. Let's try it on your finger.'

He took hold of her left hand and slipped the ring onto her third finger. It fitted as well as if it had been originally designed for her. When he'd kissed her again, he said, 'It's perfect. My mother had slim hands like yours.'

'It's beautiful, Hywel.'

'And you are beautiful. I cannot get enough of looking at you.'

She leant across and stroked his cheek. 'Thank you. You know that I feel the same way, don't you?' She looked down at the green stone. 'I wonder if it's a Colombian emerald. Colombia is world-famous for its emeralds. That would be strange.'

'And it would be a symbol of our union, a Colombian emerald set in Welsh gold – and it's the perfect colour for you.' He paused for a moment and then said, 'We need to talk, Tegan – about where we go from here.'

'I know there's a lot to consider – but is it okay for me to tell Aunt Mona and my parents?'

'Of course, it is. This is not going to be a secret – I want everyone to know.'

'Oh – I've just remembered. Mona said you're invited to the supper party tomorrow evening, if you can manage it. You know, for everyone who helped with the show.'

'I'd forgotten about that. I'll make sure I get here but I won't be able to make it before six.'

'Nothing much will happen before then. It's not just family – all the farm hands will be there and anyone from the village who helped. She said it'll be supper and a barn dance, and it's being held in the big barn.'

It should be fun, especially as they now had something to celebrate.

'Oh Hywel, I've just had a great idea – could we announce our engagement at the party?'

'I don't really –'

'We have to tell people some time. You just said.'

'All right. I just … I don't like being the focus of everyone's attention.'

'Well, you can't avoid it this time, so why don't you get your dad to come as well?'

‘I’ll speak to him. Will you ask Mona if it’s all right?’ He looked up, as if suddenly becoming aware of their surroundings. ‘Come on, it’s time to go.’

A mist was billowing down the mountain behind them. It would envelop them in a few minutes and make the walk back to the farm dangerous. Lost in the moment, Tegan hadn’t even noticed.

He stood up and held out his hand. ‘Let’s go.’

Chapter 49

By half past four, people arrived to help set up. A couple of farmhands placed two long tables, end to end, in one part of the barn, while a space was cleared for the dancing in the other. People brought in chairs, stools and benches, setting them at the table, and around the walls, along with bales of hay, in case more people turned up than expected.

'It's always hard to know how many people think they've helped with the show.' Bethan said. 'And they often bring an extra member of the family, or a girlfriend or boyfriend. So, we have to be ready for them.'

Tegan had completely recovered from her run-in with the bull. She still trembled but now, it was with happiness at the thought that she and Hywel were going to be married, and tonight would make that statement to everyone they knew. But with so much to prepare for the evening entertainment, there was no time to dwell on it. She set up a separate table for the children, placing a dozen low stools around it and then went back to the kitchen to help Bethan and Mona bring out plates piled high with cold pie, ham, cheese, pickles and lots of bread which they'd cut and buttered in advance.

‘Is that it?’ she asked, putting a plate of tomatoes from the greenhouse at one end of the table and a huge bowl of apples at the other. They were last season’s, the current crop of apples not being quite ready, but they’d lasted well.

‘Just the glasses now.’

In the kitchen, Bethan unearthed from the back of a cupboard a large cardboard box containing a great assortment of glasses, some smooth and some the classic pint and half-pint glasses with dimples and a handle.

‘We keep these for occasions like this because you always get a few breakages. No point in putting out anything delicate. The ones with the handles go to the bar.’

They walked around the table, putting a glass down at each place, and stood large jugs of home-made lemonade and cider right along the centre of the table, between the bowls and dishes. Sir George and Dickon, the stableman, were setting up a table to one side, on which were a keg of beer and a couple of flagons of cider. Clearly, some serious drinking was envisaged.

In the kitchen puddings and cakes were covered with mesh domes. Tegan looked at the first cake she’d ever baked, with its thick coating of chocolate butter icing. ‘Do you think it’s good enough to offer to people, Bethan?’

‘It’s perfect. Besides, by the time they get to the puddings, half of them will’ve drunk too much to notice what it’s like.’

The musicians began to arrive.

‘They’re not really a band,’ said Mona, ‘just some of the farm hands who know how to play.’

Tegan recognized Sam, whom she'd seen that morning working in the sheep shed. Now he was sporting a red kerchief and a hat and was tuning up an accordion.

It was very noisy in the barn, and Tegan was bemused by the intense activity, but it was a smooth operation. These people had lots of experience and knew exactly how to make it work.

A little girl tugged at her sleeve, and Tegan bent down to get to the child's level.

'Teddy,' she said, stuffing a thumb into her mouth. 'Teddy got lost.'

'So where do you think you left him? We could look.'

'Yes, in the barn.'

She must mean the second, smaller barn which was used for storage. Now they'd taken out the chairs and tables, it was probably empty and dark. She was a little thing and maybe she didn't want to go in there on her own.

'Come on, then. Let's see if we can find him.'

They crossed the yard and, grabbing her hand, the child pulled her forward to the open barn door. But someone had left the light on, a low-wattage bulb. Wasting electricity like that. It was a good thing she'd come.

'So, where's your teddy, then?'

The child dropped her hand and ran to a corner, where she scooped up the missing bear.

'Teddy!' She ran off without looking back.

'I didn't think you'd come otherwise.'

Tegan whirled around and Daffyd went on, 'I'm not invited this evening, but I knew about the party, of course.'

'You're right. I wouldn't have come.'

This wasn't fair of him, using the child like that. 'You really shouldn't have done this, Daffyd. We have nothing to say to each other.'

She was heading towards the door, but he caught her arm, making no attempt, however, to get any closer.

'Please listen, Tegan. I just wanted to apologize. I know I've behaved like a complete ba – idiot. It's just that Hywel and I, well … well, it's all in the past now. I heard your news. I came to say sorry and to wish you well.'

About to respond, she caught a flicker of movement out of the corner of her eye and, a second later, Hywel loomed up behind Daffyd.

'No!' she shouted, but he grabbed the man's shoulder and swung him around to face him.

'You bastard!'

He flung away the jacket he was carrying and landed a solid punch on Daffyd's nose, which began to spurt blood.

'Stop it!'

A moment later, the two men were rolling about on the earth floor. Bone slapped and cracked on flesh and grunts and cries filled the air. Hywel grabbed the other man's shirt collar, and began to haul him up, ready to send his fist back into the man's face. 'No! No, stop! You have to stop.'

Was he deaf? 'Hywel, stop. STOP, I said. He came to apologize.'

He was going to ruin everything. She rushed forward and attempted to pull them apart. A punch went wide of target, and she slammed back against the door post. That knocked the breath out of her, and it hurt. She pulled herself upright, and nursing her bruised elbow, she shouted, ‘Hywel, you stop this right now – or we will not be announcing our engagement this evening!’

Okay, he seemed to be listening because at last, he was dragging himself off his opponent. Now, he stumbled to his feet. Daffyd lay on his back, winded for a moment. Then he rolled over, trying to get back up.

‘You’d better go home, Daffyd.’ She hung onto Hywel in case he hit out again. ‘Apology accepted!’

‘I’m going.’

He staggered towards the door and then squared his shoulders. Both men looked battered, cuts and blood everywhere, but Tegan had the strange impression that, at some level, they’d enjoyed the fight. Given what Hywel had said, it had been a long time in coming.

They watched Daffyd leave the barn. Hywel was trying to get his breath back and was still bristling with anger. Tegan was stirred by the events, her breath coming too fast, her heart pounding against her ribs. She was angry at what had happened but pleased by the fact Hywel had not hesitated to defend her. There was something primeval about it that she also responded to.

However, there was no time to consider these feelings. When Daffyd had gone, she snatched up his jacket from the ground and pulled him out of the barn towards the house. Even in the dim light, she could see the cut on his lip and the shiny red mark that would become a bruise under his left eye.

'Cloakroom,' she said. 'Quick. I need to clean you up, you silly man. What were you thinking?'

'Defending you again, what else?' He was smiling as widely as his injuries would permit. He licked the blood from his lips and then wiped his mouth with the back of his hand. She kissed his forehead, the only part of his face clean enough.

'I can't believe you did that. You're not even sorry.'

'No, I'm not. It was satisfying, very satisfying.'

'You're going to have to drop this feud with him,' she said. 'I'm not marrying a man who spends his time brawling.' He grinned at these words, in spite of his injuries, looking far too pleased at what he'd done. 'He really did come to apologize – and I accepted, so it's finished, right!'

'Right – as long as he doesn't come back again. Ever.'

They were in the cloakroom now. She took a flannel and wet it. 'Just keep still, will you, and let me do this properly.' She washed away the blood, rinsing the cloth through and washing his face again several times before she judged him to be presentable.

'You could be a bit more gentle.'

'I had to get you clean. Anyway, it's entirely your own fault,' she added with a stern expression, but then she smiled. 'It's a good thing it's casual tonight. I hate to think what a white shirt would look like by now.'

He bent and kissed her, wincing as his lip made contact.

'Come on,' she said, 'We'd better get back before someone dispatches a search party. My uncle will be very fed up if he can't make his announcements.'

They slipped into the seats reserved for them at the table and she saw Sir George's eyebrows rise as he took in Hywel's appearance. Maybe she hadn't managed as good a clean-up of his face as she'd thought.

'What's been going on' he asked Tegan as she sat down next to him.

'A little contretemps, I think you'd call it, Uncle George. With Daffyd ap Llewelyn.'

'Ah! Least said, eh?'

'I think so.'

*

Most people had eaten and now, Sir George got to his feet. Champagne was being placed on the table, although only a limited number of people availed themselves of the opportunity. They wouldn't want that fancy French stuff – after all, what was wrong with beer and good local cider from their own apple trees? Sir George thanked everyone for their hard work and told them about some of the successes from the show.

'And now, we come to something very important to me and my family,' he continued. 'Most of you will know that I want to make a special announcement this evening. I say most of you because almost everything that happens in this place makes its way around the village in a matter of hours, if not minutes.' There was polite laughter at this. 'So, I've no doubt you're all well informed, and I hope you might like to drink a toast with us on this occasion.'

He picked up his glass.

'Lady Mona and I welcomed Tegan, into our home earlier this year and we've enjoyed every minute of her time here with us. It gave us great pleasure to discover the burgeoning relationship between our niece and Hywel Davies, a dear friend of ours, and we are delighted to learn they've decided to marry.'

He looked at the two young people and added, 'On behalf of Tegan's parents, who cannot be here but are fully aware of what is happening this evening, I welcome you, Hywel, and look forward to the time when you become part of the family.'

'Ah, thank you, Sir George. No-one could be happier about this than I am,' Hywel said, squeezing Tegan's hand.

Now Sir George turned back to the crowd, who stood waiting expectantly. He raised the glass. 'Join me in wishing them happiness together – Tegan and Hywel.'

People raised their glasses and clapped, shouted and stamped. Invited to speak, Tom Davies welcomed his future daughter-in-law and congratulated his son on his excellent taste. A few minutes later, music started up and there was a stampede to the far end of the barn. Soon, the floor was filled with dancing couples and a large number of children.

'Come on,' said Hywel, relieved the formal part was over. 'They're playing "Do You Wanna Dance." I think they're trying to tell us something.' He looked down. 'You've even got your party shoes on. Perfect.'

'I can't. I'm a hopeless dancer.'

‘Doesn’t matter.’ He scooped her up out of her chair and pulled her onto the dance floor. ‘It’s time you learned. Just watch what everyone else is doing.’

Chapter 50

On Wednesday after lunch, Tegan ran out of the house to meet Hywel as she saw him turn into the drive.

'You're early. That's lovely,' she said, giving him a hug. 'I couldn't wait for you to come. Where are we going?'

'It's a secret. I thought we needed some time together to sort out what we do next.'

As they drove along, Tegan's mind wandered over the events of Monday night, from the fight in the small barn, to the speeches and dancing, to the evening's tender end in the hayloft. When Hywel had suggested it, she'd made a token protest on behalf of his damaged mouth, but he assured her there wasn't a problem: 'My lip may not be in tip-top condition but, as far as I know, there's absolutely nothing wrong with the rest of me. In fact, I'm feeling particularly good.'

So, they slipped out into the cool night air, hot and sweaty after about the tenth dance, feeling they could leave things to others on this, their special evening. He soon had her pressed up against the barn wall under the hay loft, his body hard against hers, kissing her lopsidedly, but with just as much effect as usual.

'You know, we really do have to do this, don't you?'

His hand was working its way down her body, pressing her at the waist and then cupping her buttocks and squeezing gently, earning a breathless gasp.

'Why … why do we have to?'

'Come on, what farmer's daughter hasn't done it in a hay loft? Where's your self-respect, woman?'

He squeezed harder and she gave a little yelp.

'All farmer's daughters?'

'Absolutely. Local custom. Almost the law in Wales.'

'Well, we'll have to comply. Where do we go?'

'Let's see – oh, here's a ladder.'

'Mysteriously in the right place. How did that happen?'

'Up you go, while I get a blanket from the car.'

She climbed up and sat on a bale of hay, heart thudding as she looked down into the dark barn. Excited, curious, wanting this new experience. Wanting him. Now he came up and spread the blanket.

'Have to make ourselves comfortable.'

'You've done this before, I can see.'

'I have – those farmer's daughters, you know. It must have been ten or maybe eleven years ago.'

'Ten or eleven farmer's daughters?' she said. 'That's rather a lot.'

‘No, I don’t think it’s been that many. Ten or eleven *years* since I did this. I was sixteen at the time, and … all I can say is, I’ve learned a lot since then. I tend to prefer a bed these days, but there’s nothing like this experience.’

She lay back and watched him out of half-closed eyes. She could smell his sweat faintly after the dancing, a musky smell mixed with cologne. He was always so clean, the scent of soap the first thing she’d notice when she got close. This was different, exciting, and it stirred something within her.

‘What if someone comes, if they hear us?’

‘Won’t matter. They couldn’t know who it is – and they certainly won’t come up to investigate.’

‘Sure?’

‘What? – disrupt a time-honoured custom like this? Certainly not,’ he said, gently kissing her lips. ‘But I could pull the ladder up if it makes you feel better.’

A moment later, he was back, tugging up her dress, admiring her long slim legs in the moonlight. ‘They’d probably just be disappointed they didn’t get here first. Prime spot.’ He contemplated her, taking a firmer hold of the material. ‘Shall we take this off?’

‘No, I’d feel naked here, without my clothes.’

‘That’s sort of the point.’

‘Oh.’ Her breath was coming quickly as she responded to his caresses. ‘I’ll leave it to you, then.’

The dress soon lay discarded in the hay along with his trousers. Her nipples hardened as he moved across her. His mouth came down, first on one and then the other, and he sucked until they stood proud.

'Ow, you're scratching me!'

He stopped and looked down on her. The loft was full of shadows, but he removed something from between her breasts. 'Here we are!'

Flinging the offending straw away, he pulled her on top of him and then his hands returned to her buttocks, kneading and giving little pinches which were more than enough to fire her up. More than enough.

'I … I want …'

'What do you want?' he asked, his breath coming fast.

'… you inside me.'

It was the first time, she'd felt confident enough to say something like that, to push things in the direction she wanted. A moment later, she'd slid onto her side and was guiding him between her legs. A sweeping sensation was already building as he entered, more than ready. It all happened much more quickly than she'd yet experienced, and now, the sensation exploded and concentrated itself in her thighs, a wonderful, powerful feeling she'd not even imagined possible.

'I like that you did that,' he said as he fell onto his back and slowly brought his breathing back under control. 'I liked that very much.'

*

They dropped down onto the A4, heading towards Chepstow, and Tegan thought about that evening months ago, when Hywel had picked her up at Abergavenny

Station. He'd been coming home from the little market town then. She'd been miserable and feeling betrayed by Angharad. The silly girl was now in deep trouble, with her father having to assure the court that he'd keep her under control, or she'd end up in jail. They'd imposed a fine as well, although the amount had not been disclosed. How things had changed since that day in Newport.

But Chepstow was not his goal. Soon the land began to open up and they could see the new Severn Bridge in the distance. She drew in a sharp breath, awed by the sight. She must have crossed it with her parents months before, but it had been dark, and she hadn't taken in the details.

'It was built five years ago. It's been a great thing for Wales – really opened the country up. One day, the motorway will get to us. Even so, for the first time, we're not just a little backwater anymore.'

It was good that he was interested in his country and aware of what went on outside the small world of the farm.

The bridge was magnificent, with its two massive towers and the long tension cables that supported the roadway. A few moments later, they drove onto it, and it was as if they were hovering in the air as they sped across, the wide estuary glistening in the sunlight far below. The tide was right out, and brown and grey sandbanks poked through the surface of what water remained in the channel.

Finally, they arrived in Bristol, and Hywel was still laughing at her because she'd panicked about not having her passport to get into England.

'This is a huge city,' she said as they drove in. 'It feels exciting.'

‘I don’t know it that well. I don’t often come here but I thought you’d like it.’

They walked down through the centre, past the Hippodrome, where a musical, “The Yeoman of the Guard” was being advertised. A long queue had formed outside, for what must be a matinée performance.

‘So many people. It’s noisy and smelly, as well.’

‘Yes, that’s the dock area.’

‘But look how close that it is to the shops and theatre.’

They stopped a while to watch as one of the great cranes swung into action, off-loading cargo from a big boat. The machinery ground slowly and clouds of smoke issued from a steam train that was ploughing by, along the far side of the floating dock. Everywhere, small working craft plied back and forth over the water.

It was certainly busy, but the area had a tumbledown appearance, the massive industrial sheds in such a state of disrepair that they looked abandoned, while dilapidated warehouses lined the waterway, as far up the dock as she could see. Tegan was glad when they turned away and came to the cathedral.

‘Can we go in? I’ve never been in a building that looked as old as that.’

‘It’s about a thousand years old, I think, but I don’t know much about its history.’

Massive pillars supported the arched roof with its intricate carvings and there was a strange play of light. It was such a wonderful, huge space, so they stayed far longer than they'd intended. Outside once again, Hywel saw her eyeing the public library.

'I can see we have to come back here when we have more time. We can't do it all today.'

She looked more closely. There was something charmingly mediaeval about it and yet it clearly was much more modern than that. Yes, she did want to come back to this wonderful place.

They stayed a few moments longer, looking at the pale stone building from the outside. It was linked to an ancient gateway, just a few yards from the main doors of the cathedral. Suddenly, a huge swarm of boys in a dark coloured school uniform poured out from behind the library onto the wide stone apron, and another group of boys in long red robes hurried towards the cathedral.

'Why are they dressed like that?'

'They'll be choir boys. There's probably a school attached to the cathedral. That happens quite a lot in Britain.'

This was all so interesting, so different. She wanted to suggest they go inside and listen to the singing, but Hywel had a goal in mind. It would have to wait until next time.

So they strolled across College Green in front of the great semi-circle of the Council House, past the tinkling fountains, and turned into Park Street. Lined on both sides by a myriad shops and cafés, it stretched steeply upwards, straight as an arrow, an intriguing invitation to explorers.

Chapter 51

It was too hot. Hywel's long legs devoured the steep slope, but Tegan refused to be defeated and she pushed on, keeping pace, her face turning a deep pink colour.

'Hey, slow down.'

'Sorry.' He stopped and took her hand, not even breathing harder than usual.

A short road now led off to the left, and the Cabot Tower was signposted. A moment later, they could see it, and they followed a path that wound up to its base, where they stopped. Exhausted, Tegan laid her jacket in the shade and threw herself down to cool off. Hywel sat beside her.

'I've got an astonishing piece of news. You're not going to believe it.'

'What's that?' She propped herself up on her elbow and looked at him, unable to imagine what the news could be.

'It's Dad – he's been conducting a relationship with Emma Williams, the district nurse.'

Tegan burst out laughing. 'Conducting … oh, Hywel, you sound so stuffy and disapproving! What's wrong with that? It's wonderful. Don't you want him to be happy?'

‘

‘Of course. Of course I do. It’s just a bit sudden. I go away for a weekend and, suddenly, he’s getting married.’

‘From what you said, he’s been on his own for fifteen years. It’s not that sudden.’

‘Well, I just hadn’t expected it, that’s all. He says they’ve had a thing going for about three years. Three years – and I never even noticed.’

‘That’s not surprising at all – you had other things on your mind.’

Hywel looked at Tegan. ‘You think I’m being silly, worrying about this, don’t you?’

‘Actually, yes, I do. She’s a good woman – and hardly a gold digger, is she?’

‘Not that, no. I don’t think there’s any gold in our coffers.’

‘So don’t worry about it. If she wants to marry your father, it’s because she cares about him. Did he tell you anything else about what they’re going to do?’

‘He says he’s moving out of the farmhouse and into the little place I showed you the other day. He’s going to live there with Emma when they’re married.’

‘Oh, she has that beautiful garden. She’ll miss that.’

Hywel laughed. ‘I’m sure she’ll start another one, although it may be a bit of a challenge, up there on the mountain. Dad says they’ll soon find a tenant for her house. It’s well looked-after, so it shouldn’t be difficult.’

‘

He was lying on his back, looking up at her with a thoughtful expression. ‘I get the feeling Dad’s clearing out of the main house deliberately, for us.’

Ah, yes. They did have to discuss this.

‘And is that where you’d like us to live?’

‘Yes, of course. I know you wouldn’t want to live with my dad – neither would I once we’re married. But you saw how the other place isn’t even visible from there. We’d have it to ourselves. There are lots of changes I’d like to make and I’m sure you’ll have a few suggestions.
What about –?’

He was getting excited about their future which was wonderful, but he was ignoring something that was so important to her, as if it didn’t matter at all. Tegan gave a heavy sigh and Hywel stopped speaking.

‘What’s wrong?’

‘Hywel, have you even once listened to what I’ve been saying to you over the last few months?’ She sat up, and there was a dangerous glint in her eyes. ‘Have you? Do you remember I talked about taking over from my dad at home? In a year or two, when I’ve learned how to run things?’

‘Well, yes, but you’ve now said you’ll marry me. You even said you wanted to. I distinctly remember that – and I didn’t hear you contradicting Sir George the other night.’ He snatched up her hand. ‘Look, here’s the proof.’

His smile was beginning to waver.

‘

‘I do want to marry you, *mi amor*, more than anything, but that doesn’t mean I stop being me. Have you ever thought we could do it the other way around? That you could come to Colombia and live with me there?’

They were facing each other. His colour was unusually high, his eyes filled with bewilderment and fear – the situation had changed. He had to do something, and Tegan understood he didn’t know what move he should make. She had a terrifying moment during which she thought she might lose him by insisting on this, but she had to pursue it. If they didn’t sort it out, their whole relationship would be doomed. Hadn’t she been through this with Luís? And failed to state her case until it was far too late?

It wasn’t so much about exactly where they would live, more that he must take her wishes into account and not just assume she would follow without question wherever he chose to lead.

And looking into Hywel’s face, she saw he’d also understood how serious the moment was.

‘The farm, Tegan, my farm. How can I abandon it? It’s been in the family for over three hundred years, well before your great-grandfather even got to South America. How can I walk away from that?’

‘I know it’s important but it’s not yours, it’s your father’s. What about him? Why shouldn’t he continue to run it? Why shouldn’t he and Emma run the farm together?’

‘Because it’s too much for him. It’s been too much, even with me there, working flat out, and there’s no money to employ the proper size of workforce. But you and I together, we can change all that.’

‘

‘Yes, we can.’

She was silent for a long time, thinking over how she was going to put the suggestion to him. Men – good men, that is – seemed to be so sensitive to anything that touched on their integrity, and Hywel was no exception.

‘I wonder …’ she began, trying to find the right words.

‘What?’

‘Well, I have some money. I wonder if it could be of any use to you. Since it’s just sitting in the bank. I could –’

‘You could what?’ He’d reddened again and she couldn’t miss the anger radiating off him. ‘I am not accepting charity from your father, Tegan. I’m not sure what impression you have of me, but it goes against everything I consider important, against … honour,’ he said, unable to find the word he wanted. ‘I couldn’t do it.’

‘Honour! Hywel, you sound like some twelfth-century knight, not a twentieth century businessman.’

‘What do you mean?’

‘For a start, I didn’t mention my father and secondly, I’m not offering you charity. I wouldn’t dream of it. I’m trying to help.’

‘Well, that kind of help is not welcome.’

‘You’ve completely misunderstood. I’m making you a business proposition.’

‘I won’t accept money from your father.’

She sighed again. He was so intransigent, not even considering what she might mean by her last words. At the same time, it was good to have the proof that he was marrying her for reasons quite unrelated to the possession of wealth – not that she'd ever believed otherwise.

'For Heaven's Sake, Hywel, I'm talking about my *own* money.' She raised a hand as he made to interrupt. 'Please. Please listen to me. I have a little money, a small inheritance from my grandmother. And money I've made myself, breeding horses, nothing to do with my parents.'

He made to speak and then snapped his mouth shut. At least he was letting her say her piece.

'*Abuela* tried to teach me about what can be done with money beyond simply having it, because she said wealthy women are always at risk of being used and she wanted me to control it for myself, to understand how it works, to be independent. So, she taught me, and I did learn.

'She left it to me with instructions to invest it in something I could feel passionate about. I knew we'd arrive at this point eventually, so I've thought hard about this and worked out all the financial angles. And the thing I feel passionate about is your farm. So I am proposing to invest it in that.'

'But, Tegan, we can't just …'

'It's an investment in our future – *our* future, Hywel – instead of investing in something someone else is doing. And it would be no different from if I *did* choose to invest in some business elsewhere. At least we know about this business, so my money will be safer. Remember, you said you were going to get the bank to lend you money?' He was silent.

'You did, didn't you?'

'Yes, but – '

‘

‘To improve things, right? There’s really no difference if you take their money or my money. And there’s no guarantee that they would lend it, is there?’

‘Well, no, not if they don’t like what’s in the accounts.’

‘We can use our own money instead. Our money, Hywel.’ She waited a moment for that to sink in. ‘Or, if you prefer, we can keep it as my money and expect a return on it. And your dad or you can pay it back as time goes on – because it is a business and you do want it to pay its way, and so do I. You didn’t know I had any money of my own a minute ago. It makes no difference to me. It’s just sitting in a bank, waiting to be put to use.’

He was quiet for so long, thinking through what she’d said, that she began to doubt the outcome. Was he coming around to her way of looking at things?

‘What if it doesn’t work and the farm doesn’t start to make money?’

At least he was thinking about the angles.

‘Why shouldn’t it? You told me about the lambing shed you wanted to build and showed me the plans. Didn’t you say the important thing was being able to leave the sheep on the farm in winter, instead of taking them down the valley, so you wouldn’t have to go out in the snow every day to supplement their feed? That the numbers of lambs will go up if you have a proper place for lambing? And I read through the figures you had for the bank manager.

That all made sense to me. You see, I was well taught, and I haven’t forgotten anything you said.’ He stirred uneasily but didn’t say anything.

‘

‘But to make something grow, you have to invest in it and that’s what you haven’t been able to do. If we put in some really up-to-date equipment and employ people to do the physical work, if we modernize, it won’t be too much for your dad – and it will start to make a profit. He might be prepared to manage it.’

‘He might, at that,’ he said, beginning to see where this was going. ‘We could even work with our neighbour, Colin Johnson. I’ve been talking to him about how we can improve things. It pains me to say it, but Daffyd was right, you know, about small farms. The future is in larger units or specialisation.’

‘If your dad doesn’t want to do it, maybe Mr Johnson could be persuaded to take on the day-to-day management of the two farms and your dad could work on increasing his rare breed flock, as well. I actually think that would be a good way to go.’

‘You have an opinion … on sheep?’

He was smiling now, looking a little less strained.

‘Not an informed one, I grant you. But I saw how much interest he had at the show from various people – and he sold every one of those lambs. Maybe it wouldn’t be possible to live from that business alone, but it has to be worth developing as a side-line.’

Tegan stopped talking. She was probably going to get him to agree. But had she been too forceful in clearing away the obstacles? Hywel had to want to do this himself.

‘I’m not saying it has to be this way, but will you at least come on a visit with me, to my home, Hywel? My parents have things they want to do together. We could take over the management of their farm, say for six months once we've reorganised things here with your dad. That'd give you time to work out whether you could live there or not.'

He still wasn't saying anything, just listening to what she had to say.

'I swear, if you don't like it, if you really feel you can't, we'll come back here and I'll be happy to be a Welsh farmer's wife – as long as you allow me to invest my money in the farm, that is. Because I am *not* going out in the winter snow to feed sheep – on the mountain or down in the valley! Not when I have the means of changing that. And neither are you.'

'If we did decide to live in Colombia, we could keep the main farmhouse for us, for visits,' he said. Finally, he was giving serious consideration to what she was proposing. 'Yes, I think it could work. It depends on Dad and Emma.'

'Not really, Hywel. If he doesn't want to run the farm, we can employ a full-time manager, maybe your neighbour, maybe someone else. But I don't see that happening. He's as keen as you on making a go of things.'

'Yes, I think the accident really set him back, but he's already seeing things differently.'

We need to look at the legal side of things if he's thinking of marrying again but there's no reason that should be a problem.'

Hywel lay back, gazing at the blue dome of the sky with the little white clouds scudding across. Tegan remained sitting, hugging her knees and said nothing. He had to decide for himself.

‘

‘You know,’ he said finally, ‘I’m really slow on the uptake. I just didn’t know what to think when you said that, had to get my head around the idea. But what I do know is that I’m marrying a clever woman. A clever and lovely woman I adore.’

He came upright and pulled her into his arms. She closed her eyes and shivered in anticipation of his kiss. It was as if the stand-off had heightened the sexual tension between them.

‘I was going to suggest a show,’ he said a little later, ‘but we’ve left it late, and I do have to go back tonight.’

‘Let’s find a place to eat, instead,’ said Tegan. ‘I’m starving. And this time, it’s my treat.’

Chapter 52

Tegan stretched across and grasped Hywel's hand, thinking how the weeks were rushing past.

'It's been a truly wonderful day.'

He stretched out a hand as the horses slowly came to a halt, and kissed the tips of her fingers, pulling her closer. The beasts stood companionably together while their riders shared a deep kiss that left Tegan's lips tingling.

'I'm just waiting for the moment when I have you by my side all of the time,' he said as they pulled apart and began to move on. 'That can't come soon enough for me.'

'For me too.'

The glow of well-being and satisfaction that wrapped her around came from spending a whole day out of doors with the man she loved. And from knowing how much she was loved.

They'd ridden the trail right over the mountain to the English border and beyond, a treat they'd promised themselves months before. A late October sun had shone benignly on them as they enjoyed a leisurely picnic by a

‘

tiny tarn, and then made love in the red and gold glory of late leaves that formed a soft carpet beneath them.

Only now, as they drew close to home, she began to feel the chill in the air and looked up. The sky was cloudless, promising a cold night and maybe a frost the following morning. Soon, she would experience her first winter in the Northern Hemisphere.

Slowly, reluctant to break the spell, they took the horses back to the stables, and gave them a quick rub-down, before going into the house via the back door.

*

Something had happened. Tegan felt it as she stepped into the kitchen, which seemed to be full of people, most sitting around the table with cups of tea in front of them, as if they'd all been waiting for Hywel and her to return. Mona broke off her conversation and came hurrying over to give her a hug. This was about her, she knew it. Her family.

Her father.

‘I'm sorry, Tegan, but I've got some bad news. Your mother telephoned.’

Tegan's heart gave a great thud and began to pound, making her short of breath.

‘Dad!’ she gasped. ‘It's Dad, isn't it?’

‘He's all right for the moment,’ said Mona, ‘but things have taken a turn for the worse. They want you to go home.’

Her brow felt clammy and there was a buzzing in her ears. She was going to faint. Someone sat her in a chair and pushed her head down towards her knees. It was Hywel and she held onto his hand as if to a lifeline.

I knew it couldn't last.' Her mouth was dry, but the words were coming now. 'I knew Mamá was keeping something back – I could hear it in her voice when we talked the other day.'

'Don't blame your mother, Tegan,' said Mona. 'I think she's finding it difficult to accept this is really happening. She needs you.' But Tegan scarcely heard this.

'They said the operation was successful, but I didn't believe it. I never believed it. They said the cancer could come back, and now it has.'

She sobbed, breaking down completely. Hywel was down on his haunches in front of her, stroking her hand.

'Tegan, *fy nghariad*. I'm so sorry. But we have to get you home as quickly as possible. You need to see him. And he will want to see you.'

He held her close, and she drew the comfort and strength she needed from his embrace. He wasn't saying it was nothing, that her father would get better. Despite her agony, she was grateful that he knew to be honest with her.

*

It was shortly after five two mornings later, and the sharp cold bit at Tegan's skin. Those pearly grey lines on the horizon must mean the night was coming to an end, though it was still an hour until dawn. They'd be leaving any minute now. But the journey was long with several changes on the way, and she wondered if she would get there in time to see him. She had to stop thinking like that because there was nothing she could do about it.

She looked around at the assembled group. All this, she was leaving behind, Mona and the farm, all these people who'd formed a part of her life for more than half a year now. She tried hard not to focus on the fact that it might be months before she saw Hywel again.

How cruel life could be – for this to happen after their wonderful day. But at least they'd had that time together, and every minute glowed in her memory. She should hang onto it because it would help her through the difficult times ahead. A cool wind now blew but even in the chilly dawn, she recalled the caress of the warm sun. And the caresses of the man who loved her, and whom she loved. Tears threatened again and she dabbed at her eyes.

'I'm sorry, Mona. I've only just thought of it, but how are you going to manage in the office? I've let you down.'

'Oh my darling girl, don't fret.' The older woman's hug comforted her for a moment. 'You just need to look after your mother. Mrs Evans at the post office, her girl is between jobs at the moment, and I'm sure I'll be able to persuade her to stand in for you. Your place is beside your parents at this time.'

'So, don't think about it anymore,' said George. 'Mona will manage.'

In his rather bluff, kindly way, George was a comfort.

'Won't you be coming over, Aunt Mona?'

'No, Tegan. Your father and I had a very long conversation back in April. We've said our good-byes.'

Tegan's despair grew at this evidence that her father had already faced up to this moment, and fresh tears poured down her face. Mona had known she could not take the time and maybe find the extra money to travel across the world to see her brother. She wiped her eyes, trying to deal with these harsh realities.

George's Jaguar was standing at the front door with the boot open. It was a luxurious, dark blue vehicle which dated from five or six years earlier. Hywel had wanted to drive Tegan to the airport in his Land Rover, but George told him the huge car would be more reliable, especially as there was an early plane to catch – and that Hywel was welcome to come along.

Tegan picked up the single suitcase she was taking with her. Most of her possessions would stay here at the farm. Because she would be coming back, of course she would. George stowed it away for her and closed the boot, telling her to keep her coat on because it would take a few miles for the car to warm up.

Hywel was going to be late. Why hadn't he arrived yet? She couldn't possibly leave without seeing him – surely, he must understand that she couldn't survive all this time away, without a final good-bye. A black cloud descended on her mind, as she saw how truly awful being divided from him for weeks or months at a time would be. Divided by the Atlantic Ocean. Being on different continents. Was it even possible to endure such a thing?

There was a distant engine, the sound swelling as it approached the farm. Everyone had heard now, and they stood around the front door, waiting in silence. She calmed down. He was here. How could she have doubted him?

Now he was, coming up the drive. A moment later, he'd pulled up and hurried over to her.

'Thank Goodness you've come.'

He held her close and said, 'You didn't really think I was going to let you leave without saying good-bye, did you?' Still holding her, he turned to George and added, 'If you're sure it's OK, Sir George, I've arranged things with my father, so I'd like to come up to London with you and see Tegan onto her flight.'

That'll be much better for her,' said George. 'I'm happy to be the taxi driver, but you'll have to come back by train. I'm staying up in the capital.'

'Then drive to the station first, please, and I'll follow, so I can leave my car there.'

*

Many hours later – she didn't know how many – Tegan was gazing unseeingly out of the tiny porthole window at her right shoulder. Having the window seat was completely wasted on her, except that it made it possible to turn her back on the other passengers.

Her good-byes over and done with, she existed in a state of acute distress, caught between the agony of leaving Hywel – for who knew how long? – and the terror of what was likely to happen with her father. Somehow, she had to accept that her father might die.

*

A whole twenty-four hours had passed. She had no memory of the journey and the several changes she'd had to make en route, but she'd obviously done the right things at the right times. Her mother, driven by Julio, had come to meet her in Cartagena. Now she climbed into the family car.

'I was so scared to leave him,' she said, 'in case something happened while I was away from the house. But I thought at this moment, you needed me more. And that nurse is very competent.'

They clung to one another in the back seat, both giving way to tears, while Julio drove sedately through the city centre, and headed towards the Santo Domingo Valley.

In a way, during the flight, she'd been in a protective cocoon. Now, she would have to face harsh reality.

Chapter 53

Gone. She was gone. The smell of her perfume clung to his clothes, or maybe it was all in his mind. All he could see were the tears rolling down her face. He'd held her as long as he could, until the last call for the flight and, even then, he'd had to wrench himself away, his heart dying within him as she disappeared down the corridor towards the plane. She didn't look back. He'd told her not to because it would only make it more difficult.

She'd done what he said but he thought, if she had turned to look, he'd have run to her and … what? He couldn't stop her going. Nor would he have wanted to. And there was no way he'd have been able to accompany her.

So, she'd gone, and he'd stood there, staring down the empty corridor for long minutes. Finally, a woman in uniform tapped him on the arm. 'You'll have to leave, sir. A new queue will be forming in a few minutes.'

*

Hywel got to his train with only two minutes to spare. It had a mixture of the new carriages, open all the way along with a central passageway, and the old, compartmentalized coaches. He jumped onto one of the latter and worked his way along the corridor that ran alongside until he found an empty compartment. He didn't want to make polite conversation. He didn't much want to do anything, just get this journey over with. At least, when he was back and had work to do, there'd be less time to think.

But who was he trying to convince? No amount of work would allow his mind to let go of this sense of desolation. Oh God, they'd got it so wrong; it was easy to plan a grand life, divided between countries, when they were lying side by side on the fragrant hillside, when they'd just made love. Together, they'd felt invincible. This horrible reality now showed a completely different side to things.

She wouldn't be thinking about him, of course. Her mind would be full of concern and fear for her father. And afterwards, she would need support. And who should she turn to but him?

She'd need him and he should be there, not trying to run a farm five thousand miles away.

He should go across to Colombia and stand by her side, help her with the multitude of tasks that would suddenly land in her lap, things she couldn't just walk out on. How long would all that take? Months at the very least, especially if she couldn't find anyone to manage the farm.

It was a huge place. It wasn't as if Tegan could leave her mother, racked by her own grief, to do it all on her own. He was needed. He must look at managing the situation. And the first thing was to talk to his father. Now he'd made a decision, his mind eased a little and, settling into a corner, he slept for the first time in forty-eight hours.

*

Hywel went to find his dad straightaway because this was not something he could put off. If he was going out to Colombia, there would be a lot to arrange. And he was still concerned about how his father would react.

‘You need to look at the farm in a different way, Hywel. This is your future we’re talking about, so stop feeling responsible for me. I know what I said when I was laid up, but I *was* in pain, and it all seemed too much then. A lot of things have changed since. I’m not quite ready to give up yet, you know.’

‘I didn’t mean it to sound like that, Dad. It’s just … well, you were finding things difficult. It’s our farm. Whatever Daffyd might say, you’re surely not ready to give it away.’

‘Yes, it’s our farm – and that means there’s nothing wrong with me running it. You’ve injected the necessary money, thanks to Tegan. She deserves to get something for her investment, and it’s up to me to make it work. She needs you, son. In a few months, we’ll have everything running properly. We’ll be employing more people. Emma and I can manage. You need to have a life of your own.’

‘But Dad …’

‘No – I’ll not say any more, except that it’s not up to me. Go away and think about it, about what you want for yourself and for Tegan. Just tell me when you’ve decided.’

Hywel suddenly realised his father was releasing him from what he'd always considered to be his obligations, giving him the freedom to choose what he wanted. And he knew exactly what that was.

Chapter 54

Colombia, South America. October 1965

Tegan looked at her father and acid seemed to rise in her throat. It was even worse than she'd imagined. She took a deep breath, banishing the little girl she had once been, the one who had always run to her father for comfort and understanding. Because if she didn't do that, she'd break down and she'd be no use at all.

'Dad?'

The lump in her throat was so big, she couldn't have said another word. He was lying on his bed, cradled in a mass of pillows, his face to the wall. The room had a strong smell of antiseptic with an underlying note of decay, which frightened her, emphasising how fast he was approaching the end. Now, he turned towards her, and even that small effort seemed to exhaust him.

'Tegan?'

He took a moment to find the words and when he spoke, his voice was weak, not much above a whisper. 'I'm so pleased you're here. But I wish you didn't have to see me like this.'

How had things gone so far, so fast? He'd always been thin, but strong and sinewy at the same time. Now, the bones protruded through the wasted flesh and his face was a pasty, yellowish grey. It wouldn't be long. Thank Goodness she'd got here in time.

She hurried over and buried her head on his chest, holding him as tightly as she dared, his arms so thin she thought the bones might snap if she applied too much pressure.

'Dad, I love you.'

The tears threatened yet again – but tears wouldn't help either of them.

*

'It all happened so quickly,' said her mother when she came down later to find her daughter.

They walked out onto the veranda and sat, side by side, at a low table. Pilar followed with a tray and placed in front of them glasses of cold papaya juice bulging with ice. Tegan took a sip. She'd had nothing to drink for hours, nor yet taken the time to freshen up, driven only by the need to see her father before it was too late.

'He had grown thinner,' her mother conceded, 'but he seemed strong and cheerful, really he did, and he insisted there was nothing wrong. Even last week, he went riding – on Monday, I think it was.'

The words were tumbling out and Tegan was heartbroken that her mother should feel so much guilt for not knowing how bad things were. Anyone would try to hope for the best and she knew from when the cancer had appeared the first time, when she'd still been living at home, how aggressive it had been, how much her father had hidden it away from them. She stretched across the table and took her mother's hand, squeezing it gently.

'Not your fault, Mamá. You wanted to believe he would pull through because you love him.'

The older woman looked at her daughter and said, 'You do understand? I buried my head in the sand because I couldn't contemplate life without him. You know what? I still can't. Is that the reaction of a sane woman?'

'The reaction of a person who loves someone deeply.'

They were both quiet for a while and then her mother said, 'That afternoon, after he'd been riding, he complained of pain and went straight to bed. But he was on the go again the next day, so I didn't pay enough attention.'

She began to cry again. 'I kept on hiding away from what was happening, not wanting to recognize it. I was really good at not seeing how much weight he'd lost. Then, three, four days ago, he collapsed and I … I thought he'd died. I couldn't get him up off the floor and had to get help. That's when I called you.'

Poor Mamá – how she must be suffering. Her skin looked grey, washed out, with pale blue veins showing through. And her eyes were red-rimmed. How had she never really taken account of her mother? How had she missed her mother's needs while she was growing up?

It had always been Dad, a larger-than-life character, who grabbed her attention. But now, she had to change because, somehow, her mother was going to have to survive this. And who better to support her than Tegan?

She patted her mother's hand and then pulled her close, holding her trembling body, letting her cry until the sobs had subsided. Then, her mother sat up and wiped her eyes.

'Sorry,' she said in a nearly normal voice. 'I've been crying for days. I don't seem to be able to stop myself.'

'Mamá, you don't have to make excuses for that – and you don't have to tell me anymore if it's too painful.'

'I do. I need to talk. Your father has always been my sounding board, the person I shared ideas with. There never was anyone else, from the first moment I met him.'

Tegan thought about Hywel and the confusion of their lives at the moment, and she felt a deep ache of longing. So much had happened in the last two days that she'd single-mindedly pushed everything aside to concentrate on getting to see her father. But that was now. Afterwards, there would be a lot to sort out, many decisions to take.

Her mother gave a deep sigh, gathering herself to get to the end of the story.

'Julio carried him up to bed. Just picked him up as if he were a child. And he's been there ever since. And …'

She became silent.

'… now I can see him fading hour by hour. Oh, what am I going to do?'

There was nothing Tegan could say but she stayed where she was, hugging her mother tightly, and gradually, she calmed.

Things were in a holding pattern, and it was strange how these circumstances had forced them together, so that they were talking seriously, almost for the first time. Now, Tegan felt that she was beginning to know and understand her mother.

Given that full-time care was necessary, they'd brought in a nurse, and when Tegan went upstairs later, the woman must have heard her because she came out onto the landing.

'He's sleeping, *señorita*, and he doesn't seem to be in pain at the moment.'

'I just wanted to make sure he's all right.'

'It might be better to let him continue to sleep, so he'll be stronger for later, when your brother comes.'

Tegan turned away, nodding her understanding.

'Call me … call me if anything changes.'

What could she usefully do? It was stifling inside the house. What a contrast to Wales, with its crisp, late-autumn cold and the gold and red of dying leaves. She opened a window on the landing, to allow air to circulate, but a faint smell of cattle entered and quickly, she closed it again.

It reminded her she'd hardly given a thought to the ranch. That would be a way in which she could usefully occupy herself because there didn't appear to be anything else that she could do up here. The house was running smoothly, as always. It felt strange to have no specific tasks, but someone needed to continue the work, and she could contribute. She had to do something to pass this agonizing time.

*

Back out on the veranda, her mother had gone, and Pilar was clearing the table. She looked up as Tegan came in. '*Doña Bronwen está tomando una siesta*.'

It would do her mother good to rest. Maybe it had helped to relieve her mind, talking about the events of the last few days, and now she would be able sleep properly. Tegan went down the steps towards the stable block.

She would look for Alfonso and see what he'd been doing. He was supposed to be managing the day-to-day running of the ranch for her father, but she remembered the feckless, smiling cousin who never settled to anything, and she had no faith in him, dreading what she might find, despite her mother's praise for him. Had she been in a fit state to make a judgement?

Finally, she ran him to earth in the estate office where he was talking to a serious-looking man in steel-framed glasses, whom Tegan recognized as the vet.

'Sorry,' she said, backing out the doorway, wanting to talk to her cousin on his own. 'I'll catch you later on.'

'No, it's okay. Come on in – we're just finishing.'

They stood up and Alfonso turned to the short, black-haired man.

'I think we're done, don't you, Jorge? Let me introduce my cousin, Tegan Lewis, just back from Gran Bretaña.'

'Of course. We have met.' The vet got to his feet and gave a polite, little bow. 'I am very sorry about Don Juan,' he said, giving her father the name the locals used. 'We all have great respect for him.'

'Thank you.'

A moment later, he was gone, and the cousins embraced, before sitting down.

'It is good to see you, Tegan. I'll not ask how you are. I know it can't be good. But you just concentrate on your dad because we've got everything under control here, between Julio and me. And that includes your horses.'

'*Gracias*, Alfonso.'

This was so *simpática,* so good of him. There was a new seriousness which she didn't associate with the cousin she'd known all her life.

'I didn't think working here was something you'd enjoy, but Mamá says you've been brilliant.'

The young man looked slightly perplexed and said, 'I didn't expect to get on so well, either. It was just filling time, to be honest. Plus, Papá was finally getting tough about what I was going to do with my life.'

Tegan nodded her understanding and said, 'It took me a while to realise most parents just want what's best for their children – but I finally got it.'

'Yeah, well, it took me a *very* long time – about ten years longer than you, Tigre.' He'd given her the nickname when she'd been a little kid and he, a swashbuckling twelve-year-old. 'I can't pretend otherwise, but I have changed. I didn't think I'd like working here at all, but that just shows you how wrong you can be. I've been thinking of maybe going back to college and studying to be a vet. That's why Jorge and I were talking just now. If I'm going to do it this year. I'm going to have to decide quickly.'

This didn't sound good for the future of the ranch, but it was great he had this positive attitude. For the first time ever, it sounded as if he was taking control of his life. They talked about the everyday details of his work and, an hour later, they'd been through everything concerning the practical side that Tegan considered important, information which would be essential for her to pick up if he were no longer there. As she left to pay a visit to her mare, Bonita, Alfonso said, 'If it'll help, I'll stay for a while.'

'Please do, Alfonso. Please stay on just now, even if it's only a couple of weeks. We need time to sort a few things out. But don't let it get in the way of what you want to do.'

She mustn't put pressure on him, but maybe there was a possibility here, a way to manage the future. It was something to think about.

Tegan walked away. Alfonso, a vet? That was going to take some getting used to. He did seem completely sincere.

But it would be great if he could be here for a week or two longer, while she got back into the swing of things.

Would Hywel be able to stay when he came over? That was the biggest question, and the answer could be several months away, while he got things sorted out back in Wales. Would he even want to stay? A huge cloud settled on her, and the misery of the thought was like a physical pain. How could she bear to be separated from him for so long? The simple answer was that she couldn't.

She squared her shoulders. If Alfonso decided not to stay, she'd have to find someone to replace him, so that she could return to Wales. The search for a farm manager was always complicated. Selecting the right person could be an arduous process, always supposing there was someone suitable available. They'd already learned that the man who'd stood in for her father earlier in the year had been taken on elsewhere, so there was no point in going back to him. And some people didn't want a permanent post.

So, what if Alfonso could be persuaded to be their new manager? Would he agree to defer his entry to the university for a year? He was eight years older than Tegan and should have been the perfect choice. But, the child of wealthy, indulgent parents, he'd frittered away those early years when he should have been learning and he'd have a lot of catching up to do. On the other hand, he did seem to be coping well. But, if he persisted with the wish eventually to become a vet, he was still not going to provide a long-term solution.

Of course, *Mamá* had been very much involved with the administration and had been working with Alfonso, since they'd returned from their European trip. That would have helped him to grow into the role. Maybe he would even change his mind and become a professional ranch manager instead. Tegan had a lot of faith in her powers of persuasion, but she had to let him make up his own mind. It was a lot to take on board.

As she wandered down to the stables, she realised some good advice was needed. If her father was up to it, she'd discuss it with him. It might be good for him to talk about the ranch instead of concentrating on the state of his health. Probably, everyone had been keeping things from him in the mistaken idea that they should, that he was too weak to cope. But Dad's brain had seemed sharp enough when the pain was tamped down. Maybe he'd relish the opportunity to discuss the matter, and she couldn't think of anyone more likely to have some commonsense suggestions.

*

Idris and Carmen arrived that evening. The family sat together around the table after supper, and Tegan looked around. How subdued it all was, so unlike their usual lively discussions and the gentle ribbing, older brother style, that Idris always indulged in when they met up. When they'd arrived, he'd caught her to him and planted a large kiss on her cheek.

'Getting married, *hermanita*?' He gave her a hug. 'I'm so pleased for you, little sis. I can thoroughly recommend the married state – with the right person, of course.'

But uppermost in everyone's mind was the knowledge that it could only be a few short weeks at the most for their father before the end.

As the meal drew to a close, Tegan was watching her brother and sister-in-law. There was something subtly different about them, a suppressed excitement and happiness that was at odds with the situation, but she couldn't quite work out what it was.

'We'll have to go back on Friday morning,' Idris said eventually, 'but we'll visit as often as we can.'

'It's okay,' said Tegan. 'I'll ring you if there is any change, if we feel you should be here.'

'But we wanted to see you, *Mamá,* to tell you something really important: you're going to be grandparents.'

Ah, that was it. Tegan clapped her hands and went to kiss them both. 'And I'm going to be an aunt!'

This positive news cheered everyone up.

*

Later, Tegan telephoned Hywel, and they had a long conversation. Thank Goodness he'd put the telephone line in as soon as the loan had been set up.

'I'm coming over,' he said. 'I can take a couple of weeks off.'

'Hywel, you can't. What about the lambing shed? You've got to have that ready in time for the winter or everything you've done will be set back.'

'It's well on its way and Dad says he can handle it. He's very much better, a changed man. I do think having Emma around has made all the difference.'

She smiled for the first time in several days. 'Well, that's not surprising. You do understand how important women are, don't you?'

'I have come to appreciate that,' he said, laughing. 'In fact, the shed should be finished before the end of the week. Joe's going to carry on working with us and he's persuaded his friend from the next valley to come over. I interviewed him yesterday and we'll be taking him on.'

'Friend?' she said. 'Joe? I've never heard him say more than two words to anyone!'

'Probably a drinking partner but yes, he does have one,' said Hywel, chuckling. 'So, I'm arranging a flight, and I should be with you within the week. I'll ring you as soon as I know about times.'

'Oh Hywel!' Tegan found the tears, which came all too readily these days, were coursing down her cheeks. 'You've made me laugh and now, I'm crying. Thank you. I can't wait to see you.'

If only Dad could hang on long enough to meet him.

Chapter 55

Exactly a week later, Tegan was waiting at Cartagena Airport. She'd parked the car close by and walked into the arrivals' hall, but the terminal was baking hot. She was early, and there were no benches or seats of any kind, just one or two people standing around. She wiped sweat from her forehead and clamped her broad-brimmed hat back down, aware she hadn't yet got used to the climate again. Perhaps, she'd be better off outside.

But there, the stones of the gravelly road pushed up painfully into the soles of her shoes, the heat percolating through the thin leather. The air was thick and heavy, and it was too hot out here in the open, just as bad as in the building, an unpleasant, sticky heat. She rubbed the skin on her forearms, trying to calm the irritation that was already springing up. When had she become so sensitive? She'd be better off inside after all – where she could at least monitor what was going on.

Well, a few groups of people had begun to gather, that was something. Had that clock stopped working? She went to find another one, to check. But no, it showed the same time. As did her watch.

A street vendor with a tricycle stall entered by the far door, and one or two people waved him over to order empanadas. Moments later, the overcooked fat was sizzling loudly as he dropped in the little pastries, and the smell wafted in Tegan's direction. She hadn't had lunch and had barely touched breakfast in her desire to get away to the airport, but she turned away, sickened, unable to face the idea of food.

From far away, came the drone of an aeroplane, and suddenly, there was a muffled announcement. She didn't quite catch the words but there was a flurry of movement, and people were now hurrying towards the doors that led from the runway. She followed.

Gesturing to the converging crowd to move back, a uniformed official slowly pulled the doors open, in anticipation of the new arrivals. The plane was already down, and people craned their heads, trying to see who was coming. Tegan's mouth went dry. He had arrived.

*

Four hours later, Tegan pushed open the door of her father's bedroom and Hywel followed her inside. The whole place was bathed in the orange sunlight of the late afternoon. She walked softly across the old boards of the wooden floor and peered down at the figure in the centre of the bed.

'Dad.'

He lay very still. Her pulse picked up and she felt the familiar banging of her heart against her ribs, a sensation she'd experienced several times over, in the last few days. It happened every time he didn't immediately respond. Had she lost him in the hours she'd spent in Cartagena? She couldn't bear the thought and turned in distress to Hywel who laid his hand on her arm.

'Wait. Look, he's waking up.'

'Tegan? You've come back.'

She swallowed and got her words in order. 'Yes, Dad. And look who I've brought with me. Dad, this is Hywel, my fiancé. I wanted you to meet each other.'

Hywel took hold of her father's hand which lay on the counterpane and shook it gently. 'Hello, Mr Lewis.'

Ieuan Lewis raised himself a little in the bed and looked hard and long at the young man who now stood with his arm protectively around his daughter's shoulders. Finally, he said, 'Take care of Tegan, that's all I ask of you.'

'I will. I love her.'

The older man slid back on the pillows and closed his eyes, as if that was what he had needed to hear.

'I'm tired. Better … leave me now.'

*

'I can't bear to see him like that. Yesterday, he was giving me advice about cattle and today, he can hardly open his eyes. He has no strength left,' she wailed.

His arms went around her, and he held her until she calmed.

'Come on, we'll go outside.'

The sun was going down quickly and would set in a few minutes. The air, which had lost the fierce heat of the day, now caressed and cooled her skin and dried the tears on her cheeks, giving some measure of relief.

But there was no way to escape the dread as her father's death approached, nor could she forget that he was in great pain, despite the drugs that had been prescribed for him. This was a hard way to go, both for him and for the family. The image of his skeletal frame, with its stretched, yellowed skin, would be with her for a long time.

They walked out of the yard to the far side of the barn. Horses snuffled and blew quietly nearby, in comforting acknowledgement of their presence, as they went to sit on the bench. It had been placed against the back wall of the barn, to give a view across pastures and on to the distant mountains. The latter were dark shapes by now, with only, at the very top, that rapidly diminishing glow of orange.

It was curiously calming to sit there, leaning into one another and holding hands as they listened to nature settling for the night. The chorus of the ever-present crickets increased minute by minute. The sound came in waves, rattling drily to a crescendo like desiccated seeds in a pod and then receding to almost nothing, only to start all over again. Large insects, mostly moths looking like huge black butterflies, flew to their inevitable death on the lights of the veranda. Meanwhile, the land stretched out in front of them, a vast empty space. The sky darkened inexorably, and suddenly it was night.

'I think he's happy to have met you,' she said finally. 'He feels he doesn't have to worry about what will happen to me.'

'No, he doesn't,' said Hywel, possessing himself of her hand and carrying the fingers to his lips. 'Because I'm going to take care of you, Tegan. And he knows that.'

His arm tightened across her back as he pulled her close and then kissed her gently. She felt a stirring, the beginning of desire, and would even have wanted to push things forward, but it felt strange and inappropriate. Her own needs would have to wait. She looked at him to see if he had experienced the same thing.

'You have to let him go and be strong for your mother,' he said, reading her thoughts. 'She needs you at the moment. Later, we can plan for ourselves.'

When a gong sounded in the distance, Tegan got up. 'That's dinner. We must go in.'

Chapter 56

What were all these people doing here? The rows of black-clad figures looked like strangers to Tegan, but they must know her father somehow. The service was taking place in the morning, and by noon, they were at the graveside. It was the culmination of two days which had been among the most difficult of her life. Her mother was tough, to find the strength and purpose to do what was required of her.

'I've done all my crying,' she'd said.

She was tired, though, and Tegan suspected it was only the demands made on her that kept her going.

In accordance with local custom, the casket had remained open for the two previous days, held on a trestle table in the cool aisle of the church, and monks had come to watch over it and pray. Incense had burned constantly and had somewhat hidden the beginnings of decay but, in this climate, the burial could not be delayed.

Even during the night, mourners had come past, to look in the coffin. To pay their respects to Don Juan, beloved by the ordinary people who had benefitted from improvements to their lives that he had brought about.

There were many who genuinely mourned him and felt bereft. As she'd watched them pass around the coffin, she'd felt great pride in her father's achievements. A stranger from a foreign land, he had given care and attention to his adopted community.

Her parents had no religious belief, but everyone was Catholic here, and the family had learned to adapt generations before. When Tegan managed to lift her head above the misery that inhabited her, and take in what was going on around her, she was astonished at how her mother somehow remained composed and even gracious, understanding and responding to other people's needs.

She had deep admiration for this strength, because she herself was in despair. She was grieving, she supposed. A weight bore down on her shoulders, seeming to compress her lungs, so she could take only shallow breaths. She gazed at her hands. Was this her skin? It looked old and dried out. And these must be her limbs. But they seemed unsuited to bear the weight of her body. She'd cried a lot. Crying must be good since people did so much of it in these circumstances. If so, she'd been doing the right thing. But it hadn't made her feel any better.

She hadn't known what to expect, but she thought that grief was about love. And she had loved her father.

No amount of anticipation of the event had prepared her for the reality. Now the coffin was being lowered into the ground and, with it, a piece of her heart. Soil and small stones began to thud on the coffin lid. She was done and she wanted to leave, to hide herself away somewhere, but there would be people back at the house, friends offering condolences, wanting to drink to his memory, to tell the good stories. She couldn't escape yet. Hywel squeezed her hand. They'd talked little in the last few days. She'd been deep inside herself, but he'd seemed to know what she was thinking, to know that all he could do was be strong for her, so that she could continue.

There was her brother now, coming towards her, looking not much better than she felt. She ran across to hug him. With a delicacy she had not shown before, Carmen held back.

'You'll get through it,' Idris said. 'Just a few hours to go now.'

'I know. And it's much more difficult for Mamá. But she's so strong.'

'She's going to need you, Tegan,' he said, 'after – when everyone's gone. It'll be harder for her then. Please stay a while. We'll come back as soon as we can.'

'I will,' she said.

*

Finally, the people had all gone. The house was quiet now, except for the creaks as night came, and the wooden beams contracted in the cooler air, and settled.

'I've had enough,' her mother said. 'I need to go to bed.'

It was only eight o'clock, but there was no doubt she wanted to be on her own. Tegan accompanied her upstairs.

'Mamá, you –'

'I'll be all right, darling, don't worry. I just need some time to think, work out how to go on from here. Go and keep Hywel company, why don't you? There's nothing you can do for me just now, and with you helping me, that poor young man hasn't seen much of you in the last few days.'

It was good advice, and she found Hywel sitting on the veranda, a small glass of beer, scarcely begun, on the table before him. He rose and said, ‘Want to walk?’

‘And talk.’

‘Come on.’

Chapter 57

They picked their way down the stony track that led to the *posso*, a small reservoir on the farm that her father had designed and helped to construct. He'd wanted more water storage than could be held by the tanks that had been put in decades earlier, to supply the house and the animal troughs, and some of the workers' houses.

She remembered that time when she was a small child, standing on the bank, looking down to where the men were digging out the hole. Her hand had been tucked into her mother's and she'd closed her eyes, trying to imagine it filled to the top with the hundreds of thousands of gallons of water that would turn it into a small lake, but she couldn't. It was just dry, brown earth, and they had to wait for the rainy season to start the process of filling it.

And yet, just a few months later, there it was, as if it had always been, a testimony to her father's creativity. Two years of rains had been necessary to fill it to the top, although they'd begun to use it towards the end of that first year. It had been a massive project and had transformed the ranch, a highlight of her father's life. Oh God, she would miss him so much!

And soon, Hywel would be leaving. She couldn't bear the thought. 'Hywel, I'm so sorry but I'm going to have to stay here a short time, a few weeks. *Mamá* needs my help while she picks up the running of the ranch. But Hywel, *querido*, I cannot do this long term. I thought … I thought I was stronger, but I'm not, so I've started the search for a manager and, as soon as I've found one, I'll be free to –'

'Do you think that's the best solution for the ranch?'

'No, not really, it's not ideal. The management should stay within the family, but a woman on her own is at a disadvantage in this country. I've already tried to persuade Alfonso to stay, but I don't think he will. He's not said no yet, but he's set on a career as a vet. It's taken him years to work out what he does want to do, and I can't make him feel bad about refusing to stay – or worse, be the reason he abandons his plans.'

She grasped his arm, pulling him around so that they faced one another.

'I know you have to go back, *querido*,' she went on, 'but I promise you, the moment I've sorted it out, I'm coming back to Wales. I promise.'

She was gazing up at him, trying to read his expression, willing him to understand that staying here for the moment was something she had to do, not what she wanted. What if he felt she didn't care enough? She couldn't bear it if he thought the ranch was more important to her than he was.

'You will wait for me, Hywel, won't you? You won't give up on me?'

'Silly girl.' He pulled her close, so that her face was buried in his chest. He stroked her head and then ran his fingers through her beautiful hair, while her heart thudded hard against his.

'Whatever makes you think I'd go away and leave you to it? Haven't I given you enough proof that I love you? Didn't I tell your father I'd look after you.'

'Yes, but I thought you were trying to reassure him.' She laughed a little tremulously. 'It won't be for very long, I promise.'

'It won't be for any time at all – I promise you.'

'What do you mean? I can't leave now.'

'Tegan, I bought a one-way ticket. I'm not going back, so you can let Alfonso go as soon as he wants to. I'm staying. I'll be helping you manage the ranch.'

She was startled and she pulled away as a wave of emotions hit her: delight; relief; and then, anger.

'But why … why didn't you say? Why did you let me think you'd be leaving? That wasn't fair. How could you do that?'

'I had to hear you say what you just did, that our relationship mattered to you more than anything else. You've always worked things out very logically, and you're a brilliant businesswoman, and very persuasive. I've seen all that – and benefitted from it – but I needed you to say it, that it matters as much to you as it does to me for us to be together, not just from time to time, but always. And now you have.'

'You didn't trust me? I'd never try to trick you into believing something that isn't true.'

'Please don't be angry. I do trust you, but it's important for both of us that we're doing this for the right reasons and that we're honest with each other. Listen – if I hadn't trusted you, *fy'ngariad*, I would have made sure I had a return ticket.'

Tegan was silent for a while, trying to see things from his point of view. Finally, she accepted what he'd said.

'I know you'd be making a huge sacrifice, giving up on your farm. Are you sure you can do this?'

'With your investment, yes. You've made that much easier for me than it would have been. Of course I'm attached to our land, but now I realise that's all it is – a piece of land. I can leave it behind. It's you I care about.

'I found that out the moment you left. I knew it as you walked down that corridor towards that plane, knew there are more important things in life than the family farm, that I can always start again. Most of my worry was about Dad, but all that's changed. And maybe he and Emma will have a child who can eventually take over. Who knows?'

He obviously had given it a lot of thought. A few weeks earlier, he wouldn't have been able to imagine such a thing.

'So you see, it doesn't matter, Tegan. Because my life is here in Colombia with you. *Rwy'dy garu di.'*

He was watching her, and when she looked into his eyes, she saw his love, and she moved towards him.

*

A long time later, they broke apart.

'You really will stay and help me manage the ranch?'

It still seemed too wonderful a possibility to quite believe it.

'Yes, I will.'

‘We’ll have to get married. In this country, it wouldn’t be fitting to live together, not even for a short time.’

He grinned; already, she was tackling the practical details. ‘I thought we’d agreed on that.’

‘Well, I mean, we’ll have to organise it and do it more or less straight away.’

‘I took the liberty of talking to your mother to see how she feels about doing anything so close to the funeral, and she agrees it can be soon, as long as we keep it small, out of respect for your father.’

‘You do realise, don’t you, this is Colombia. Everyone will expect to be invited, so I think it may be somewhat larger than you imagine.’

‘That’s not a problem. I think it might be good for her to be involved in the organisation, in building for the future. It will help her, not to be thinking about your father all the time – to have things she must do, I mean.’ He said nothing for a moment and then added, ‘Of course, if you’d like a big society wedding, which you deserve, we’d have to delay a while.’

‘Now, who’s being silly? Do you really think I’m that sort of girl?’

No, he didn’t. She was beautiful, intelligent, sometimes foolish and often wise. And most of all, he knew without a shadow of a doubt that she was the woman with whom he wanted to spend the rest of his life.

‘Did I tell you I love you?’ he said. ‘I don’t care what sort of wedding we have. It’s being with you that matters.’

A little while later, he added, ‘I’m glad you don’t want a big affair because I really do not want to wait.’

‘And you absolutely hate being the centre of attraction, I seem to remember. This is a very neat way around the problem,’ she said, teasing him.

‘So, let’s get it organised as quickly as possible. We’ll line your brother up to give you away and we’ll be all set.’

*

And, six weeks later, they were married.

Did you enjoy this book? If so, please take the time to give it a rating on Amazon. Good ratings bring books to readers' attention.

Further books by Mary Georgina de Grey

Then the Earth Moved is a contemporary romance published by The Wild Rose Press in 2023.

Talented designer Isla Bruni is keen to widen her experience before setting up her own interiors business, so she accepts an exchange with a top studio located in an Italian hilltop town. She doesn't trust Italian men – after all, hasn't she had good reason? But irresistible, sexy entrepreneur Edmondo Benedetti turns her carefully ordered life upside down. How can she realise her ambitions without sacrificing love? Only when she's thrust into danger does she begin to understand what is important.

The past is the past. Yet, if secrets buried there resurface, could they destroy her future?

Praise for Mary Georgina's novel:

'It's a classic romance … but it's so much more.'

'What an antidote to the murder and mayhem … that I usually read! I wasn't certain if I'd like the genre. How wrong I was. This book is a gem, which will carry you away,

'She has a style all her own … I was reluctant to set this book aside until the conclusion, entirely caught up in the lives of its characters.'

' … a touch of Victoria Springfield and Sue Moorcroft.'

'A strong recommendation from me – a book I really hope others will try and enjoy as much as I did.'

'An evocative and wonderfully written novel.'

Then Time Stands Still, a contemporary romance set on an archaeological site on the outskirts of Zaragoza in Spain, due to be published later in 2024.

Archaeologist Dr Amancia Harding has looked after her family for five years. Now it's time to take care of herself, drop the less-than-wonderful boyfriend, and relaunch the career that's going nowhere. A chance to lead a team on a dig in northern Spain is a dream come true.

Her good intentions are thwarted when she meets Max. Damaged by war in Ukraine and a tragic event in his past, he fights the attraction he feels for Amancia; it's not only that it forces him to confront things he finds too painful, there's also the gulf between their backgrounds, and the clash of cultures.

But they must work together. Ambitious and fiery in character, can they recognise that compromise is sometimes necessary to find happiness?

Other publishing Credits

Short Stories for Young Adult

2015 Collection du Fantastique (2 collections)
Award winner 2015

2016 Algunos Thrillers en Español (2 collections)
Award winner 2016

Short Stories for Adults
2016 Retribution (The Dark Half of the Year)
2023 With Malice Aforethought (Grasping the Nettle)
2023 Some other Kind of Love (Grasping the Nettle)

Flash Fiction
2021 You're Hired
2021 Paxman Challenged

Dates for your diary:

If you'd like to hear Mary Georgina speak, dates will be posted on her Facebook page:

Mary Georgina de Grey Author

And her website:

www. marygeorginadegreyauthor.com

You can also sign up for her newsletter through the website or email.

marygeorginadg@gmail.com

Printed in Great Britain
by Amazon

60692289R00208